CHERRY BLOSSOM BLUES

A NOVEL

VIRLANA KARDASH

Cherry Blossom Blues
Published by Virlana Kardash
Ontario, Canada

ISBN: 978-1-0688039-2-5
FICTION / Romance / Suspense

Cover and Interior Design by Victoria Wolf,
wolfdesignandmarketing.com, copyright
owned by Virlana Kardash.

For Mary, who held my hand every step of the way across the miles and over the years.

CHAPTER
ONE

IT WASN'T A BAD CASE, as far as cases went, until Susanna Bailey found the dead man. Had she slowed down, she may have sidestepped that instant where, in the blink of an eye, the whole trajectory of her life shifted. But she had not.

And everything had already begun changing a day earlier. Because that's how life is.

The morning's traffic snarl just past the Arlington National Cemetery had her running a few minutes late. In the lobby of the Washington, D.C. law firm where her deposition was to start in five minutes, she rushed through the metal detector at the security check and jumped into the elevator as the doors were shutting. She needed today to go smoothly. The boss had called her into the office less than a week ago when that prevaricating lawyer from Florida blamed her for losing one of his exhibits. For a court reporter about to set up and run the Maryland branch of their court reporting agency, this was not good.

Tension bit into her shoulder as she hit the eighth floor button and attempted to smooth down her hair and check her make-up in the elevator mirror. And it was when Susanna was trying to dab a touch of concealer onto the faint scar on her cheek that she realized she was not alone.

She looked over to find a man watching her, his look discreet but appraising. His eyes held hers, but no smile crossed his face, and he averted his gaze. She turned away but then found herself taking another look despite herself. Brown hair. Solid build. Sort of rumpled like his suit. Faint frown lines creasing his brow. Definitely fine looking. And though she recognized the quality of the gray suit he wore and the expensive silk of his tie, he nevertheless struck her as somehow disheveled, hastily thrown together.

"Lovely day," she murmured as she tucked the concealer away nonchalantly and her eyes went to the elevator panel.

"Is it?" he asked.

"Hell, no," she mumbled, surprised. "Not really."

She felt him looking at her, really taking her in, and when she ventured another glance, she saw traces of a smile flickering in his eyes. Their gaze held for a beat, and she looked away, down at his hands, hands that did not match that suit, she realized, rough and strong, capable-looking hands. And she wondered what it would feel like to have those hands on her skin. Heat rushed into her cheeks. Oh. It had been a while since she'd noticed a man.

He followed Susanna out of the elevator and headed for the receptionist's desk while she hurried off down a hallway hung with modern art. When she entered the boardroom, the Department of Justice lawyers, the witness Mr. Nashta, and his lawyers were all there. Their greeting was polite but impatient. She apologized quickly as she sat down at one end of the conference room table and turned on her steno machine and laptop. The witness sat down on her right, and the examining lawyer from the Department of Justice, John Pike, on her left.

"When you're ready, Madam Reporter."

She nodded as her fingers settled onto the black keys of her steno machine. This was the second day of the deposition, and she hoped they would wrap it up early. She needed to get started on her government security clearance paperwork today. Without it, she couldn't move forward with the Maryland branch. The kind of work they were hoping to get there demanded it.

Mr. Pike reminded the witness that he was still under oath, and Susanna shifted in her seat to a more comfortable position as she started to stroke the words on her machine, her fingers warming up.

"Remember to keep your voice up, Mr. Nashta, and give me a chance to get the complete question out before you start your answer," Mr. Pike half-smiled, revealing a mouthful of tiny, sharp teeth, "or else the court reporter will start kicking us under the table."

Chuckles from everyone and an obligatory smile from Susanna. The lawyer's words were misleadingly soft-spoken and light as he adjusted the straining buttons on his suit jacket. But Susanna knew him for who he really was — smart, fast, and deadly as a shark. The government attorneys were trying to pin down some sort of wrongdoing in the execution of a defense contract, and with John Pike out for blood, Susanna knew the witness didn't stand a chance.

No sooner had they settled into the rhythm of the questioning than the boardroom phone buzzed. A Department of Justice lawyer got up to answer it and motioned to Pike.

"Let's go off the record." Mr. Pike pushed away from the table, and a huddled conversation among the DoJ attorneys ensued.

Mr. Nashta turned to Susanna. "Traffic?"

She nodded as she glanced quickly at her phone before turning it off.

"I'm never late for anything," Mr. Nashta said and drank from the glass of water in front of him. "I always take the Metro," he added with a self-satisfied smile.

"Not so easy when I've got all this equipment to lug around." She smiled back. Some witnesses wanted to chat during breaks. It helped with their nerves.

A knock on the door interrupted them, and when Susanna looked up, her breath caught. The man from the elevator walked into the boardroom. The Department of Justice attorneys surrounded him, and they all shook hands before John Pike turned to the others in the room.

"This is Robert Crowell, Department of Defense, Military Sealift Command. He'll be joining us today."

"Why is the Sealift Command here?" The main defense attorney shot to his feet. "Wait a minute, Counsel. We weren't told about this."

"Neither were we." Mr. Pike sighed with apparent effort.

After a whispered exchange, Mr. Nashta and his lawyers nodded their agreement, and everyone sat back down. Robert Crowell found a seat at the far end of the row of Department of Justice attorneys and took a look around the room. When he saw Susanna, he paused. Their eyes met in recognition, and they both averted their gaze at the same time.

As Susanna turned away, she caught the fragment of a smile. She studied the boardroom table before her, taking in the rich brown gleam of wood that whispered of decades of careful polish. That man had the most expressive eyes she had ever seen. A stormy gray blue, dark as a starless sky, dark as the depths of the ocean. The deposition started up again, and Susanna focused on the testimony and the words appearing on her laptop screen as she wrote them on the steno machine in realtime.

"Mr. Nashta, you were telling us about the military photo interpretation keys; is that right?" Mr. Pike looked up from his notes at the witness. "Would another name for these be stereograms? Go on, please. You hadn't finished explaining."

The witness mumbled something unintelligible.

Susanna glanced at him. "I'm sorry. I didn't get that."

"Books of aerial photographs and instructions that help

a photo interpreter make out certain things in those photos. That's all."

"Well, Mr. Nashta, help us a little. What certain things?" John Pike asked.

"Certain things." Mr. Nashta reached for the glass of water in front of him. "Like geological things. On the ground. Like parks. Or maybe mountains."

"Mountains?" Mr. Pike's impatience grew. "Mountains? Or aerial photographs of military facilities?"

"Objection. Leading," Mr. Nashta's lawyer cut in.

Mr. Nashta swallowed. "Could be any of those."

"And you understood the highly classified nature of these stereograms, did you not?"

No response.

Susanna looked up at the witness, surprised by his hesitation. After the previous day's testimony, she knew Mr. Nashta to be a man of many words. Now he seemed reluctant to answer.

"You had to pass top levels of clearance to work on this project; isn't that right? And the defense contractor gave you the necessary training to understand what you were looking at; isn't that also right?"

"I don't remember." The witness's face colored.

Mr. Pike rolled his eyes. "Are you on any medications that may hinder your memory or your ability to testify truthfully this morning, sir?" It was one of those questions that the lawyer didn't really want an answer to, and he went on before Mr. Nashta could respond or his lawyer object.

"These photo interpretation keys are not available to the civilian world, are they?" He paused for a theatrical beat. "Please speak up, sir. I didn't hear you."

Susanna didn't understand the jumpiness she was picking up from the witness this morning. He fidgeted in his seat, his eyes darting to and from Robert Crowell. This was a completely changed witness from yesterday. She saw Crowell watching him and wondered why he would be the cause of the witness's unease.

Mr. Nashta turned to his lawyers, who seemed as surprised by the sudden change in him as the Department of Justice lawyers were. "Can I have a break, please? I'm not feeling well at all. We've been over all this ground yesterday. I don't have all the time in the world, you know."

"We're in the middle of a question," John Pike snapped, refusing to stop.

Susanna forgot about Robert Crowell and focused on getting the words down as her fingers flew over the keys of the steno machine. Mr. Nashta's voice grew softer and softer with every answer. The room grew warmer. Mr. Nashta's deodorant kicked into overdrive, and his lawyer reached into his jacket pocket for a couple of aspirin. Susanna's attention drifted to the large boardroom window as she wrote. At the beginning, Washington had held little appeal for her. She was never drawn by the aura of power that the city was supposed to hold. To her, it was more the bureaucratic capital of the world.

But slowly it grew on her. And Michael, whose easy

charm had won her over and brought her down here, had shown her the loveliness of Virginia and Maryland, the Eastern Shore and the Chesapeake Bay, the pretty little towns dotting the countryside. Had the National Geographic not sent him on a photo assignment up to Canada, their paths would never have crossed at a Metallica concert in Toronto and she never would have become his wife. It was funny how life worked that way, messing with the plans you've made, more a cosmic roll of the dice, a ball of random chance and chaos. But there was something to be said for that too.

On the other side of the table, Robert Crowell shifted in his seat, and his gaze wandered from the witness to Susanna Bailey. He studied her surreptitiously, at his leisure, taking in the long, auburn hair, the mouth, inviting, sensuous and full, and the tilt of her head as she squinted her eyes in concentration. Around the same age as him, he'd guess, somewhere in the wilds of her forties. His eyes lingered. She was the kind of woman who could make it hard for a man to keep his mind on task. Good thing he was not that kind of man.

What was it about her? She had looked at him, for a moment their eyes had locked, and something had passed between them. Impossible. She was way more than lovely, no doubt, but distractions were costly, and women were not scarce. Just do your job and get out. Introspection led to dangerous waters, and it wasn't good for his health. And yet.

He pulled his attention back to the witness and the questioning. The DoJ lawyer John Pike shifted his bulk in the armchair, his eyes not leaving Mr. Nashta's face.

"And these keys would be of assistance to you if you were trying to make out a missile silo or, for example, a certain kind of Navy surveillance ship?"

"I told you already all this stuff, Mr. Pike. They could give you an overview of anything — weapons system or vessel or location — whatever you shot. But this case here is about timeliness of delivery. And I keep telling you we delivered this contract on time. Why don't you hear me?" Mr. Nashta was almost hyperventilating now.

Bingo, Robert Crowell thought and discreetly pulled out his phone and checked his messages.

"The missing or misplaced interpretation keys contained what kind of information, Mr. Nashta?" Mr. Pike asked.

His lawyer's hand shot out to stop him, but Mr. Nashta elbowed him aside. "What missing keys? I never said anything like that. I really need a break."

"You were asked to interpret stereograms that contained images of tank deployments on the ground; was that it?"

Mr. Nashta's mouth opened and closed like a furious little guppy. "I don't know anything about that. You're confusing me."

Robert Crowell watched Mr. Nashta thoughtfully. Not a bad job, but prey always sensed the end drawing close even if only subconsciously. It was almost too easy sometimes, or maybe he'd been at this too long.

"Then why don't you tell us what you know about Diego Garcia, Mr. Nashta."

Without another word, the witness shoved back from the table and stormed out of the room. His lawyers hurried after him.

John Pike turned slowly and looked at the Department of Justice lawyers and Robert Crowell with a pointed smile and a wink. "This is recess, then."

Crowell kept his face expressionless. Did satisfaction really come that easily to the big fish of the DoJ pond, or was it all just part of the show? He got to his feet, and they all filed out of the room together. He wasn't glad about the recess, but he was sure his job here was almost done.

Susanna Bailey shook out her hands, pushed her chair back, and rolled her shoulders to loosen the kinks. This unexpected turn of events would set them back timewise, but she still hoped they might finish early enough that she could get started on her government security clearance today. She opened a bottle of sparkling water and walked to the wall of windows facing K Street and looked down onto Franklin Park. The morning's sunshine was gone, and rain streaked the windows. March in D.C. Springtime. Michael had died in the spring.

Never had she felt so alone as those first years after he was gone, nor so dead inside. But somewhere along the way, she realized she was still alive because missing him hurt so much. And then much later, she started wanting to feel good again, whole, happy even. She was still here. She wanted to live. So she worked harder and stayed busier and hoped that was the way back. And now she had the fresh challenge of starting up the Maryland office, and happiness was at the end of that hill she was sure. She drank until her reverie was broken by Mr. Nashta's return.

He was still fidgety, sweating, uneasy. "Oh, Miss Susanna, there you are. That awful man Pike was asking for you."

She turned to see him running a blue plastic comb through his hair, then fluffing the top with his fingers. "Myself, I find that man to be overly demanding." He shoved the comb into his suit pocket and straightened his tie. Susanna looked at him, a question in her eyes.

He shrugged. "Don't ask me, but it was something important. I would definitely assume that."

"He knows where I am."

"No, no," Mr. Nashta said. "He needs you at the receptionist's desk, something about the courier or something."

He must have misunderstood something, but no matter. She locked her computer and closed the screen. She could use the brief walk. But out in the reception area, she didn't see Mr. Pike anywhere. Passing a large, gilt-framed mirror on her way back, she slowed, straightened her suit, and checked to see that makeup still covered the scar on her cheek. In the boardroom, Mr. Nashta was on his phone. He turned to Susanna with a start and crammed the phone into his battered briefcase.

She said, "I didn't see Mr. Pike anywhere."

"Not to worry, I'd say." He seemed distracted and started to pace the room. "Who cares?"

"Are you feeling all right, Mr. Nashta?"

"Why do you ask that?" He fumbled around in his suit pocket and wiped his palms on a balled-up handkerchief. "I'm absolutely fine."

He didn't look fine, but she understood. Testifying was stressful for a lot of witnesses. When everyone returned to the boardroom, the deposition proceeded to drag on for most of the day, much to Susanna's dismay. Finally at half past four, Mr. Nashta insisted on breaking.

"I am feeling most unwell, Mr. Pike. Fully unwell. I am not willing to go on."

Mr. Pike addressed Mr. Nashta's lawyers. "We were hoping to finish this up today."

"Do I not have a say here?" Mr. Nashta demanded, looking around. "Huh? Since when has this American citizen lost his rights?"

Robert Crowell leaned in and spoke in hushed tones with the Department of Justice lawyers. They agreed to finish up the deposition the following morning. Relief washed over Mr. Nashta's face, and it seemed he couldn't get out of there fast enough. As the lawyers huddled, Susanna packed up her things and left the boardroom. When she came into the lobby, Mr. Nashta glanced at her as he jumped into an elevator. She hurried over to catch up, but the elevator doors closed in her face.

Surprised, Susanna waited for the next one, and when she stepped into it, she heard someone calling out, "Hold that elevator, Mr. Nashta." It was not a request so much as a command.

She froze as her fingers hovered over the button.

A strong hand stopped the doors from shutting, and Robert Crowell stepped into the elevator.

CHAPTER
TWO

HE LOOKED AS SURPRISED TO SEE Susanna as she was to
see him.

"Oh," he said, nonplussed. "I was hoping you were
Colin Nashta."

"Sorry to disappoint."

He jabbed at the elevator buttons. "That didn't come
out quite right."

Their gaze tangled, and she looked away as the elevator
doors shut, but she could feel his eyes on her hair, her cheek.
Her hand went to her scar before she could stop herself, and
she forced it back down to her side.

"Mr. Nashta didn't seem his usual talkative self today,"
Robert Crowell said evenly.

"Didn't he?" Susanna looked straight ahead. "I'm sorry,
but I can't talk about the witness in a case with you."

"Of course. Definitely. We wouldn't want to compromise your impartiality," he said, "would we?"

She took a good look at him then, and a slow smile spread across his face. It started in his eyes and went to his mouth. It looked genuine, warm even. Was he flirting with her? It was the last thing she expected, and it took her aback. She turned away and sensed him follow suit.

When she risked another look in his direction, he caught her eye again. But she saw no smoldering there, no innuendo. There was nothing salacious about it. When he smiled again, she felt herself break into a grin in response. Sweet Jesus, this was somehow too intimate. But it felt nice, she had to admit. It would be better if someone spoke. But what to say?

"Why are you smiling?"

"Same reason you are," he said.

She laughed. "Well, my mother told me never to make assumptions about what was going on in other people's minds because it was usually something bad."

He chuckled but stopped when he saw her face. "Really?"

She nodded.

"You don't believe that, do you?"

She shrugged a shoulder. "I don't know."

"Well, my mom always said tie your shoelaces, cracker-jack, or you'll fall flat on your face."

The elevator doors opened and a heavyset man in a yellow shirt stepped into the elevator, pushing a sandwich cart in front of him. He wedged in between Robert and Susanna and glanced at each of them. It was as though a gust of reality blew in on his heels and chilled the air between them. The warmth drained out of Robert's face, and his look became closed and unreadable again.

The sandwich man snuffled and coughed and shifted his weight, and when the elevator opened on the ground floor, he pushed the cart out ahead of him. "Another day, almighty dollar," he muttered under his breath. "Lighten up, people. It's just a frickin' job."

A smirk crossed Robert's face as he followed the man out and held the elevator doors for Susanna. And somewhat awkwardly, they headed for the exit together.

Robert cleared his throat. "So what attracted you to court reporting?" he asked her. "It's a tough job."

Susanna expected him to hurry off without another word, but he was looking at her intently.

She slowed down as around them people bustled past and through the revolving glass doors to K Street beyond. "Okay." She paused, collecting her thoughts. "I guess the opportunity to help put the world to rights in my own tiny way."

He stopped, and Susanna glanced at him. "What? I know it sounds stupid."

"No. I guess I wasn't expecting that, a real answer. That's all."

Susanna blushed. "Interesting witnesses, intriguing cases sometimes. As court reporters, we're the guardians of the record."

They headed out of the building together, and he asked her, "If it's not in your transcripts, it didn't happen?"

She nodded. "We're responsible for a verbatim record of all the testimony in a case, of everything that transpired in a deposition. It helps lawyers build their cases for trial, and it gives judges and juries an accurate record of the evidence. Without that certainty, the legal process doesn't work."

"But don't witnesses lie?" He surprised her with his question.

"More than I ever would have imagined. It gets you down sometimes."

The sidewalk flowed with people hurrying home at the end of the work day. They moved off to the side to avoid getting bumped into. He didn't seem in a hurry to leave.

Flustered, she said, "But it's still a better justice system than any others out there. I just wish people didn't lie quite as easily, cover up so much in self-interest." She met his eyes. "I wish they would do the right thing more often. It's important."

He looked at her as if seeing her for the first time. "Is it?"

"I think so. Maybe if lawyers reminded witnesses of the penalty of perjury more often, it might make people think twice about lying under oath if they knew they could go to prison for it."

"Wouldn't it help if lawyers didn't coach their witnesses in the art of evasion?" Now he was teasing her, with the start of a smile in his eyes. "Or in those mighty lies of omission?" he added.

"Mr. Crowell, I'm a realist. That would be asking for too much."

He laughed, and when his eyes didn't release her, Susanna was glad of it. There was something there that drew her in and made her want to take a step closer to him. She realized she was enjoying herself. What the… She'd always thought that part of her had died along with her husband.

"There are lots of bottom feeders in the legal business. That's true," she hurried to add. "But there are also some heroes out there. And they're the ones that help you keep the faith." And she suddenly felt like an idiot for being so open with this complete stranger.

Why was he looking at her like that? He seemed to have lost his professional decorum the same place she'd lost hers. "Thank you," he said, and a warmth flooded her.

"For what?" she asked, and they both looked away at the same time.

He took his time replying, and when he did, all he said was, "Sounds like a pretty good job, Susanna Bailey." He said her name as if trying to commit it to memory, and without another word, he turned and hurried away through the traffic across K Street and in the other direction.

Susanna watched him go as her mind whirled with what had just happened or not happened between them, and she wondered if he had been as surprised by it as she. There had been a spark she hadn't felt in years, but she instinctively suppressed it. That part of her life was most definitely over, her broken heart dead and buried, and that was where she intended it to stay.

The next morning found Susanna at her steno machine with the lawyers assembled around the boardroom table on either side of her. But Mr. Nashta was late. Robert Crowell wasn't there either. Amid the shuffling of papers, tension in the room mounted as the minutes passed. When people started getting up from the table and milling around, Susanna decided to pop over to the café across the street for an espresso, canvassed the room for requests, and left.

Outside, the smell of wet sidewalk greeted her as she rushed across K Street, tugging at the waistband of her suit skirt as she went. Damn. She refused to give in to the siren call of the next size up. Her suit was getting as uncomfortable as her morning routine sometimes felt – slipping into that proper mindset, the proper attire, the proper business frame of mind. She hurried past Franklin Park to the café, inhaling damp, earthy spring air and car exhaust. She'd try to squeeze a run or a walk in this evening. Dogwoods shivered in their pink glory, and the wind hurtled empty cups and stray newspapers around her feet. She saw some men out of the corner of her eye, sitting on a bench, facing in toward the small park. A soppy, torn leaf slapped her on the hand, making her jump, and she shook it off.

She reached the café and was opening the door when something made her turn and look back. Two of the men had gotten up from the bench and hurried away, leaving the third still sitting. Susanna went through the café door and then stopped short. Of course, she thought, recognizing him. That was Mr. Nashta. She stepped back out into the street. It was definitely him, sitting there on the park bench like he hadn't a care in the world. His collar was turned up, and the wind was dancing with his hair. What was he doing, she wondered as she hurried towards him. Didn't he realize what time it was?

As she approached him, she called his name, but he didn't seem to hear her.

"Mr. Nashta, good morning. It's after 10:00. Everyone's waiting for you."

She reached the bench and hesitated. "Mr. Nashta?" She tapped him on the shoulder, and he fell over heavily. Susanna started, and her mouth went dry.

"Mr. Nashta?" She bent closer to him, tried to lift him back into an upright position, but he slid out of her grip and fell off the park bench with a soft thud onto the matted, dead grass. Her heart jumped. She knelt down beside him and tried to pull him into a sitting position, but her hands shook so hard she couldn't get a good grip on his jacket. She thought she heard someone shouting, but it barely penetrated the fog of fear enveloping her.

And then Robert Crowell was standing above her. "What are you doing here?" he demanded, panting a little and out of breath, surprised to see her.

She faltered as she looked up, recognizing him. What was he doing here? "It's Mr. Nashta, the witness."

"Get away from him," Robert said as he did a quick scan of the area.

Susanna's limbs wouldn't move. "He's either very drunk

or dead. I don't know what happened." She could hear her own voice rising in panic. "I don't see any blood but —"

Robert grabbed her and pulled her to her feet, made sure she could stand. Then he bent down over Mr. Nashta, checked for a pulse and, finding none, quickly patted down the body. He pulled up Mr. Nashta's jacket sleeves as if checking for a wristwatch, went through his pockets, slid his fingers over the inner lining of his jacket, then up and down his pant legs. He lifted each foot and examined the sole of the shoes and cursed when he didn't find whatever he was looking for.

Susanna stood watching him, not understanding what was happening, what he was doing.

When he was done, he got up and focused his attention on her. "Are you all right?" he asked, the harshness leaving his voice. "Look at me. What were you doing here anyway?"

She couldn't answer. At this moment she couldn't even remember her name.

He lifted her chin slowly. "Look at me," he insisted.

Her eyes met his. "He's dead, isn't he," she said.

"It's okay," he said. "You're okay." He put his hands onto her arms. Her body trembled under her suit, but he held on, steadying her, his eyes not leaving hers, and gradually the shaking lessened and she could move again. And she realized that he was reluctant to let go of her.

"What happened to him?" she asked, feeling his hesitation.

His glance swept the park quickly before coming back to her. "We will find out." His voice was quiet and strong, though she sensed the urgency beneath. And his demeanor helped calm her down, soothe her. He wasn't freaking out at all, as if this was all in a day's work for him. He smiled slightly as she met his eyes.

"Better?" he asked.

Susanna nodded. And it was then that she became fully aware of him again and of his attraction to her, all of it seeping into her awareness as she stood over the body of a dead witness by the sidewalk on K Street.

"Good," he said. "I have to ask you something. Did you see anything on Mr. Nashta's body, any papers or anything?"

She answered no.

"What about his watch? Or cigarettes?"

"What?"

"Was there a watch on his wrist when you found him?"

"His watch?" She looked at him, uncomprehending.

The wind was picking up, blowing gray storm clouds over the park. Robert pushed the hair out of her face. "Never mind. It's not important. Listen, you'd better get back."

"The police," she started to say as she fumbled around in her purse for her phone.

Robert pulled his own out of a pocket. "Don't worry. I'm on it. Go on."

"But the police, they'll have questions."

"I'll take care of it. This is my job. It's okay," he repeated as he propelled her away from Mr. Nashta's lifeless form and from the group of people starting to gather. "Go let the lawyers know what's happened."

He nodded when she threw him a backward glance, and as she crossed K Street, the first raindrop fell on her cheek. Inside the law firm, the news of Mr. Nashta's death left the lawyers in a state of consternation and a flurry of phone calls. Through the blur of shock, Susanna wondered aloud if someone had called Mr. Nashta's family or if he even had one, but no one seemed to hear. She glanced out the window at the scene unfolding in Franklin Park below. The rain had started in earnest, and there were police down there now and people with all sorts of equipment. She could make out some kind of black tarp covering Mr. Nashta's body.

"That poor man," she murmured. "Never late for anything." Her hands went to the windowpane, but the cold glass made her start. Did he have a heart attack? He did seem a little uneasy the previous day. But if he was feeling ill, what was he doing out in the park? The police would want to talk to her. Two men. There were two men with Mr. Nashta when she had first spotted him. She'd have to tell them about that.

She was turning away from the window when she noticed Robert Crowell off to the side, some distance from the scene. He was pulling up the hood of his jacket against the rain, and he was involved in what looked like a heated discussion with another man and a woman. He had told her not to worry, that he would deal with things. Was that out of concern and kindness to her? She swallowed hard. Shock tasted metallic in her throat. As she watched, Robert jumped into a dark-colored car and sped off, followed by the other two in a black, unmarked van. She turned away.

Once more death had come calling with a wink and a jeer and left her reeling.

Susanna didn't remember leaving the law firm. When she got to her car, it took all her strength to heave her equipment into the trunk and ready herself to battle the never-ending traffic. The city smelled of rain and damp. Shivering, she pulled out onto Constitution Avenue, past the looming granite monoliths that lined the street, past the White House and the Washington Monument. Overhead a military helicopter descended in a deafening roar to nearby Fort Myers. Through her windshield, she watched straggling groups of wet tourists being whipped about by the wind as they wandered among the blooming Japanese cherry trees lining the banks of the Potomac River. She couldn't remember the last time it was actually warm for the Cherry Blossom Festival.

Her mind went back to the park. What had Robert Crowell been doing there? The traffic started to move, and her car merged into the flow over the Roosevelt Bridge and into the Northern Virginia suburbs.

This morning there had been three men sitting on a bench chatting, and now one of them was dead. And he just happened to be the witness in the case she was doing. Oh, great. Wait until the office found out about that.

CHAPTER
THREE

SAFELY AT HOME, SUSANNA STEPPED out of the crumple of black crepe suit at her feet, into the embrace of her jeans and an old Metallica t-shirt, and forced herself downstairs to make something to eat. Finding a dead witness wasn't an everyday occurrence in the life of a court reporter. She needed to hang on to some semblance of routine after the day's shock. Patent and trademark work, construction disputes, government contracts, medical and corporate malfeasance, stock market fraud, an assortment of the more pedestrian yet insidious crimes and offenses, that was what made up her daily bread and butter. In the kitchen, her eyes swept over a shelf full of beautiful, glossy cookbooks, most of them unsplattered and unused, and stopped at the flashing light on her phone.

She was one of the few holdouts who still believed in a landline and answering machine as well as a cell. She listened to her message as she opened the fridge. It was empty but for a box of baking soda and a packet of cellophane-wrapped tomatoes.

"Hey babe, it's Gracie. Don't forget mani/pedi poker night. You're bringing nail polish this time. Everyone else has the food part covered. Is Farida coming or not? Call me."

In the cupboard Susanna found some packages of spaghetti, and as the pasta cooked, she gazed out the kitchen window at the bamboo swaying in the neighbor's yard. She hadn't realized that Robert Crowell was some kind of investigator. Hadn't they said he was from the Department of Defense? The Japanese maple that she and Michael had planted their first year here was leafing out, purple and magnificent now. As she stirred the strands of spaghetti, her mind leapt from thought to thought, unable to focus on any one thing. She rifled through the drawer for scissors to cut up some basil from the plant on her window sill.

Her eyes fluttered shut as she inhaled the pungent green aroma. Oh, damn you, Michael. For the first year after his death, it had caused her actual physical pain to roll over in bed at night into the empty space beside her. No warm male body. Not even the smell of him after a while. And with him had vanished the other dreams – making babies, growing old together. She took out the cutting board and started chopping up some tomatoes. Damn you. Growing up, she had been certain that if she only reached that mythical state of sane adulthood, having slain all fire-breathing dragons, she would get her chance at playing happy families. And she had gotten close.

They bought this home together in an old, pretty neighborhood of giant trees and gently rolling hills, lovely despite being filled to the gills with bureaucrats, lobbyists, and defense industry types. It was called Falls Church, and it sat around a small lake in which you could swim and boat and fish. And then Michael had died of an aneurysm, sudden and unexpected, leaving Susanna in pieces and dissolving her world into something liquid and unrecognizable. But she had buried her shattered heart and made her peace with all that. So where was this coming from today? She would have loved to talk with him right now about what had happened. That was all.

She pulled the strainer out. "I'm a woman of great resilience and strength," she muttered as she strained the pasta, hoping the words sunk in as she said them. "Great resilience and strength." Only 51, but right now she was feeling older than a century. She would call Gracie back or have a glass of wine with Farida. As she reached for the olive oil, the doorbell buzzed, making her jump and sending the bottle crashing to the floor. She hadn't been expecting anyone. Grabbing for some paper towel, she glanced out the window and saw an older man in a suit. Looked like he was collecting for charity. She threw some paper towels onto the spill and hurried to the door.

The man smiled at Susanna as if they were friends,

flashed a badge in front of her face, and whisked it away before she could get a look at it. "How are you, dear? Good evening. I hope I'm not interrupting dinner."

Dear? She was instantly on guard, thrown by his condescending tone. "I didn't quite get —"

"Do you mind if I come in?" He pulled out a hard-backed binder and flipped it open.

Susanna hesitated. "Well, actually —"

"Not to worry, not at all. I'll just get right to the point here, if you don't mind." His manner was courteous, his hair was white, but his voice was hard as slate. "I'm from the Defense Security Service, and we're making inquiries about some of your neighbors. Two doors up, actually. Just routine. And I was wondering if you wouldn't mind answering a few questions about them?"

"My neighbors?"

"Two doors up. Brown house with that big old magnolia on the front lawn. Nice Audi. You know the one? We're making inquiries, you know, habits, hours they keep, things like that. Routine stuff."

"I don't know them at all," Susanna said. "They're hardly ever around."

"Is that right?" The smile stayed on his face as he checked off some boxes on his pad. "Of course, anything you can tell me will help. For instance, what time do you see them coming home in the evenings?" He looked at her, waiting for an answer. Was he doing a security clearance on somebody? Is this how they were done? Did it really involve government agents snooping around the neighborhood, asking random neighbors questions? It felt creepy.

"Who did you say you were with?" she asked him. Or maybe this was something else.

His smile was so sincere it struck her as sinister. "Nice accent," he replied. "You are a U.S. citizen, aren't you?"

She laughed out loud at his non sequitur. "No, actually, I'm not."

"Really? Whereabouts, if you don't mind —"

"I'm Canadian, but you haven't answered my question."

"Oh, I see. Well, thank you very much, but you shouldn't have wasted my time." He turned and started scribbling in his binder as he walked back to the street.

Wasted his time? Apprehension settled around Susanna like a prickly blanket as she watched him. What the hell was that about? In this town, it was always hard to pin the source of your unease to something concrete, she thought as she mopped up the spill on her floor and sat down to eat. Washington D.C. was like a large, constantly shifting mirage. You never could be sure that what you were looking at was actually what was going on. It was an unsettling experience, one of the things that bothered her about living here, that sense of parallel realities. And it was something she'd not experienced anywhere else.

After a few mouthfuls of lukewarm pasta, she pushed the plate aside. The morning's shock was wearing off, and a deep exhaustion drifted over her. The guy's visit reminded her that she had yet to tackle her own government security clearance application. She had to get to that. But maybe she'd call Gracie back first about poker night. Or go for a long walk. She decided the best option was to lay her head down for a second to consider her choices more fully. Just a quick second.

A cold, colorless dawn found Susanna asleep at the kitchen table. She shifted and fell off the chair, banging her head on the granite floor. Disoriented, she sat up in the gloom, wincing, looking around, and pushed away the hair plastered to the side of her face. Rubbing her head gingerly, she considered whether crying was an option. Then the thought hit her that she was late for work, and she scrambled to her feet. But when she saw the previous night's dinner congealed on the table, it all came back to her. There was no job to rush to because Mr. Nashta was dead.

Soon she would have to call her office and fill them in on what had happened, but it was still early. Dragging herself up the stairs stiffly, she ached for the comfort of her bedroom and more sleep. She wondered if she was suffering from PTSD. Her body hit the bed, and her last thought before drifting off was of the mysterious Robert Crowell. The insistent buzzing of her cell phone woke her up what seemed like mere minutes later. A warm morning beckoned at her window as she put the phone to her ear.

"What in the world happened with your case yesterday, Susanna?"

"Oh, shit." She was instantly alert. "Morning, Randolph." As she yawned and stretched and got out of bed, she realized that she was actually feeling better.

"Are you all right?" Randolph Bush asked. His concern was almost convincing, until he didn't wait for her reply. "When we didn't hear from you yesterday, we didn't know what to think. I'm not pointing fingers now. Dead witness, not your fault."

Susanna could hear the calming intake of breath before he went on.

"But one has to pause. Is this kind of news good for the growth of the agency?"

"Thanks for your concern, but I'm fine," Susanna said sarcastically. She put the phone on speaker mode, pulled on some fresh clothes, then headed downstairs to her study, the phone cradled in her shoulder as she filled him in on the previous day's events.

"Well, that explains the phone call I got a couple minutes ago," he said. "Someone from the Department of Justice, asking if Madam Reporter Susanna Bailey would come down to the judge's chambers at the Alexandria, Virginia courthouse. Apparently, the judge on their case has squeezed in some kind of emergency meeting, and they thought their case was about to be dismissed. Of course I didn't know what they were effing talking about."

She imagined the scowl on his face. A veteran reporter himself, Randolph Bush ran a smooth, efficient operation, kept close tabs on all the reporters and their assignments, and he didn't handle unexpected bumps in the road well.

"And they were sure the judge would have a few questions for the court reporter who found the body," Randolph went on, emphasizing the last couple of words with displeasure. "'What body?' I inquired politely and was told that the reporter would be able to explain everything."

"Sorry I didn't get a chance to call yesterday, but I was wiped out." Susanna started to unpack the Nashta job and organize it for her scopist-assistant Farida Rafik, who would be editing it. "I was beyond exhausted. Must have been the shock. Do you think I might have PTSD?"

"Your jokes are not funny this early in the morning."

"Not joking."

"And I've got a load of stuff on my plate to get to." An undertow of anger pulled at Bush's tone, and Susanna sighed. His worry for her was touching, she thought sourly.

"Hey, don't we have our Maryland office meeting this afternoon?" she asked. "I've got it pretty well worked out." Taking her papers out of her bag as she listened to him, her eyes fell on something in the bottom of the bag, in among all the paperwork. She pulled everything out to get a better look. And froze.

Randolph Bush was still talking. "We've got to reschedule that, and you have got to get on over to the courthouse pronto, Susanna. I know it's short notice, but I just got the call myself. By the way, I hope you've sent in the paperwork for your security clearance."

Susanna stared down at the two, eight-by-eleven aerial photographs. These were stereograms. This is what they had been talking about in the deposition the last couple days.

Her heart jumped into her throat, choking her. She turned them over in her hands, not understanding. But there were no exhibit stickers on them, as she had first suspected. So she hadn't accidentally taken home evidence from Mr. Nashta's deposition, which would have been impossible since every exhibit was marked "Highly Confidential" and remained in the lawyer's possession at the end of the day. She turned them over frantically again. So where did these stereograms come from, and how did they get into her bag?

"Susanna? Hello?"

She managed to suck in a breath.

"Susanna? Are you still there?"

And what the hell is this? Susanna turned over the tiny memory stick that had been taped to the back of one of the stereograms. This is definitely not mine either.

"Susanna?"

She broke out in a cold sweat as she stammered, "Oh, sorry."

"Get on over there. Judge's chambers, second floor." He paused. "And then afterwards, go take yourself a couple days off... because I care."

She didn't bother with a smart retort. "No, no. I'm fine."

"That's an order. We'll deal with the Maryland office when you get back. You could use the break, Susanna."

"I'm... I'm on my way."

She quickly put everything back into her bag and shoved the bag into the back of her closet. She would figure this all out later.

Inside the imposing old Alexandria courthouse, the meeting was already in progress in the judge's chambers. As Susanna slipped into the room, a couple of the lawyers turned and nodded. Much to her surprise, Robert Crowell was there as well. He looked at her briefly before turning back to the judge, who was writing something at her desk.

The judge handed him a sheaf of papers. "Military Tribunal, soon as possible." Then she turned and looked at Susanna, not certain who she was.

One of the Department of Justice lawyers stepped in. "Your Honor, this is Ms. Bailey, the court reporter. She's the one who found the witness's body in Franklin Park. She and Mr. Crowell, Officer Crowell —" His eyes went to Robert Crowell, and he didn't finish his sentence.

The judge motioned Susanna over to a chair in front of her desk, and Susanna sat down and proceeded to answer her questions. Robert moved off to the side of the room, but his eyes didn't leave Susanna. She stole a glance at him, and this time he acknowledged her with a barely perceptible nod.

Struggling to bring her attention back to the judge's questions, she described the two men with Mr. Nashta on that bench and everything else she could think of about the previous morning. Unbidden, the stereograms she had just found came to her mind. Should she tell the judge about them? Susanna froze. Maybe not. What if the judge thought she had stolen them? That was crazy of course, but the judge didn't know her. Oh Jesus, her office would find out. No, she had to think this through. She would stay calm and answer only the specific questions asked at this time.

When Susanna was done, the judge thanked her and asked all of them to give her a few minutes. There was an empty courtroom next door where they could wait for her. She would join them momentarily with her decision. Giving the judge a slight nod, Susanna stood up, started to move away, and backed into someone. She turned to apologize and came face to face with Robert Crowell. She practically jumped back, and her heel caught on a chair leg. She stumbled, tried to regain her balance, and her foot shot out, clipping him hard on the shin, and sending her sprawling to the ground.

Blinking, she bit back a yelp of pain. "How embarrassing. I'm so sorry." She was an utter mess of nerves at this point. It felt like her whole life was falling down around her. She had to keep it together.

Robert got down beside Susanna to help her to her feet. The unexpected kindness she saw in his eyes flustered her even more.

"Thank you," she said, feeling like a complete idiot. "My heel must have caught — did I hurt you?"

He chuckled. "No."

"Are you okay?"

He stopped midsentence and considered her, and she felt herself blushing under his gaze.

"Hell, no," he said in an undertone, echoing her words from the elevator the first time they met.

She stared at him. "Oh, my," she whispered. He wasn't supposed to say that.

"What about you? Are you okay?" he asked her.

"I was in a hurry. I wasn't paying attention. Too much stuff on my mind." She paused. Was he looking at her legs? "I apologize again," she added.

"I'll live," he said and reached out a hand to her.

As their fingers touched, Susanna almost pulled away. Invisible sparks flew. What was going on here? He stopped as well. Their eyes locked, a building awareness of each other all over again. No, no, no, this could not be happening.

When they realized the lawyers from the Justice Department were standing above them, waiting, Susanna let Robert help her to her feet. Then someone called to him, and he was gone.

CHAPTER:
FOUR

ROBERT CROWELL FROWNED as he stepped into the court-room, thankful for the cool, dark interior, the quiet hum of emptiness that permeated the room before the lawyers started to file in. What the hell had he been thinking? Had he lost his fucking mind? In the midst of an operation? Susanna Bailey was a witness, for God's sake. This whole job was taking longer than planned, and the suits were getting more annoying by the day. Or was he just getting sloppy? That was a possibility, and did he even care? He was supposed to be long gone by now, and that bastard Nashta was not supposed to be dead.

He sat down and loosened his tie and tried to focus on the hushed conversation of the lawyers around him. He had a mission to finish, and he would finish it cleanly. And then he would move on to the next one. Or hang up his spurs if he chose. Except nothing awaited him on the other side of burnout, so why bother. But he'd never veered off course like this before. It was not like him.

The strongest urge to lean over and kiss her had overcome him back there on the floor. Susanna seemed to be unaware of the effect she was having on him. Like some testosterone-fueled kid, he hadn't been able to keep his eyes off her legs. He guessed that a good twenty-four hours locked away in an excellent hotel room with her would probably scratch that itch, cure him well enough, but he already sensed that wasn't who she was and that she wouldn't take such things lightly.

Nor could he ignore the fact that he had found her in Franklin Park clutching Colin Nashta's lifeless body. She was involved in this. His gut told him no, but that probably wasn't his gut talking. He just needed to be done with this job and get the hell out, not start getting personal here. He'd been down that road before, and it hadn't worked for him. That's just the way life went.

But there was something natural and unstudied about Susanna that made her insanely appealing, and it was driving him to distraction. It made him want to get to know her, to figure out how to tease a smile out of her again. He was a sucker for sexy smart and liked the veiled strength he saw there and that vulnerable something that she worked so hard to hide. It was a heady mix that had him losing his focus, and it had been clouding his judgment since they met.

He would have to do something about the situation, and fast.

Out in the courthouse hallway, Susanna drank coffee out of paper cups with Mr. Nashta's lawyers, and they commiserated briefly about poor Mr. Nashta and the funeral arrangements and the spiraling crime rate in Washington, D.C. And were the garbage collectors on strike again because did you see how much trash there was in Franklin Park? Something had got to be done about that.

And then they headed into the darkened courtroom to wait for the judge. Susanna slid into a wooden bench in the back row and scanned the cavernous shadows. It was a shame the city didn't keep up the insides of these majestic old buildings as nicely as the exteriors, she thought. It was always such a letdown when you came inside only to stumble upon a rundown '70s flashback.

She spotted Robert among the Department of Justice lawyers. He was huddled and whispering with one of them. Always whispering. The policy of keeping secrets. It's what kept the wheels turning in Washington, D.C. She took in his fine black suit, the crisp white shirt with the top couple buttons undone, the tie hanging loosely, and his dark hair just flicking the back of his shirt collar. And she had the strongest urge to run her fingers gently over that spot on the back of his neck and kiss him there. Then she would grab a fistful of his hair in her hand. She shifted on the courtroom bench. There was something dark and primal in that man that whispered to her, coaxing her out of a deep sleep, awakening feelings she hadn't expected to be feeling at this point in her life.

As if sensing Susanna's eyes on him, Robert turned and caught her watching him. Best to ignore him, she decided, blushing. But she didn't turn away like she intended to. She smiled at him instead. And he smiled back. And they stayed that way for she didn't know how long, held in some magic space where time had caught on the fabric of reality. And the next thing she knew, he was on his feet and walking toward her. Flustered and suddenly nervous, she was aware of the way his eyes moved over her as he approached, and now somehow her light spring dress and bare legs left her feeling too exposed, defenseless.

When he reached her side, he bent down and murmured in her ear, "I need some fresh air. What about you?" And before she could answer, he took her by the hand again, and she let him. Her breath caught in her throat. What was he doing? She felt his hand start to loosen his hold on hers, and she pressed her fingers gently against his to stop him. "Fresh air, yes," she agreed.

Pulling her to her feet, they walked out of the courtroom together as a few lawyers glanced their way. In the hall, Robert looked down at her hand, still firmly caught in his. "Do you have a problem with this?" His voice was soft and hard at the same time, and it made her belly do a tiny somersault. His eyes searched her face, and then he said, "Good."

He hurried them outside and down the steps to the cobblestoned courtyard where people stood smoking and chatting in the noonday sun and a vendor sold hotdogs and tacos from a sidewalk cart.

Robert cast around impatiently. He seemed to be looking for a more private spot.

"Did anyone find out what happened to Mr. Nashta?" Susanna managed to ask as her heart fluttered and jumped.

"Yes — no." Robert stumbled thickly over his words and cursed under his breath. "Let's just say it wasn't a heart attack," he said, still holding her tightly by the hand as he led her around the corner to the side of the courthouse. There was no one here. It was peaceful and still but for the birdsong raining down on them from the yellow and white magnolia trees that lined that side of the old building. Robert's eyes didn't leave Susanna as he pulled her over to the wall, up against the warm, rough brick, and she met his gaze.

It was that moment of no turning back, and Susanna recognized it like an old friend. He took her face gently in his hands and kissed her slowly on the mouth. And then more greedily as his body pressed against hers. And she found herself drowning in the hunger and abandon and luxury of it. She didn't remember ever being kissed quite like that before, and her whole body responded. It was beautiful, intoxicating. She felt drunk on the strength of his need and the closeness of his body.

Her hands moved under his suit jacket and over his chest. And in that moment, she didn't care where she was. She needed to feel the heat of his bare skin under her fingertips, and nothing else would do. Searching frantically for his shirt buttons, she felt something beneath his shirt and stopped. Hard plates, cold, ungiving. And she pulled back. It startled her out of her desire. Was he wearing some kind of body armor? A bullet-proof vest?

Before she could catch her breath, Robert let her go and stepped back with a violent shake of his head, as if trying to snap out of the spell that had fallen over them.

"We better get back inside." He grabbed Susanna's hand in his again but didn't meet her eyes. "What the fuck am I doing? I'm sorry. I've never done anything this stupid before."

"Don't be sorry," she started to say. "Wait a minute."

Without another word, he hurried her back into the building, back into the darkened courtroom, and she didn't even have a chance to gather her thoughts or pull herself together. Susanna poured herself into the seat in a daze, and Robert hurried back to the front and planted himself down next to the Department of Defense lawyers, his back to her again.

Susanna's body trembled, her mind whirled. What the hell just happened? She tried to corral the unspoken words and sensations clamoring for attention. Unexpected as it was, that kiss had felt like a tiny life raft in the midst of a stormy sea. But which bloody rule book did this guy play by?

The judge came into the courtroom and told the assembled group that, based on the facts as they now stood, she had decided to stay the proceedings in this venue and pass the file on to the appropriate body, be it the Intelligence Tribunal, the Military Court, or otherwise. The lawyers buzzed with subdued excitement while Robert Crowell sat quiet and pensive in their midst. When the judge excused herself and left, everyone started to file out of the courtroom. The lawyers acknowledged Susanna as they passed. Robert didn't even look in her direction.

She was taken aback and for a fleeting second thought she had imagined what had happened between them, but she could still taste him on her lips. She groaned aloud and practically dug her nails into the bench in front of her. There was no doubt that she was, in fact, still fully alive.

And she also remembered what Robert had intimated, that Mr. Nashta had been murdered. Why would someone want to kill Mr. Nashta? She had seen him with her own eyes, sitting on that bench, chatting without a care in the world. It was crazy. After a while she realized she was the only person in the courtroom and got up and left. Coming down the courthouse steps, she headed for the elevator that went down to the parking garage under the building.

The words flew past Susanna's ear like the faintest breeze, and she barely caught them in time. "Remember, little one, it is in the shelter of each other that the people live." She glanced around. No one was there. And for the smallest millisecond, a memory stirred in the recesses of her mind. Big Dave Bailey? Did she just hear his voice? She must really be tired and confused if she was hallucinating about her good ole da, that drunken Irish ne'er-do-well she hadn't seen in decades.

This had definitely been one long day. Stepping out of the elevator into the underground parking garage, she headed for the attendant's booth to drop off her parking ticket and pick up her keys and stopped in her tracks. Robert Crowell stood in the dim light, speaking with the parking attendant. Both men turned when they heard her approach.

"Come on. Let me walk you to your car," Robert said as she joined them.

Susanna found herself at a loss for words. He took her car keys from the attendant. The urgency she had sensed in him earlier was gone now. His voice was quiet, gentle, and his fingers brushed the small of her back as they headed for her car.

Oh, don't do that, she thought and stepped out of his reach. She felt his eyes on her the whole time. When they got to the car, she had to lean against it. She was aware of engines starting somewhere, tires rubbing against concrete, and the beating of her heart. After a while she looked at Robert. There was a jumble of thoughts in her head, and she couldn't decide which was the most important. "My name is Susanna. Susanna Bailey."

"Robert Crowell." His voice barely audible. "And I do believe we've met."

She smiled despite herself. This guy was heady stuff.

He watched her shift from one leg to the other. "I'm sorry about what happened earlier," he said. "You can punch me if you want. I deserve it. I'd understand."

"My pleasure," she murmured but didn't make a move.

Searching her face, he leaned closer and brushed her cheek briefly. She could smell his skin again, delicious lingering traces of the morning's aftershave. He seemed to hesitate, and she heard his labored breath as he took a step back.

"Listen, I have to go. I just needed to apologize and make sure you were fine."

"What?" She could only shake her head in confusion.

"You don't want this, Susanna." He looked away, took his time. "I put the world out of my mind for one brief minute, pure and simple. You did that to me. Thank you. But the world is insistent, still waiting. I shouldn't even be here right now."

"Why?" She looked at him. "What do you mean? Why did you need to make sure I was all right then?"

He glanced around the dimly lit garage and then back at her. "It doesn't matter. I really have to get out of here," he said but didn't move.

She studied him. "Are you a cop or something?"

"No. Why do you ask that?"

"You're wearing a bullet-proof vest. I felt it."

"I'm not a cop, no. The Kevlar I wear, cops can't afford."

"So are you married, Robert? Is that it?"

"That's who you think I am?" he asked, and he looked taken aback. "No. Divorced. Are you married?"

"Widowed."

"Oh. I'm sorry."

"It's been a while. One day he was 50 and thought he'd be around forever. Next day he was dead," she said dryly. "And I'm still here."

"You shouldn't be alone, Susanna Bailey," he murmured.

She reached her hand up to the nape of his neck and took a fistful of his hair between her fingers, and it felt as good to her as she had imagined it would.

"Neither should you, Robert Crowell." She let her hand drop.

An amused look scratched the surface of his face, but Susanna saw the struggle in his eyes. He moved closer to her again until his body was warm and hard against hers and his fingers caressed the palm of her hand. Her skin drank up his touch. She hadn't understood until now how much she missed that part of her life. Robert bent his head toward her, and she thought he was about to kiss her, but he stopped himself before his mouth reached hers, and he practically moaned aloud as he pulled away.

Muttering under his breath, he reached behind her, unlocked her car, and opened the door for her. "Get into your car so I don't have to worry about you. And I've got to get out of here. I truly am sorry." He pressed the keys into her hand, turned and headed for the exit.

Susanna couldn't believe it. She wanted to jump on him and beat him with her fists.

"You are the biggest idiot I've ever met," she called after him, but he was gone.

Good riddance, she thought. She didn't need more complications in her life. She may have been confused about things, but he was a damn fool.

She got into her car and slammed the door shut as hard as she could.

CHAPTER:
FIVE

"I CANNOT BELIEVE MR. NASHTA IS DEAD." Farida Rafik swept a curtain of glossy black hair behind her ear and dabbed the last of her crusty bread around the salad bowl, soaking up the dressing. "It's shocking." She stared at Susanna as she chewed methodically.

The warm, buttery aroma of chocolate croissants and profiteroles caressed their senses as it wafted through the Corner Bakery Café on L Street and mixed with the low hum of conversation around them. Susanna nodded at her friend as she brought a napkin to her mouth. "The girls want to know if you're coming to mani/pedi poker this month. Bring booze or a potluck dish. And lots of spare change."

"I'll think about it. Do you want to share a lemon square?"

"I have to tell you something," Susanna muttered through a mouthful of chopped salad. She cleared her throat and pushed her plate aside.

"Actually, I might come to poker night." Farida let out a long, satisfied sigh. "Maybe we should forget the lemon square. I'm stuffed. Iced coffee?"

"I don't care."

"Oh, I forgot. You're off coffee, aren't you? You're the anti-coffee now. Tea, then?"

"Sure. Fine. But listen —"

Farida got up and headed over to the counter to order their drinks. The jewel tones of her sari glimmered in the soft light. Susanna took a quick look around the café before taking a manila envelope out of her bag and pulling out the two stereograms she had found among her things earlier. When Farida returned with their drinks, she lay them out on the table in front of her.

"These are aerial photographs. Stereograms. Two of them."

Farida looked at them, momentary confusion crossing her face, and picked them up.

"Don't look so blank." Susanna pushed her tea aside.

"Hold your doggy. I'm sensing a little frustration, nervous tension. Relax, will you?"

"I am very relaxed," Susanna hissed. "Aerial photographs, Farida."

Farida stared at her. "Yes, I can see that you are very relaxed." She held the aerial photographs up to the light to

examine them. "Wow, stereograms." A stack of gold brace-
lets jangled as they shifted on her arm. "I have been editing
your transcripts. I know what these are. Where did you get
these?" She paused, and her eyes grew wide. "Shouldn't they
all be marked highly confidential?"

"I found them in my bag the day after Mr. Nashta was
killed." Susanna leaned closer in. "But no exhibit stickers
on them. Look. I've never seen them before."

Farida locked eyes with Susanna. "So how did they end
up in your bag?"

Susanna shook her head as she took the two stereograms
from Farida and slid them back into a manila envelope and
back into her bag without taking her eyes off Farida.

"So give them back," Farida whispered.

"Give them back to who?"

Farida's eyes grew wide. "The lawyers, I suppose."

"Oh, okay. Great idea. And then they'll think I stole
them. Do you know what kind of trouble I'd be in? And
why would the lawyers put these into my bag anyway? That
doesn't make sense."

"You're right. It doesn't." Farida thought. "By the way,
did your security clearance come through yet?

Susanna could only shake her head.

"Oh shit," Farida murmured. "If someone thinks you
stole them, you can wave goodbye to that."

"No kidding," Susanna practically hissed.

"This is not good. You shouldn't be in possession of
highly classified government documents. What about Mr.

Nashta or his lawyers? Drink some tea. It's good for the nerves."

Susanna took a sip of her tea. "What about them? Mr. Nashta interpreted aerial photographs of military stuff on some kind of secret computer systems. That's all I know about it. He wasn't running around stealing these things and throwing them into court reporters' bags. This lawsuit was about late delivery on a contract, as far as I could make out."

"Are you absolutely sure of that?" Farida studied Susanna for a moment and then pulled her laptop out and placed it on the table. "Nashta was quite knowledgeable, wasn't he?" She turned the computer on and slid closer to Susanna. Around them, the crowd of diners was starting to thin.

Susanna moved the plates and glasses aside. "You've been editing the transcripts. You know as much as I do about this."

Farida said, "How about the judge? Give them to her."

"Oh, great, okay. And how will I explain it to her when I don't even know how they got into my possession. You think she'll believe that? There goes my security clearance for sure. And I can wave goodbye to the Maryland office."

"That's true," Farida said. She pulled her laptop toward her and retrieved the Nashta transcript and started scanning through it. "Look. Here." She pointed at a line of text. They were looking at aerial shots of military facilities, things of interest to the military."

"Uh-huh. Down further," Susanna prompted, her eyes on the screen. "Listen to this answer. 'You have to use the photo interpretation keys and the aerial photographs together to be able to identify what you're looking at. Without these keys, the aerial photographs are pretty worthless. They're put together to aid a photo interpreter in identifying a particular kind of thing, like naval ships or airfields or geological features on the ground.'"

"So he was the photo interpreter, looking at military – probably highly classified — photographs."

"And the things in my bag are definitely aerial photographs," Susanna said.

"Right," Farida said. "You somehow are in possession of two aerial photos. But these are not stereograms because stereograms are the whole package, the whole book of information — the photo interpretation keys and the aerial photos put together to interpret these photographs."

Susanna took a breath. "Actually, that wasn't all —"

"So Mr. Nashta works for a government contractor," Farida went on, "doing this big military contract."

"Used to work," Susanna said.

They looked at each other. "He worked, past tense, on this big military contract," Susanna lowered her voice, "and the government was suing his company."

"For being late delivering on the contract and for doing a bad job to boot," Farida added, untangling strands of glossy hair caught in one of her hoop earrings. "So the military takes pictures of all kinds of secret stuff from the sky –"

"Wait. Look at this." Susanna pointed further down on the screen. "Answer: These photo interpretation keys, also known as PI keys, were books that were prepared by the military."

"Yeah, we got that part. The photo interpretation keys are the code books that help you decipher what's on those aerial photographs."

Susanna read on. "Some are available in the civilian world, but that's much less common."

"Right. Secret military code books," Farida said, "not available in the civilian world." She paused as she looked at Susanna. "I have three words for you – illegal, military, secret scary."

"Thanks. Just the reassurance I needed."

Farida mouthed the word "Sorry."

They stared at each other.

"Maybe it was Nashta that dumped those things in your bag."

"Why in the world would he do something like that? That doesn't make any sense. The man is dead now anyway."

"Nothing about this makes sense." Farida's eyes narrowed. "Wait a minute. What were you about to say earlier?"

Susanna hesitated. "You think those photo interpretation code books could maybe be kept on a little computer memory stick?"

Farida raised her eyebrows slowly. "Why do you ask?"

"The pictures weren't the only things I found in my bag." Susanna paused as a waiter came by and started to clear off their table. Susanna glanced up at him. Circles of sweat stained the armpits of his shirt. "Thanks very much. That was delicious," she said to him.

He grunted something they couldn't understand and hurried off, the plates balanced precariously on his arm.

"And I thought I was having a hard day." Susanna frowned. "Let's go through this step by step. The government said the contractor was late in delivery of a contract."

"And the contractor is countersuing and saying, 'We did the job. Pay us our money.' And that's about all we know for sure."

"It seems like everyday stuff, Farida. Murder just doesn't make sense here, does it, if it's just two sides arguing about paying a bill? You don't kill over that."

"I guess it depends how outrageous the bill was. Ha, ha. But what were you saying about a memory stick?"

"There was a little USB flash drive in the bag with the stereograms. And I swear to you it's not mine either."

"So what's on it?"

Susanna shrugged. "Do you want to venture a guess?"

"The bloody photo interpretation keys," Farida whispered. "I'd bet money on it. It's the keys to interpret those two aerial photographs." She shook out her long hair and then grabbed it, twisting it into a knot at the back of her head and snapped a clasp over it. "It would be good if I was wrong, but as we both know, I hardly ever am. Ask Sanjay."

Susanna didn't bother smiling. "I need to get rid of these things. I've got to get rid of it all."

"Calm down," Farida said. "Listen, maybe Mr. Nashta's

death was just a random mugging in the park. Happens all the time."

"Or maybe not." Susanna shook her head. "The worst part is I have no idea where to turn, who to even give this stuff to without somehow incriminating myself."

"Honestly, Susanna, you need to slow down. Don't let fear push you into a misstep. Don't give it to anyone right now. Mum's the word. Let's think about this before you jump."

"You're right. I've got to think this through."

"Don't return it to just anyone to be rid of it. That may get you into even more trouble. Remember, at this point nobody knows you have it. Right?"

Susanna hesitated. "I don't think so."

"So that's good. And that's the way we want to keep it. Caution is what I'm saying."

Susanna took a deep breath.

"We will figure it out," Farida said. "I'll help you. Don't worry. We stay silent until we can figure out what to do. You can't afford to jeopardize your security clearance."

"And maybe Mr. Nashta's death had nothing to do with the lawsuit at all," Susanna nodded. "This is D.C. Right? Bang, bang in the park. Not that rare."

Farida shrugged as she sat back in her chair and looked around the restaurant. "I don't know what's going on, Susanna, but you must remain circumspect. You don't want to get sucked into whatever the heck this is." She paused and studied Susanna's face. "Wait a minute. What else are you not telling me? I know you too well. We've been friends for too long for you to hide anything from me."

"Well, there was someone else at the deposition I didn't tell you about," Susanna said slowly, not sure how to even express the turmoil of her thoughts over what had happened with Robert.

Farida's eyes moved beyond her and a smile lit up her face. "Over here, Sanjay," she called out with a wave.

Susanna turned to see Farida's husband, a big man in a bright sports jersey, motioning from the restaurant doorway. "Car's double-parked out front. Don't want to get a ticket." He waved to Susanna. "Hello, Susanna. See you soon, I'm sure."

She gave him a quick wave back.

Farida closed her laptop and packed up her things. "We'll talk very, very soon, like tomorrow." She gave Susanna a hug, and as she headed for the exit, she glanced back over her shoulder. "I'll e-mail the first day's transcript to you tonight, when we get home from the game."

And with a wave, she disappeared out the door with Sanjay. Susanna watched the door close after her. Luck had definitely been smiling on her when it sent Farida into her life, her editing assistant and friend all in one lovely package.

She started to gather her things together when she noticed that she had forgotten to actually give Farida the final day of Mr. Nashta's deposition still to be edited. Grabbing the brown manila envelope, she jumped up and rushed out the bakery door and caught them just as their car was pulling away from the curb. Farida rolled down her window.

"Last day of deposition," Susanna said, breathless. "Sorry about that." She pushed the envelope through the window. "It's a five-day delivery."

"Thank goodness one of us still has our wits about us." Farida laughed as she took the package.

After Susanna waved them off, she slipped back into the Corner Bakery, waved the waiter over and paid the bill. As she dropped her wallet back into her bag, she did a double take. The stereograms in the manila envelope were gone. Her heart started pounding until she realized her mistake. She had unwittingly given Farida not only the transcript to edit but the mysterious aerial photographs and the computer memory stick as well.

CHAPTER:
SIX

THE POLICE OFFICERS FLASHED their badges at Susanna
as she opened the front door. She blinked from one to the
other and glanced to the curb where she saw their District of
Columbia police car. Bad dreams always left her with a headache, a nasty little memento to keep her company through
the day. Before Michael's death, she'd never dreamt at all.
Not good, not bad, nothing. Just a big, restful nothingness.

"Susanna Bailey?"

"Yes."

"We're here to ask you some questions about the inci-
dent in Franklin Park."

"Would you like to come in? Sorry, but I just woke up."
She went to pull her robe around her and saw that she wasn't
wearing it. She had slept in an old t-shirt of Michael's, something she did whenever she needed comfort, and now she

tugged down on it uncomfortably. The cops' eyes went to her bare legs, and she rolled her eyes in resignation.

"We need to ask you some questions about what you remember from that day," said the younger of the two as his eyes slid up her legs to her face. She turned, and they followed her into her living room as she debated whether to run upstairs and throw on some clothes.

"This won't take long, and then we'll be out of your hair."

"Oh. All right." She motioned them to a couple of overstuffed armchairs and sat down on the couch across from them. "Thank you. I've got to be at work at noon." The morning sun streamed into the serene, soft gray room through a wall of windows and warmed her face.

The younger cop sat down, cleared his throat, and pulled out a notepad. The older one moved around the room, taking his time, looking at the built-in bookshelves that lined one entire wall.

"Nice place," he said. "I'm a bit into the antiques myself, but I like the way you did it here, sort of mixing them up with modern stuff. Very nice. So tell us how you knew the victim, Ms. Bailey."

"I didn't know him. He was the witness in the case I was doing."

He stopped pacing. "Lawyer, huh?"

"No. Court reporter."

"Oh, yeah?" They both looked at her with renewed interest.

"Tough job."

"Not as tough as yours," she said.

"I guess you could say that," the younger one agreed. "So you do criminal?"

"Civil."

"Court?"

"Depositions."

"Didn't think so. I would have remembered if I'd seen you in the courtroom."

Susanna flushed.

"So tell us exactly what happened from the moment you left your home that morning and how you ended up in Franklin Park," the older cop said as he sat down on the comfortable armchair across from her.

By the time Susanna had gotten to the end of their questioning, she was glancing at the clock.

"Listen, I can't be late for work. If you don't mind —"

The young cop nodded as he snapped his notepad shut. "We wouldn't want to keep some lawyer waiting now, would we?"

She smiled, and her head ached.

He winked. "One last question, though. Did the victim look ill at all the day before, the day you were in the deposition with him?"

Susanna gave this some thought. "No. More ill at ease, I would say."

As they stood up, the officers handed her their cards.

"We may be calling you down to look through some books. Could help you recall a face maybe. Never know."

Susanna got to her feet, her head throbbing. "No problem."

"If there's anything that comes to mind later on, don't be shy. Anything at all."

"I'll remember that." She glanced at their cards as she led them to the door and watched as they climbed into their cruiser. Her thoughts went to the mysterious memory stick and aerial photographs. She needed to get them back from Farida as soon as possible, and then she needed to return them to someone, but she needed to do it as discreetly as possible. She paused, considered. Nah, these cops were busy hunting down Mr. Nashta's killer.

Stepping out of a hot shower, Susanna felt better. The bathroom smelled of her shampoo. She caught sight of herself in the bathroom mirror, and after an initial impulse to turn away, she stopped and looked back at her reflection. She took off the towel on her head, and her hair tumbled down, curling from the steam and brushing past her shoulder blades. The scar gleamed softly on her cheek. She sighed. Her's was an "un" body, she thought, un-tucked, un-nipped, un-lipo-ed, slowly and gracefully claiming the advantages of age. How well this body had served her, how much it had done, how sweet the pleasure and satisfaction it had given her over the years. How could she ever look at it disparagingly or with an unkind eye? She wrapped herself into the softest of robes and went to get ready for work.

An aspirin, a couple coffees and a chocolate croissant later, and Susanna let the door slam behind her and headed to her car. She was backing out of her driveway when her foot jammed down on the brake. Empty liquor and wine bottles filled her recycling bin to the brim, glinting in the sun, winking at her. Not again. She stopped the car and hurried to the curb. Why would anyone sneak out at night and dump their empty liquor bottles into her bin?

She looked at the house next door and saw that her neighbor Bill Strong's bin was empty. Again. Was he the one doing this weird thing? She had the strongest urge to go knock on his door, but then she remembered the bunch of gas-station carnations he'd left on her doorstep after Michael's funeral, and she paused. Perhaps the man was drowning sorrows of his own. But why dump his empty bottles on her? She didn't know what to think. Looking up and down her street, the gracious old street gazed back, silent, unperturbed. The sun streamed through the tall trees, cutting sylvan swaths across her lawn. But unease nipped at her, and she hurried back to her car as fast as her heels allowed. Oh, why even bother asking? Any place else this would be odd, but in Washington, D.C. it just came with the territory.

The witness was suing his insurance company for harassment. He was convinced they were harassing him so that he would drop his claim against them, and he knew that their work was being aided by an evil devil dog that followed him on the streets and scared the living daylights out of him.

Susanna kept her eyes averted, focusing on the black

keys of her steno machine as she took down the testimony. Over the years she had learned it wasn't safe to establish any sort of eye contact with witnesses such as these. You never knew whether they understood that the court reporter was looking at them to catch their words more clearly or whether they mistook it for a personal interest or some kind of attraction. In the past she had been offered club passes by shady nightclub owners and rides home from bodybuilding firemen, but she knew of fellow reporters, for whom such attention hadn't been as benign.

With loud excitement and much adjusting of his eyeglasses, the troubled man described the insurance company's nefarious methods, which he said involved using immigrant heavies sent to scare him and intimidate him, most of whom were Russian or Pakistani. But he was sure there had been a Korean involved in one particularly nasty attack. Thankfully he had been able to outwit them all through violent harangues and, when necessary, forceful attacks on the devil dog.

He banged his hand on the table, making Susanna jump, and waves of fear and indignation rolled off him. He would not give up his lawsuit, he shouted. The insurance company owed him. When Susanna finally came out of the examination room three hours later, she let out a long sigh of relief. Spotting the office manager Pat Halliwell behind her desk, she discreetly rolled her eyes in Pat's direction.

"Rough one, was it?" Pat asked.

Susanna mouthed the words softly, in case the witness was nearby. "The devil dog made me do it."

"Oh, dear. One of those." Pat waited until the witness and his lawyer left the offices and then called Susanna over with a wave of her hand. "I heard what happened with the Department of Justice case. How awful that must have been for you."

Susanna shrugged. "You could say I've had better days."

"We need to go for a drink and get caught up. I want to hear every detail. As a matter of fact, there's a couple investigators here to see you about that case right now. I put them in room 3."

"What? But I saw them this morning. They were at my house."

Pat shrugged her shoulders. "Maybe these ones are different. How many police agencies have we got in this town? Half a dozen or more." She got up from her desk and pulled her cashmere sweater more tightly around her. "Everyone's got to make a living. You know, maybe they're the Park Police. They get involved in criminal investigations all the time."

Susanna's heart skipped a beat. Maybe the two cops had somehow stumbled onto evidence of the missing memory stick and stereograms and were now here to arrest her. But that was ludicrous. They were here about Mr. Nashta's death. That's what interested them. Oh, she should have gotten rid of that stuff right away.

"Don't worry. They seemed nice enough." Pat looked at Susanna's pale face and touched her on the arm as they walked over to room 3 together. "By the way, we've got a couple Maryland office locations to go check out. Have a look at your calendar, and let me know what day works."

Susanna gave her a nod as she stepped into room 3, and Pat shut the door after her.

Robert Crowell and the woman beside him looked up as she came into the room.

Susanna stopped, momentarily stunned. "What are you doing here?" she blurted out before she could stop herself. Robert looked at her stone-faced as if he didn't recognize her and then back down at his notes. She had nearly forgotten how attractive he was, and she didn't like being reminded of it now. It was the last thing she needed.

The woman at his side looked from Robert to Susanna and then stood up and offered her hand. Her sober blue suit and taupe nail polish whispered "government investigator" subtly but unmistakably. Susanna shook the woman's hand and sat down at the table across from them, trying to calm herself. The woman smiled.

"My name is Meredith Perth. I'm from I-S, Intelligence Services."

Susanna could hear the woman's stomach growling.

"And this is Robert Crowell, also from I-S," Ms. Perth added.

"I-S?" Susanna looked from one to the other. Robert wore another of those suits that cost a couple weeks' wages and was worth every penny. But this time when she looked at the suit, she thought it looked like it didn't belong to him at all.

Robert discreetly slipped his phone into his inside jacket pocket and looked at her levelly. Why was he acting as if he didn't know her? And why did he have to look so goddamned good, she thought, though it wouldn't hurt if he'd get a haircut or at least comb his hair once in a while. Susanna wasn't sure what she wanted to do more, slap him or kiss him again. And then she realized that he probably felt the same way about her. This wasn't fair. He'd had a chance to prepare himself. She hadn't, and she really didn't want to be here.

He looked at her as if to say that he didn't want to be here either. The arrogant bastard.

"The D.C. police already questioned me this morning," she said.

"We're not the D.C. police," said Ms. Perth.

"Well, who are you?"

"As I just said, Ms. Bailey, we're from Intelligence Services, I-S, D-o-D." Ms. Perth enunciated every word as if Susanna was hard of hearing.

Susanna shot her an angry look, though her anger was really directed at Robert. Intelligence Services and Sealift Command were worlds apart, weren't they? Who exactly was this guy?

"D-o-D. Department of Defense," Ms. Perth added in a condescending tone.

"Oh, that I-S? D-o-D, I-S. I see." Susanna's words dripped sarcasm even though she knew the endless acronyms went hand in hand with government service.

Ms. Perth glanced at Robert. He nodded for her to continue, but she hesitated.

Robert said to Susanna as he tried to catch her eye, "Ms. Perth is going to ask you a series of questions, and if you'd answer them to the best of your knowledge, we'd really appreciate it."

"And what exactly is your job here?" Susanna asked him, exasperation getting the better of her. "Who are you?"

He looked as uncomfortable as she felt.

"Mr. Crowell is the senior investigating officer on this case." Ms. Perth raised an eyebrow as she spoke, glancing from Robert to Susanna and back to Robert.

"What case? Mr. Nashta's death?" Susanna asked.

"Look, Ms. Bailey," Ms. Perth said, "let us ask the questions, and you just answer them. That will really move things along."

Susanna looked directly at Robert. "But you were there, Robert. You know as much as I do."

Robert shook his head imperceptibly, refusing to be drawn in.

Ms. Perth shifted in her chair. "Let's make a list of found items in the vicinity of the body. You list them off, and I'll jot them down."

"I don't understand. I didn't find any items," Susanna said. "I found the poor man's body."

"All right," Ms. Perth said, breaking into her thoughts. "We need to think about this."

Susanna stared at Robert. He looked her straight in the

eye, as though saying, "*I told you you didn't want to get into anything with me. Okay?*" And he raked a hand through his unruly hair. *This is getting dangerous*, his eyes warned her. *Can't you see I'm in the midst of something?*

So you have to pretend you don't know me, she thought.

This is work, his eyes said. *Leave us out of it.*

"Oh, please," Susanna said out loud, startling all of them, the words leaving her blushing almost as soon as they were out of her mouth.

"Pardon me?" Ms. Perth choked on her words.

Robert turned to Ms. Perth. "Perhaps Ms. Bailey is apprehensive or confused by the situation, which is understandable."

At least he was willing to help her restore a modicum of her dignity when he didn't have to, Susanna thought as her cheeks flamed with embarrassment. It was the least he could do.

Ms. Perth coughed and scraped an impatient pen across her notepad.

"Perhaps narrowing the questions down would be the thing to do," Robert added softly.

Susanna looked from him to Ms. Perth. "I'm sorry. Go ahead. Please ask your questions," she said and went on to answer much as she did earlier in the day with the D.C. police. When she started to describe her concerns for Mr. Nashta's family, Ms. Perth stopped her.

"Let's stay focused on the issues here. Tell us one more time exactly what you saw on or near Mr. Nashta's body or in the vicinity of his body when you got to the park?"

Susanna realized that there was something here more important to these people than Mr. Nashta's murder, and the enormity of the situation started to sink in. What exactly was going on?

"I've told you already. I've told you everything I remember," she said to Ms. Perth. "Is this whole thing here about Mr. Nashta's death, or was that just an irrelevant inconvenience?"

No one spoke, and Ms. Perth glanced at Robert. Their momentary silence was all the answer Susanna needed, and she pushed back from the table.

Ms. Perth said, "If you would just answer our questions, this would go a lot faster."

"But I have been answering your questions," Susanna protested, getting to her feet.

"Well, perhaps if —"

"I have nothing more to tell you."

Ms. Perth's mouth dropped open, but Robert threw a cautioning arm out to stop her.

"Never mind," he said. "I think we're done."

Susanna left the room without giving him another glance and shut door behind her with greater force than absolutely necessary.

CHAPTER:
SEVEN

WHEN SUSANNA FOUND A PARKING SPOT on Farida's cobble-stoned street, night was falling. A breeze off the Potomac was warm on her skin and had the American flags hung over various doorways flapping gently as she hurried up the brick sidewalk. Sanjay and Farida Rafik shared their Old Town Alexandria home with two daughters, three goldfish, and a riot of pink and orange azaleas in the tiny patch of earth in front of their red brick row house.

It was almost dinner time in the Rafik household, and Susanna and Farida stepped out the back door together after Susanna exchanged quick hellos with the family. She was here to retrieve the mysterious memory stick and aerial photographs.

"Everyone knows that kids love pierogies for dinner," Ramsha called after her mother as the two women headed into the long, narrow Rafik backyard. The moonlight that greeted them was weak and misty, barely illuminating the narrow cobbled path.

"Get back in the house right now, or I'll give you pierogies," Farida yelled at her youngest as Ramsha tried to follow them out into the dusk of the garden.

"Why do we always have to have korma? I am so sick of it," Ramsha moaned.

"Not another step, lady. You tell dad to get dinner on the plates, and we'll be back in a second. And you put out the napkins."

Susanna and Farida waited until they heard the screen door bang shut and Ramsha's complaints recede into the kitchen. Then Farida clicked the flashlight on, and they made their way through the shadows to the end of the garden and the old potting shed that had been there since the days the Fathers of Confederation called this neighborhood home.

The flashlight beam fell on the white plastic bag in Susanna's hand.

"Are you sure we should leave it here?" Susanna looked undecided. "I don't know if that's a good idea."

"I didn't even know I had the stuff until you came over in a panic," Farida told her. "Look, no point you taking it back to your place. Seems like there's a lot of cops buzzing around you now. If they find this, they might think you stole it."

"But I didn't. You know that. They wouldn't know what it was anyway."

"I know that, but you know how some of these cops can get. Give them the slimmest notion, and they run with it whether it makes sense or not. I think this is the way to go."

But images of Farida being hauled away in handcuffs in front of her husband and daughters sent a shudder down Susanna's spine. "I don't want to get you involved in this whole thing. You've got your family to think of. Maybe I'll just take the bag and throw it into the trunk of my car until I can figure this out."

"Oh, that's a great place for it," Farida laughed. "Now, get quiet and help me. No one will ever find it here." She cleared some cracked clay pots and a half-empty bag of potting soil from a rotting wooden bench in the corner of the shed, and together they hefted the old bench aside as quietly as they could. Farida felt around in the darkness for a shovel, and they took turns digging a hole in the dirt floor, coughing as they inhaled dust and dirt.

Farida whispered, "We bury it and forget about it, at least for now. That's safest."

Susanna was surprised to find the earth give easily from the pressure, and the smell of warm earth and mustiness settled like an old blanket around them as they worked.

"So we've got the Department of Justice lawyers, we've got Mr. Nashta, and we've got Nashta's lawyers, three parties, one of whom most likely stuffed these aerial photos and memory stick into my bag," Susanna whispered as she dug. "Question is why would they do that?"

"Maybe they didn't want to get stuck with something

they shouldn't have had in the first place," Farida whispered back as she rolled up the sleeves of the brown cable-knit sweater that covered her beige sari. "Maybe they stole it."

"Yes, maybe they stole it. So if you look at it that way, the most likely candidate would be Mr. Nashta, wouldn't he?"

"The guy at the bottom of the heap? No way. He was just doing his job. From reading the transcripts, I don't think he had any idea what was going on. Hey, slow down. We're not burying a body here. I think that's deep enough."

Susanna straightened up and winced with pain as she looked at Farida. "You think this is a foot deep?"

Farida took the shovel from Susanna's hands. "Of course it's a foot. Never mind. Give me that blasted bag. Let's get this done already."

She shoved the plastic bag into the hole and started covering it with dirt. "It was probably the government lawyers who did it, hiding evidence they didn't want the other side knowing about."

"Come on," Susanna scoffed. "You know lawyers wouldn't do that."

"Oh, really? You can bet on it when there's lots of money involved." Farida hissed as she shoveled dirt onto the plastic bag.

"Your faith in humanity is refreshing, Farida," Susanna whispered sarcastically.

"Everyone's got a price, Susanna. Everybody. There was a show on last week, and I saw —"

"Farida, please —"

"Susanna, how can you be so naïve? Is that a Canadian thing, or is it just you?"

"Nice to see you've got such a level head on your own shoulders," Susanna said.

"Mark my words, Susanna."

"Let's just get this done and get out of here."

"Yes, mark my words," Farida deadpanned, looking at her friend. "I'm sensing some irritability. Rough day at the office?"

"Something like that."

When they were finished, they looked at one another. "What's different?" Farida stopped and stared at Susanna. "Wait a minute. What's going on – I mean other than all this craziness? There is something different about you, my friend."

Susanna shrugged her shoulders. They shoved the bench back into place and hurried along the dark path to the house. At the back door, Farida turned on the hose, and they washed the dirt off their arms and hands as they heard Sanjay heading toward them from the kitchen.

"I'm coming, San," Farida called out. Susanna gave her a hug and motioned her into the house. She could hear Sanjay at the back door as she headed for her car.

"Where's Susanna? I thought she was here for dinner?"

By the time Susanna got home, it was pitch black outside, and she wished she had remembered to turn on the front-door lights. Nothing was worse than coming home to a dark and empty house. It's not that she was afraid of anything, but the trees in Virginia grew tall, and the shadows they cast fell long and deep.

A soft rustling of insects pierced the quiet as she walked up the path to her door. Somewhere someone opened a window, and faint music carried on the night air. She stopped to listen, looking up at the stars scattered across the black velvet of the sky. "Don't worry about a thing. Every little thing is going to be all right."

She smiled. It was Bob Marley, sitting up there on one of those stars, serenading the night. Sweet as a lullaby. As she started to relax, a sharp crack of twigs startled her out of her reverie and sent fear prickling up her spine. Then something moved in the inky darkness, and she nearly jumped out of her skin.

"I didn't mean to scare you."

Susanna peered into the dark. Robert Crowell got up from the door stoop and came towards her. She took a step back as she recognized him.

"Hello," he murmured.

"You're kidding me."

"Did I frighten you?" He tried to touch her hand, but she moved out of his reach.

"How did you know where I live?"

"Are you going to keep me out here all night?"

"What are you doing here?"

He paused, shifted his weight. Silence filled the darkness between them. He shoved his hands into the pockets of his jeans.

"You're not going to help me out, are you?" he muttered with a half-smile.

She didn't answer.

"I came to apologize for this afternoon. It wasn't fair to take you by surprise like that." He was going to add something but stopped.

She watched him.

"I don't know what I'm doing here. How's that?" He looked at her, his gaze steady and unwavering. "Maybe I'm carrying around more regrets than any man ought to, and I didn't want you to be another one of them."

"Did you kill Mr. Nashta?" she asked and saw the surprise on his face.

"No, of course not."

"Are you sure?"

He laughed, relaxing a little then. "I work for the Department of Defense, not the CIA." He paused a beat. "That was a joke, about the CIA."

Susanna didn't say anything.

"I didn't kill him," he said, "even though the bastard deserved it."

"Pardon me?"

"Are you going to invite me in now?"

She had to admit to herself in that moment she didn't want him to leave. "Is this a business call?"

"Definitely not."

"So this visit is part of the personal services you offer every witness?" She saw her sarcasm hit the mark and was

77

unnerved by the momentary, unexpected vulnerability in his eyes. Or was it just her imagination?

"I never felt the need to apologize before," he said. "This time I did."

"How did you know where I live?"

"In my line of work, it's not a hard thing to find out."

"Oh."

He smiled a little at that.

She looked at him, her distrust mixed with desire, and tried to still the pounding of her heart. Uncertainty coursed through her. She wanted this man more than anything she'd wanted in a long time, and yet now that he was here, seemingly hers for the taking, she wasn't sure. What was he really doing here? Was she safe? She remembered the kindness in his eyes that was real. She clutched her house key more tightly in her hand.

She said, "If you're here to ask me more questions, I don't know what else I can answer other than what you already heard this afternoon."

"Susanna, I'm not asking."

"I see." This part of her life was supposed to be over. Why wasn't her body agreeing with her?

"Do you?" he asked.

Was it elemental, then? Pure and simple. Two grown-ups with a healthy desire for each other. Nothing more and nothing less. Just what the doctor ordered, and it would do her a world of good. It felt as if she was awakening from a deep sleep that had befallen her with Michael's death. That scared her too. It came with disappointments and complications and hurt and you always paid a price. Nor did Robert strike her as having the time or necessity for such diversion. What did he need from her, need enough to find her here tonight? The thought chilled her. Was it her that he wanted?

She took a deep breath and tried to push aside all the thoughts that crowded in. Keep it simple, she told herself. Two people with a raw hunger for each other and not a lot to lose. And even though theoretically it sounded pretty good, she hesitated. She was not a woman conversant in the language of casual sex. Yet she felt there was something more here than that. And she could see it in his eyes too. An unguarded, nameless something that he thought he was keeping tightly under control. She sensed a man at the end of his rope and not even knowing it. And though she probably should have, she sensed no danger from him.

He stood before her, all that intensity, but patient and easy now. Waiting for her to decide. And tired. He seemed so very tired. He was wearing jeans and some kind of old t-shirt. She hadn't seen him like that before, unprotected somehow and vulnerable without the armor of expensive tailoring. But it didn't matter what he wore, he struck her the same way. He took her breath away without trying.

"So you're not going to help me out here." His voice was quiet and firm, and he nodded his head. "Nothing ventured. Nothing gained. I think I should leave now."

And when his eyes released her, Susanna's gaze traveled downward, stopping at his hands, and her heart beat faster still. And she knew she would be a fool to turn away a gift like this. It wasn't often that the skies opened up and hurtled down presents.

"Would you like to come in for some tea or a drink or something?"

When his smile came, it took its time in coming, and her heart almost stopped for a beat.

He watched her fumble with the key and said, "Can I help you with that?"

She looked up at him.

"You mean you don't already have a key to my front door?" she asked pointedly, and turned and unlocked her door and let him into her life.

CHAPTER:
EIGHT

ROBERT CLOSED SUSANNA'S DOOR behind him and looked around. Her place was light on furniture. What was there looked expensive but comfortable. No clutter. Custom-made bookcases. Overstuffed sofa. Lots of breathing room. It felt safe. That was good. And it smelled good too. Bergamot? Oranges? Something like that.

Susanna went around switching on lamps and drawing curtains, and he stood watching her. He wanted to reach out and stop her. He had an urgent need to take her in his arms, but he held back. Everything about this woman felt right to him, and that was a feeling he seldom had about anything.

She finally stopped and turned to him. The smile she gave him came out shy, not seductive. God, he could lose himself in her, he realized, and he was not a man who could afford the luxury of getting lost. Yet here he was letting down his guard, slipping, and he didn't give a damn. That courthouse kiss was supposed to have satisfied his interest in her, but it had the opposite effect. He hadn't been able to stop thinking about her or the need for one more, perhaps in the hollow of her neck or on the curve of her breast. That damned kiss had only made him want her more, made him want to map every single inch of her with his mouth.

When she had looked at him back in her court reporting office earlier after he'd steered her out of her embarrassing slip, the look in her eyes had been almost unbearable. He saw her hurt, and it broke his heart. Fuck. That meant he still had one. And he'd been hit with the urge to help her out back there, to apologize, to take away her discomfort, to make everything okay for her. Shit. And he knew he couldn't leave things like that. To be not as bad was suddenly important. To look into this woman's eyes and see something good was essential.

But he was also fucking exhausted, and he couldn't remember when he'd last slept more than an hour or two. It had to be affecting his judgment. But maybe the world wouldn't end if he put work out of his mind for a heartbeat. He had found Susanna next to Nashta's body in the park, but she had clearly been ignorant of anything to do with the case, or so he told himself tonight. Still, he shouldn't be here now. And yet.

"I'm going to be absolutely honest with you," Susanna said.

He looked at her. "Good."

"I'm a little scared. Nervous."

"That's okay. That's a smart thing," he said, drinking her in. She was brave to admit it, and her bravery was endearing.

Susanna glanced around the room, and spotting a photograph in a silver frame, she went over and turned it face down on the table. "Michael shouldn't be watching. My —"

Robert smiled slowly and watched the blush spread over her cheeks as he said, "No, he shouldn't. I wouldn't stand for it." He looked down and shifted his weight. She was lovely, more lovely than he knew he deserved, and she brought out a tenderness in him that he hadn't expected and didn't know he possessed. The feeling was a foreign one to him, and it took him by surprise. He wanted to open up a bit but was bound by protocol not to reveal anything, not to give her the explanations she deserved. He paced the bookcases instead, ran his hand along the spines of volumes, pulled out a book here and there, and glanced at it before replacing it on the shelf.

"What are you doing, Robert?"

A flicker of a smile played across his face. "Well, what I want to do is just go over to you right now and take you in my arms, but I'm not going to do that. I'll just go sit right over there and wait for you to come to me." He motioned to a staircase across the room, which he assumed led to the second floor. She gave him a hard look that made him chuckle as he shook his head. "Susanna, you make me laugh. Do you know how lovely you are?"

"Oh, you are a confident bastard, but you know that."

They stood in the living room, each safe at their own end for the time being. Their gaze tangled until he looked away.

"This is a nice place," he said, looking around as he moved through the room. He slowed down at an antique walnut sideboard with CDs scattered across its smooth, polished surface and picked up a handful. Van Morrison, Etta James, The Pogues, Bob Marley and the Wailers.

"Ah, the classics," he said with a smile. "Nothing like a woman who appreciates good music." He paused as he picked up another CD. He showed it to her as his other hand went to his chest. "Ah, be still my heart," he said dryly. "Metallica?"

Susanna laughed. "I'm not apologizing for anything."

Why did he feel comfortable here with this woman whom he didn't really know? He felt his body relaxing, felt himself letting down his guard. Then his attention was drawn to three black and white photographs in weighty gilt frames on the wall above the sideboard. He stopped and did a double take, taken aback. The photographs hung heavy and gray with the sorrows of the world. Bruce Davidson. Robert Doisneau. Aubervilliers 1945. 100th Street East. These were modern masterpieces, dripping with the desolation of childhood, desperation, silent misery in the lines of an old man's face.

Their impact on Robert was visceral, a left hook to the solar plexus. This was not what he had been expecting. He'd come here to forget himself in this woman, not come face to face with his own insides, raw and exposed, nailed to her wall. He had to force himself to look away.

"They're amazing, aren't they," Susanna said, not seeming to catch his unease at first.

He looked at her, unnerved. "Yeah, museum-quality stuff."

"Not too many people even notice. They were gifts from my husband over the years."

He stared at her, not saying anything until he realized she was flinching under the intensity of his look. Turning away, he walked over to the staircase.

"Would you like a drink or something?" she offered.

"No." He sat down on the stairs heavily and stretched his neck and rolled his shoulders. But the weariness was back and all those heavier, unspoken things.

Susanna took a hesitant step in his direction. "So you've told me you're divorced, Robert."

"I have." He looked at her.

"Can I ask you what happened?"

Robert let out a long breath. Well, this night was sure taking a different turn. "You want to go into this now," he said. "All right. I guess you deserve to know whatever you need to know. My ex-wife was in the I-S with me."

"Intelligence Service?"

He nodded. "That's where we met, and that's where it ended. I'm not blaming the work, but it wasn't an easy road for a relationship."

Susanna asked, "So then what about Sealift Command?"

"Do we have to do this now?"

The look on her face answered his question.

"Okay, fine," he said. "But why don't you come a little closer?" He patted the step beside him, but she didn't move.

He asked her, "You don't have many pictures, family photographs I mean, things like that, do you?"

She looked surprised. "There's enough for me."

"Why?" he asked.

"I thought I was the one asking questions."

"Let's take turns," Robert said. "Where are the family pictures?"

"I don't have any except for that one of Michael."

"Why is that?"

"I don't have any family to put in the frames."

"No brothers? Sisters? Father or mother?"

"You mean the woman who gave birth to me?"

He studied her. "Okay," he said, running a hand through his hair and frowning, his desire easing its grip on him. "I hear you." And he felt again just how damn tired he was, and he couldn't remember the last time he'd seen a bed, and he didn't know if he had the strength for this conversation right now. "How about if we just lie down together and rest a little? That actually sounds pretty good right about now," he said softly.

She looked at him. "Robert, I'm so sorry. I wasn't even seeing you, all wrapped up in my own stuff. I'm not usually this bad. Honestly." She was at his side in a few steps, and he moved over so she could sit on the stairs beside him. She smelled of fresh laundry and shampoo and good perfume, and his senses drank it all in. The sweetness that curved her smile made him want to kiss her and wipe her concern away. She raised her fingers to his face, her caress tentative and gentle, as if she wanted to wipe away the exhaustion that sat heavy on him.

"I'm fine," he said, pushing aside her concern.

"I know you are." She let her hand slip back into her lap, but he took it in his.

They looked at each other for a long time, tiredness stripping away their defenses, their bodies basking in the nearness of each other.

"You're finally here," he murmured.

"I am." Her voice was low and sweet to his ears.

"I don't want to hurt you."

Susanna laid her finger over his mouth. "I know you don't."

And hesitantly their heads drew together, and their lips met. And this time the kiss was not a frenzied, hurried thing but a sensual, deep, and slow exploration that had him moaning with pleasure.

"Jesus Christ, Susanna." His voice was barely audible.

"Yeah, me too," she whispered. Pulling him by the hand, she got to her feet.

"Are you sure?" he asked.

"Yes."

In Susanna's bedroom, Robert fell back onto her bed fully clothed and pulled her with him. As she laughed in protest, he wrapped her in his arms and kissed her, and their kissing was gentle and unhurried until a languor overtook them, enfolding them in its magic, and he didn't know who drifted off and fell asleep first.

CHAPTER:
NINE

SUSANNA WOKE IN THE MIDDLE of the night, gasping for air. Her mother had been grabbing for her with red-painted nails, trying to get a firm grip. From the look on her mother's face, Susanna knew she meant business. She fought her off, breathing hard, inhaling her cheap perfume, pulling the sheets, moaning, kicking, until the image receded, losing its power, its immediacy. She bolted up in alarm. It was just another nightmare.

For a moment in the darkness, she wasn't sure where she was. Her heart was hammering like it would break out of her ribs. She looked around in a daze and released the blanket bunched up in her fist and forced herself to take a deep breath. She heard something and looked up to see Robert come into the bedroom, cloaked in shadow. He broke into a grin when he saw that she was awake. She looked down, momentarily unsure, but both of them were still fully clothed.

"I tried not to wake you." He made his way in the dark back to the bed.

"What are you doing up?" she asked.

"My gut was growling. It was either that or your sweet snoring that woke me."

"Robert," she protested with a laugh. "I don't snore."

He pushed a strand of hair behind her ear and looked at her, caressed her cheek. "I found your kitchen, but there was nothing to eat except for something moldy in a pot."

"You poor thing." Her fingers went to trace the outline of his jaw, and he kissed the palm of her hand. "I haven't gotten around to the groceries."

"I need something to eat." He sat back and studied her face.

"Me too. That's for sure," she said.

"Since you're awake, how about we go to Five Guys? Isn't there one on Columbia Pike?"

"Oh, yummy. My favorite place. Greasy hamburgers and peanuts galore. You are a true romantic, Robert Crowell."

His laugh was deep and rumbling. "It's four in the morning, Susanna. I don't know any place else that's open at this time of night. Do you?"

A sudden scraping noise made both of them jump. It was outside and close. In a flash, he shoved her down flat on the bed and dove for the gun in his ankle holster. Susanna was stunned. Before she could say anything, they heard the noise again. He put a finger to his lips to caution her.

Her whisper was urgent. "I think it's my neighbor."

He looked at her, a question in his eyes.

"My neighbor, Bill Strong. I think it's him dragging out his garbage cans or — "

"Don't move," he warned soundlessly and edged over to the window and carefully drew back the curtain an inch. Susanna got out of the bed silently.

"That's your neighbor? Take a good look."

She peeked out the window and let out a sigh of relief. "That's my neighbor."

Robert cursed aloud. "What the hell is he doing? It's the middle of the night."

Together they watched him scrape something off his car bumper, working with stealth and speed. Robert turned to her. "Are you okay?"

"Yes, but you scared me."

"Sorry. Automatic response."

"Talk about instantaneous reaction. Wow."

"Hazards of the job." He looked back out the window. "Does he do this kind of thing often?"

"Well, now that you mention it, he does all kinds of crazy stuff. Like I think he puts all his empty liquor bottles into my recycling bin on garbage day."

"How long has that been going on?"

"Oh, about a month now. Isn't that bizarre?"

"Probably not."

She looked at him.

"He's likely going through some sort of security clearance. Any idea where he works?"

"Some Third World development fund or something like that. Developing World education something. I don't know him well, hardly talk to him." She swallowed hard as she remembered her own pending security clearance application and then the weird white-haired guy at her door. But he wasn't asking questions about Bill Strange.

"Okay," Robert said. "That sounds like NSA or CIA but could be any one of a dozen or more intelligence shops in town, most of which you've never heard of, most of which don't even officially exist." He let the curtain fall back in place.

"I knew there was something odd about him. Always waving and smiling at the slightest provocation."

He pulled Susanna over and kissed the top of her head. "This town is crawling with spooks and creeps. He's probably being vetted for a higher level of clearance on the job. Someone sifting through his garbage is part of the process. The guy doesn't want them to pin a drinking problem on him, so he dumps his empties on you. Sleazy but effective."

Susanna watched him as he went and switched on the bedside lamp, bathing the room in soft light. "Most people do whatever it takes to pass a clearance. Tighten that noose a notch tighter around their own neck."

"Sounds like you're speaking from experience." She paused. "Robert, what is it exactly that you do?"

He replaced the gun in its ankle holster. "What do you mean?"

She couldn't see his face. "Where do you work? And why were you at Mr. Nashta's deposition? It's safe to assume you're not a lawyer."

"No, at least you can't accuse me of that," he said as he took her hand. "Come on, let's go eat."

Falls Church lay sleeping, a heavy breeze slow on the night air, while Five Guys Burger and Fries blazed with light and smoking fryers and the din of tired cabbies and radio static. Everything was permeated with the scent of deep-frying oil. Robert sat back in his rickety plastic chair, threw a crumpled napkin onto the pile that lay beside him on the table, and looked at Susanna.

"Ah, much better. What about you?" His grin was lazy, his voice languorous, his eyes smiling.

They sat across from each other at a small, wobbly table squeezed up against the back wall, their legs intertwined beneath it. Peanuts and salty burnt fries sprinkled the vinyl tablecloth between them. They talked as they ate and laughed over inconsequential things, contented and enjoying each other's company until outside the stars slowly faded from the sky and daybreak shimmered on the D.C. skyline.

Susanna put the last bit of juicy hamburger into her mouth and grinned at Robert. There was something very sensual about him, she thought, just the way of him, the way he sat, the way he ate, the way he wore his clothes, just the way he was. Faded jeans or tailored suit, it didn't matter. Frown lines, laugh lines, all of it. She liked the way he seemed only himself and nothing more, at home in his own skin. She found it irresistible.

"So what were you doing at Mr. Nashta's deposition?" she asked him.

"Colin Nashta stole something that belonged to the Government, and the Government needs it back," he said matter-of-factly.

She almost choked. "Stole something?" Her mind flew to the mysterious stereograms now buried in Farida's garden shed. Were they caught up in some dangerous undertow they could not begin to understand?

Robert broke into her thoughts, brushing aside her question. "You're a beautiful woman. You know that, don't you?"

Her cheeks flushed, and she looked at him, amused. "I'm way too old for your charms to work on me."

He studied her unselfconsciously. "I wasn't trying to charm you."

"We should get going," she said.

"Definitely." Robert said as he leaned forward, hooked her chair with his foot, and moved her as close to him as she could possibly get with the table still between them. "Now that we've actually slept together, I feel like we've got all kinds of catching up to do."

Oh, my. No one had ever said that to her before. She chuckled. "What are you doing?"

He took his time and leaned in and kissed her on the

mouth. She forced herself to draw back and was about to say something when he put a finger to her lips, and under the table, his other hand meandered up her bare thigh and lingered. She stared at him in amazement. If he aroused her with a mere touch of his fingers, she could only imagine what the rest of him could do.

"Your skin is so smooth," he murmured.

Sweet heaven above. Her eyes fluttered shut despite herself. Oh, this man. She wanted this man, and her body was in agreement. "Not in this place," she managed to get out.

"Let's go home."

"Home? You mean to my place."

His eyes never left her face as his fingers snapped the band of her panties hard against her skin.

"Let's get the hell out of here," he said.

Peanut shells all over the linoleum floor and the best damn hamburgers in town.

By the time they got back to Susanna's house, dawn had started its unwelcome creep over the horizon, and they hurried back into her bedroom, needing to keep the world out just a little longer.

Robert kicked the door shut and pulled Susanna to him. His kiss spread fire to the tips of her toes, and he tugged her dress off over her head and unsnapped her bra in one deft move. Groaning with pleasure at the sight before him, he went to her breasts and took one in his mouth, but she dragged him up and practically tore his t-shirt off in her hurry to undress him. Robert sat back on the edge of the bed and drew her to him. Breathless and heart pounding, she put out a hand to slow him down.

"Wait a minute. I really have to ask you a question."

"Now?" He drew her even closer.

"Do you work for the Sealift Command?" she asked, standing in front of him, naked but for her panties.

"I do." He kissed her belly. "I did." He kissed it again.

"So what is that? Do you work on a warship?"

"Not exactly. I used to. That's where I started out." His voice was low and sweet to her ears, and he left a warm trail of kisses down her belly as his mouth slowly headed south. He was sending butterflies fluttering inside her, and she found it hard to concentrate on anything other than what he was doing to her.

Letting out a soft whimper of delight, she managed to say, "But last night you said you worked for the Department of Defense, and later you mentioned Intelligence."

He stopped abruptly and sat up, making her exclaim in disappointment. His gaze traveled up her body very slowly, and he locked his eyes on hers as he slipped her panties off. She stood naked before him. "All of those are correct or were at one point or another," he said as he stood up and cupped her breasts in his hands and brought his mouth to them, and Susanna was starting not to care anymore what he did as long as he was doing it to her.

"So which is it? And why so — "

He kissed her on the mouth.

"— oblique?" she finished.

"Look, there's a lot of things I just can't tell you, even if I wanted to. I did start out in the Sealift Command, but they're not warships. They're supply ships. We delivered supplies to warships on active duty and to military posts all over the world. I was co-opted into the Aerial Intelligence Division there." Robert nipped her bottom lip. "And I do work for the Department of Defense. And that's all you need to know, and that's all I can tell you."

Susanna tugged open the snap on his jeans and unzipped them as he spoke, and he sat back onto the bed again and rolled up a pant leg and unstrapped his ankle holster so he could get his jeans off. Then he patted his lap. "Get over here," he ordered.

God, he was a confident bastard, she thought, as her body yearned to be touched by him again. He was looking at her with such pleasure that she found it hard to breathe. She had to keep her wits about her. "So why did the lawyers at the deposition say you were from Sealift Command?"

"How many times are you going to ask me that?"

"Because I would like to know whose lap I'm about to sit in. Because I like you, in case you haven't noticed."

"Jesus H. Christ," he muttered and pushed aside his holster with his gun in it and pulled Susanna onto his lap with a firm grip. "I cannot discuss this matter with you any further. Do you understand me?" His voice was as hard as she'd ever heard it, and it broached no complaint.

Susanna wrapped an arm around his neck and pecked him on the nose and then yanked on his hair as hard as she could, making him yelp. And before she had a chance to protest, Robert flipped her around, threw her onto the bed, and trapped her beneath his body. Grabbing her wrists, he pinned them to the mattress and stopped her laughter with his mouth.

The ringing of the doorbell meager hours later dragged them back to consciousness. Susanna stumbled to the bedroom window, forcing her eyes open. She squinted and tried to get a better look at the car parked outside her house. Robert groaned and pulled the pillow over his head. Then he groaned again, shoved the pillow to the floor, and sat up in the bed.

"Looks like the D.C. Park Police are here." Susanna turned around, and her heart skipped a beat at the sight of him, tossled, groggy, defenseless with sleep and sex. And somehow out of place in a sea of white duvet and soft pillows.

"I can't remember the last time I spent so much time in bed," he murmured.

And she instinctively understood that comfort was not a word he had much experience with, but the knowledge didn't frighten her. She had been in that place herself once long ago. "Welcome back, cruel world?" she said softly.

"Something like that." He gave her a crooked smile. "D.C. cops?"

"I think it's the Park Police." She looked at him with apprehension, not wanting the real world to come crashing back so soon.

"Hey, come here," he said, swinging his legs out of bed and pulling her to him. "What is it?" His eyes were gray and fathomless and full of concern.

She swallowed hard and reached for him, kissed him on the mouth and winced. Her lips felt bruised and swollen. "Ouch."

Robert chuckled. "Yeah, I know what you mean."

She liked how he was warm and his humor was dry and how he could make her feel safe and relaxed. She never would have guessed that about him. But then maybe it was time she started to trust her instincts more, she told herself.

"Why don't you get back into this really nice bed, and I'll go deal with them." Robert put his arm around her shoulders protectively, and she wanted to stay there forever, next to his naked, solid strength. There was something quiet and assured that emanated from him and beckoned to her like uncharted land. Her throat started to feel tight, and she could feel the tears starting behind her eyes. It felt good to have a man to lean on if she wanted. It had been a while. She blinked a few times and ran a hand through her tangle of hair as she pulled away from him and got up and stepped over the clothes scattered across the floor and went to find her robe.

"I'll be fine," she murmured.

The doorbell rang again.

"Okay. But don't sweat it. They're here to ask you a couple questions about Colin Nashta, about finding his body. Routine stuff."

"How do you know?"

"I need more sleep," he answered as he fell back into the bed. "I could get used to this sleep thing."

"Oh, I see. Another one of those questions you'd love to answer but just can't?" Her words were laced with sarcasm. She pulled her robe around her body. "In that case, I better hurry down."

"Wait a minute," he said, grabbing her by the sash.

She turned around.

"Thank you."

She looked at him, not sure she understood.

"For last night." He paused. "For trusting me. For all of it."

Susanna looked away. She couldn't bear the effect that he was having on her.

"You better get going," he said, but he seemed reluctant to let her go.

She pulled free and headed for the door.

CHAPTER:
TEN

THE D.C. PARK POLICEMEN were friendly, and in answer to their questions, Susanna told them everything that she could remember about that day and finding Mr. Nahsta's body and what she could remember seeing when she looked back from the coffee shop, which is where these cops' focus seemed to lay.

"You saw two men on the bench with him?"

"Yes. I saw two guys sitting beside him. And then they got up and left."

"What did they look like?"

"I don't know. I didn't really pay them any attention. You see, I didn't realize at first that that was Mr. Nashta sitting with them. And they got up and walked away in the other direction. Away from the coffee shop."

"How were they dressed?"

"I don't remember. Nothing stands out." She thought about it. "So I'd say they were probably in suits. They blended in."

"What about hair color?"

Susanna shook her head. "No."

"Light? Sandy blond?"

"It must have been dark hair, both of them, like Mr. Nashta's."

"An employee at the coffee shop told us she saw two dark-complexioned men sitting with him. Does that sound about right?"

She paused. "I have no idea. It was such a shock. I don't remember much."

"Of course. It's understandable, Ms. Bailey."

"The only thing I can say for sure is they all knew each other because of the way they were chatting," she added. "I assumed they were friends."

Then they asked about her work and what her job entailed, and she explained it to them. This was starting to feel like her new routine.

"So you're like the person that writes stuff down on that little machine thing?"

"That's me."

"Work mostly in D.C.?"

"Yes."

"Lived in Northern Virginia all your life, Ms. Bailey?"

"No, I'm Canadian."

"Oh. Nice people, the Canadians. Good beer up there.

Some decent hockey players too. Shame about the weather."

Susanna smiled from one to the other as she pulled her robe down around her legs. "I guess so. I'm not much of a beer drinker."

"How long you lived here, then?"

"Around ten years now," Susanna said, and much to her embarrassment, she could feel a trail of sperm start to trickle down her leg. She looked down in mortification.

One of the officers noticed her discomfort. "Everything okay, Ms. Bailey?"

She crossed her legs stiffly, her inner thighs growing slippery. "I need to use the powder room. Will you excuse me, please?"

They glanced at each other and back at her. "No problem."

She got up and backed away from them as nonchalantly as she could manage, her face flaming. But how to distract them? Frantically she glanced at the kitchen. Coffee. "Would you guys like a coffee or something?" She wanted the earth to open up and swallow her whole. "I'll be right back."

One of the cops shrugged. "Sure. Why not?"

"Oh, good. Just go on in the kitchen and help your-selves." She backed out of the living room. "It's not actually brewed yet, but the coffeemaker is on the counter. I'm sure you know what to do."

As she ran for the hallway powder room, she could hear one of them. "Maybe it's a Canadian thing. Maybe you make the coffee yourself up there."

Susanna returned feeling much better, calm and composed once more. "So why don't you officers speak with Robert Crowell? He'd probably be of more help to you than I can be."

"Who's that?"

She wasn't sure how exactly to identify Robert at this point. "He's the one who made the initial call from the scene."

One of the cops flipped through his notepad. "What did you say his name was?"

"Robert Crowell. He's the one who called you."

The cops looked at each other. "No, ma'am. It was one of the employees from the coffee shop who called the police."

Susanna frowned, trying to remember. The cops shrugged. "Sorry. Maybe you're confusing things. Wouldn't be too surprising after the shock you had."

She was puzzled. "Well, there must be some confusion somewhere."

"Yes, Ma'am. And it wouldn't be the first confounding thing on this case."

"What do you mean?"

The officers looked at one another, as if they weren't sure exactly how much they should be telling her. "When we went to the deceased's home, looking for his next-of-kin, we found his house had been broken into and ransacked."

Susanna's eyes widened.

"Not sure it's connected to his death. We're looking into the possibility. Anyway, we'll leave you with a number. If you can remember anything else, please give us a shout."

"Sure." She closed the door after them and hurried upstairs, her mind swirling with questions. Did Robert know about that?

When she came into the bedroom, it was empty.

She went through the house, looking for him, but he was gone. Didn't even leave a note.

Slowly she went back upstairs and sat down on her bed. The lingering scent of him still there teased her, and she moaned and fell back into the pillows. The house felt too big.

Of these few things she was absolutely certain. Robert was the senior investigating officer on the case, but he hadn't asked her anything about it while he was with her. The police agencies and Robert Crowell were after two different things, and she didn't think the police were the ones interested in the memory stick and stereograms now hidden in Farida's potting shed. And she was well fucked, in so many ways. Stepping out of a hot shower, she pulled on some black jeans and a t-shirt and went into her study, turned on the computer, typed in "Sealift Command" and waited. He could have at least left a goodbye note.

She started reading everything that appeared on her screen. "Military Sealift Command. Atlantic, Pacific, Europe, Central, Far East. Military Sealift Command operates approximately 110 noncombatant, civilian-crewed ships that replenish U.S. Navy ships, conduct specialized missions." She scanned the list of ships. Naval Fleet Auxiliary Force. Special Mission Ships. Prepositioning ships. Her eyes drifted down the screen. Sealift ships. Then she looked back up. Special mission ships?

"Sealift Command plays a vital role in Department of Defense strategy in the central command area of operations, including the global war on terrorism by operating..." So he had been telling her some truth. They were all connected. She scrolled down. "Special Mission Program." 26 ships that provided operating platforms and services for a wide variety of U.S. military and other U.S. government missions."

She stopped at "Special warfare support" and leaned back in her chair. This all fit together somehow, but she couldn't see it yet. What had Mr. Nashta done? Robert told her Mr. Nashta stole something from the government, and the government wanted it back. Robert seemed to be the one sent to get it back. He worked in some kind of intelligence organization, and Ms. Perth had said he was the senior commanding officer. Was he CIA? Now she knew she was definitely getting out of her depth. Good thing he was gone, she consoled herself. You don't mess around with those guys. Everybody knew that.

What was going on? It felt like a tornado tore through her life a couple days ago, and everything had changed, become unrecognizable. Even if she could trust Robert, what was she to say to him? "Oh, by the way, you handsome bastard, I may have something you might be interested in in your investigation, even though I can't imagine how and I don't even know how I got it. Honestly. But in any event, I don't have it. It's at my friend's house, but we've buried it"? He'd think she was certifiable. And since she didn't even know exactly who he was, that would be a stupid move.

She searched her computer screen for more information, and slowly she understood who had put those things into her bag. It had to be Mr. Nashta. She remembered his insistence that she go looking for Pike during the break. He was alone in that boardroom. She didn't know why he'd done it, why pick her, but when she thought about it, that made the most sense. She remembered how nervous he had been that afternoon.

Mr. Nashta's deposition had been about aerial stereograms and photogrammetry. She typed "photogrammetry" into her search engine. "Photogrammetry is the science of making measurements from aerial photographs taken from aircraft." Susanna sat back. Robert had been after him, and Mr. Nashta must have sensed it. So he dumped the stolen property into her bag in a panic. And then he got killed in the park? Now she was most likely the one who had what Robert was looking for, but he didn't know it yet. Or did he? Is that why he had spent the night with her? She couldn't believe that. And if he'd searched her house while she slept, he wouldn't have found anything anyway.

Even thinking it made her head hurt. She couldn't trust him. That was true. He'd only revealed bits and pieces to her. What if she gave him the mysterious stuff and then he turned around and had her arrested? After all, he'd gotten what he wanted and more. No, she'd wait on that option. What was on that memory stick and those two stereograms that the government needed back so badly? How had Mr. Nashta gotten his hands on it in the first place? And if Robert was the senior investigator, why send him personally and not someone on his staff of spies, or whatever they were called?

She looked back at the computer screen. "Special Warfare Support Ships. Missile Range Instrumentation Ships. USNS Invincible and USNS Observation Island monitor foreign missile and weapons tests that may pose potential threats to air or surface navigation. These ships also monitor domestic weapons systems and provide valuable feedback to U.S. weapons systems designers."

Could that tiny, plastic-encased piece of technology no bigger than her thumb be the cause of a human being's death? She felt a chill run through her. Mr. Nashta had seemed such a harmless man. A little long-winded, yes, perhaps. Her heart went out to him. But what did any of that have to do with the Sealift Command? She should give the memory stick and stereograms to Robert and be done with it, was probably stupid for not having done it already. None of this had anything to do with her. She went back and forth in her mind. But then Robert would think she was somehow involved. He had called Mr. Nashta a treasonous bastard. She could be charged with treason herself. Or Farida.

Why should she believe anything Robert told her anyway? She didn't even know where he worked. And he had been in the park just like she was that day, suspiciously so now that she thought about it. She would have to get over to Farida's later today. She glanced back at the screen. And even if she wanted to, how was she supposed to contact him?

"U.S. Naval Hospital ship Mercy, USNS Impeccable, USNS Victorious, USNS Loyal. Ocean surveillance ships"… on and on it went. She scrolled down. "Military Sealift Command, headquartered at the Washington Navy Yard in Washington, D.C." She had done a deposition there before and knew where that was, not a very nice part of town as she remembered it. Small world. She could call there and ask for him. She wondered if they just picked up the phone and said hello like any other office.

She'd explain to him what she had and how she had gotten it, turn it all over to him, and then put him firmly out of her mind. Would they let her speak to him? Maybe it really was as easy as picking up the phone. But did he even work there? She frowned as she got up from the computer and stretched. Or she could simply throw everything into the garbage, and that would be the end of it. Except that somebody may be going through her garbage. It was obviously of serious import to many people. Mr. Nashta had lost his life because of it.

Back on the computer screen, pictures of ships flashed in front of her, fine-sounding ships — Invincible, Impeccable, Victorious, Loyal. Mercy! She shut her computer. She needed a run. In the hallway closet, she searched for her running shoes and fought with the laces in her hurry to get outside. Her nose wrinkled. She needed more of those Dr. Scholl's deodorant insoles.

She let the door slam behind her, then retraced her steps, grabbed her cell phone, and headed out again. If Robert knew where she lived, he was sure to know her telephone number as well. She looked down at her phone. What was she doing? It was time to get back to the real world. Put that man out of your mind. She jammed her earbuds in and put on some Ramones, gabba gabba hey, and set out at a fast pace, around Lake Barcroft from Beach No. 3 to Beach No. 5 and the community gardens, then over to Columbia Turnpike, where cars streaked past endlessly, and on to Beaches No. 1 and 2 until she felt the sweat between her breasts and her muscles starting to protest.

She drank in the verdant green of the trees, the ferns and vines prettying up the houses around her, and it helped clear her sex-addled brain. She slowed to a jog on her way back home as sweat slicked her body, and she gulped lungfuls of air. This was good for her soul. What she needed was to get back to work, she thought, breathing hard as she reached her house. There were Maryland office locations to check out, and she hadn't started on her security clearance yet. She came to a stop, trying to catch her breath. Susanna looked at her house as if seeing it for the first time, serene and bucolic in its solid respectability. Then something shifted in the air, and fear crawlies scurried up the back of her neck. She spun around, feeling someone's eyes on her. But no one was there.

Her hand went to the back of her head. She was starting to get paranoid. That's what you got for living in Northern Virginia. Surveillance and defense of the realm permeated the very air you breathed, and it was very big money. Certain players grew richer by the day peddling the business of fear, but she wasn't buying what they were selling. The azaleas in her front yard beckoned to her, all frothy in their pinks and oranges, and she let her fingers travel over their woody branches. The cautious spring sun pecked her on the nose and teased her out of her morose thoughts.

She had better things to think about, like who ransacked Mr. Nashta's house and why and did the police really not get that initial phone call from Robert? She glanced around again, up and down the street as she wiped the sweat off her brow, but everything looked the way it always did, swathed in a luxury of green. Her phone buzzed, and she answered it.

"Susanna, it's me."

Robert. Her heart skipped a beat. "Oh."

"You sound surprised."

Susanna paused. "I wasn't expecting to hear from you again if you want the truth."

"Is that how it's done nowadays?" he chuckled. "I guess I'm out of practice."

She broke into a smile despite herself. Charming bastard.

"Is that what you'd prefer?" he asked.

"You disappeared," she said. She heard all kinds of noise in the background and wondered where he was.

"Listen, I'm sorry. I was hours behind the real world. It's not good when the brass doesn't show up for work."

She didn't fill the silence that followed.

"Bad excuse. I'll try not to let it happen again." He

paused. "Let's get away, Susanna. How about St. Michaels on the Eastern Shore for a day or so? I know a nice, quiet place on the river where we can stay, you and me alone. Steal a little more time together. Get to know each other better. "

This was unexpected. She took a deep breath, tried to gather her wits about her. There she'd been, accepting that she'd never see him again, and now he was here. Her time with him had been a wonderful break from reality, but she had to get back to work, she told herself. Nothing could possibly come of this, and she'd had enough heartbreak to last a lifetime already.

"No, I don't think so." She tried to keep her voice firm. "No thank you," she added for emphasis. "You didn't even leave a note." She knew that there were women who, like some men, were able to keep their emotions out of it and take their pleasure where they wanted and keep themselves uninvolved, but she was not one of those women. And she knew that, if she saw him again, she would be defenseless before him. Damn, wasn't this stuff supposed to go away when you grew up and got sensible and lived in the real world?

"No. I have work to do," she said more forcefully, in case he hadn't heard her, and she kicked her foot against the cement front step for emphasis.

"Come on, Susanna. Beg off a day's work. Give me a chance."

The damage someone like him could cause a woman was incalculable even when it was unintentional. She knew that as surely as she knew that no other man had ever come close to Robert in his effect on her, not even Michael. She started pacing her front yard from one azalea bush to the next.

"We can spend the whole day together," Robert said. "Have you ever been crabbing?"

She knew she wasn't willing to open her heart again, but hadn't she been thinking of giving him the memory stick and stereograms anyway? He had just made it easy for her. Oh, but her mind was treacherous. Best to keep the stuff buried where it was forever, end of story.

"Look, to be honest," he said, breaking into her thoughts, "I don't know how much free time I'll have on my hands in the near future. I know this is sudden and out of the blue, but say yes. We're not kids anymore. Let's not waste whatever time we have."

"That sounds ominous."

"Shit. I'm really out of practice at this stuff, aren't I?" he muttered, but his voice was teasing.

She had to smile. "We're too old and wise to get carried away like a couple of silly teenagers."

"Look, I don't want to overwhelm you, and if you're going to tell me you've got other plans, okay. I know it may seem a bit fast to you, but don't try to rationalize this away."

"Warp speed," she cut in as she stopped and looked out at the street in front of her house.

"I don't live in a nine-to-five world, and I don't have a nine-to-five job. Say yes, Susanna." He waited for her, and when she didn't respond, he said, "I can't talk much longer.

Things are getting hairy here. But don't tell me it wasn't meaningful. So if I can get away for even a couple hours with you, I'm going for it. That is, if you say you'll come."

"Robert, I'm absolutely fine with where I am in my life, and I'd like to keep it that way," she answered. But was that absolutely true, she had to ask herself. She could get some time off work. Her boss had already offered. She sank down onto the moist, spring grass, amidst the azaleas, her cell phone cradled in her neck. Supple blades of grass tickled her legs. It was exhilarating stuff when a strong man lay down his defenses before you. And with Robert, all that strength was tempered with an unexpected quantity. Tenderness? Was that the right word? Yes, she thought so. Intelligence? Definitely that too. Without that, the attraction would not be nearly as powerful.

But after Michael's death, she had rebuilt her life brick by wobbly brick, and she sure didn't need someone like Robert Crowell blowing in like a hurricane to tear things up again. It was supposed to have been a night of shared comfort, that's all. At this stage of her life, was anything more even reasonable? She had closed that chapter of her life. So why did her heart ache to be known again? She may have loved the feeling of being swept off her feet, but as for allowing real honesty and vulnerability to flow freely in her life again? Most definitely not.

"The one time I took a chance on somebody, he went and died on me," she said into the phone.

"Oh, bullshit."

"What?" The nerve of him, she thought. He was a bastard, wasn't he?

Robert's voice was low, seasoned with anger. "So who told you life was supposed to be easy?"

She hadn't expected that.

"Everyone else is supposed to get doled out the shit except for you? We're all here to die. Get used to it, gorgeous." She heard him take some deep breaths and blow them out slowly. "Sorry. You didn't deserve that," he muttered. "And that's not what I wanted to say."

"Okay." She was being torn in every direction by indecision at this point.

"But here's the thing," he said. "The fucking road is mighty long, time is always short, and the scenery flashing by is pretty goddamn dreary most of the time." He paused. "Susanna, am I mad, or is there something between us that's too good to pass over?"

She almost didn't catch his next words. They were mumbled and breaking up. She shoved the cell phone closer to her ear.

"You've got to choose to live life, in all its painful imperfection."

"What are you —"

"A fucking poet," he cut in wearily. "But I've got to get going here."

"Wait, Robert. All right. I'll come. But only if you promise to be completely honest with me from here on. About everything."

"I don't know if I can do that."

"Then don't bother showing up."

As silence unfurled, Susanna gazed at a solitary lime green fern frond amidst the sea of blue forget-me-nots that carpeted the ground beneath her azaleas. The air was pungent with wet earth, and she inhaled steadying breaths. This was best. End it now before things got out of hand. She wanted him to hang up.

But he didn't. Instead he said, "You drive a hard bargain, Susanna. I'll pick you up around seven." The line went dead.

And she heard her mother's singsong voice whispering to her over the distance of years. "You will pay, you will pay. You always have to pay the price." Had she just made the biggest mistake of her life? Did she really want to chance being known again? All her embarrassments and deficiencies and ugly bits? For her, that was a scary business, and she hadn't done it before or since Michael. That part of her life was over as far as she was concerned.

Maybe she was just hiding, buried safely under a heap of fear and self-pity. But Robert didn't know about the broken-ness that dogged her with Michael no longer around running interference, the sense that she was flawed on her own, the dark little suspicion that happiness was for others and not for her. In that moment, Susanna's decision seemed so far-reaching to her that she was certain the whole earth had shifted on its axis. But when she looked around, not a single living thing had taken notice, and she realized that the physical world around her hadn't changed at all. It just felt that way.

This was just a couple days away. Maybe she could slow down and enjoy this man for a bit. She would soak the days in and savor them. Being busy was so overrated. Her heart was going to stay closed and safe, and she would go and have a lovely time. She could do that.

CHAPTER:
ELEVEN

"HONEY, YOU KNOW RANDOLPH will approve," Pat Halliwell told Susanna over the phone. "For goodness sake, it's just a few days since you found that poor fellow's body. You need to process."

Susanna sat in her jeans and a white, cotton shirt in Farida's kitchen with a cup of Pride of India tea in front of her and imagined Pat pacing to and fro as she spoke, craning her neck to get a glimpse of the White House out the window of the court reporting firm. "Put everything out of your mind and have a nice break. Business can wait a day or so."

"Well, if you're sure then. Thanks. And give the boss man a hug for me." Susanna dropped her phone into her purse and pulled out an envelope with Farida's paycheck and handed it to her.

"Why didn't you come to poker last night?" Farida asked. "I won a manicure and a couple bucks." She showed Susanna her nails, a gleaming, glittery green. "Sea Witch Princess."

"Excellent. Look, Farida, I've got to get that bag with the memory stick and stereograms out of the shed. You're not safe as long as it's here. Neither is your family."

Farida raised an eyebrow in question, then pulled Susanna to the window that looked out onto her narrow, sunny backyard. Farida's husband Sanjay stood holding a shovel, dressed in a sleeveless undershirt and plaid shorts a touch on the skimpy side. Sweat glistened across his forehead, and he was panting with exertion. Next to him sat a wheelbarrow, a large pile of gravel, and a mound of dirt.

"He's laying do-it-yourself interlock pavers," Farida said as the two women watched him.

"I didn't realize Sanjay would be home on a Thursday."

"Flex time."

"The FBI does flex time?"

"I guess the accounting department does."

"Is he really in the accounting department?"

Farida shrugged her shoulders. "I don't ask anymore."

"I've got to get that stuff out of your shed," Susanna said.

Farida turned to her. "And how do you propose we get that shovel from Sanjay without arousing his suspicions?"

Susanna studied him through the window.

"What's the rush, anyway? Has there been any more dead bodies turning up in the last twenty-four hours?"

"No, but it's not safe for you to keep it in there. The last thing I want to do is endanger you or your family. Plus, I know who I'm going to turn it over to."

"You do?" Farida was surprised.

"There's this guy who is investigating the case." Susanna paused, thinking of Robert, not sure how to begin explaining it all. "He showed up on the last day of Mr. Nashta's deposition. His name is Robert Crowell."

"You never mentioned this guy."

"I never got around to it last time I saw you. Anyway, Robert was —"

"Robert?" Farida stopped her. "Why are you calling him Robert? What is he? A friend of yours?"

"Well, I wouldn't call him a friend…exactly."

"What do you mean exactly?"

The cooking timer went off, and Farida hurried over to her stove. "Anyway, we won't be able to dig up that stuff today. Sanjay looks to be set up for the whole day. He doesn't work nearly as fast as he thinks he does."

Susanna sat back down at the kitchen table.

"Robert turned up on the last day of the depo, but he wasn't one of the lawyers. And his being there made Mr. Nashta very nervous."

"So he was connected to the Department of Defense; am I right?" Farida turned to her. "Or was he CIA?"

Susanna hesitated. Farida was always one step ahead of her. "I'm not sure."

"But why are you calling this guy 'Robert'?"

"I don't even know where to start."

Farida studied her. "Good grief, how much can there be?"

"You'd be surprised." Susanna stared into her teacup.

Farida opened the oven door, and a toasty, buttery aroma filled the kitchen.

"Did you find out anything more about you know what — our mysterious bag of unknowns?" she asked as she pulled a pan out of the oven and set it down on the stove.

"Not yet."

"Here, have some naan. I've also got cucumber raita. Don't fight it because I know you love it. It's almost time for Sanjay's coffee break too."

"Maybe we'll talk another time," Susanna said, starting to get up.

"No way. Sit down. Pull that chair back. Sanjay's coffee can wait." Then she saw the look on Susanna's face. "What's going on with you? So it's worse than I thought. He is CIA, isn't he, this Robert man? Everyone knows you must stay away from those guys."

"No, he's not. Well, I don't think so. He said he wasn't."

"Yes, that's what they all say."

"He said he works for the Department of Defense." Susanna hesitated. "We've spent some time together. Very, very little time, really, if you look at it objectively."

"What does that mean?" Farida studied Susanna, her eyes narrowed. "What's happened?"

Susanna tried to sound nonchalant. "Not much."

"Does this explain the no-show for poker last night?"

Susanna didn't answer.

"Uh-huh. Maybe he's the one who killed that poor Mr. Nashta. Did you ever think of that? What if he's getting close to you so he can snuff you out too?"

"Oh, come on. But first he must spend the night bonking me into oblivion and making me deliriously happy? Is that the procedure? Was that part of the assignment as well?"

Farida's mouth dropped open, and she blinked rapidly.

"Are you telling me you got to know this man in the Biblical sense?" She could barely get the words out. "Have you lost your mind?"

She banged a pan down onto the stove, and Susanna attempted an awkward smile. Farida was flustered. "Oh, my God. A little modesty, please." She paused for a moment. "Of course you have to tell me everything," she added, "but wait. I hear Sanjay coming. Pretend everything is normal."

"Actually, he also told me he works for Sealift Command. He said he's in the aerial intelligence unit or something like that. So I can't be sure."

"Yes, right," Farida hissed. "Because if he told you the truth, he'd have to kill you. Everyone knows that too."

Susanna laughed, but Farida shook her head as she adjusted the shoulder of her green and gold sari with impatient fingers. "I'm all for you getting a life again. You're too young to be dead, but does it have to be with a fellow like this? Seriously. You are my dear friend, and I know you to be a smart and relatively sane woman, but this is…unusual of you, to say the least."

"I know. But —"

The back door banged, and Sanjay walked into the kitchen at the same time as Susanna's cell phone went off.

"What's unusual?" he asked as he wiped the sweat off his face with paper towels. Susanna busied herself in her purse, and by the time she had found her phone and had it to her ear, the line was dead. Farida watched her as she put the phone back in her purse, and Susanna shrugged her shoulders in response. Sanjay looked from one woman to the other.

Susanna said, "Hello, Sanjay. Let me ask you something. And I know this is completely out of left field, but indulge me, please."

"If this has anything to do with my car, the answer is no," he said. "In case you've forgotten, the last time you and my lovely lady wife borrowed it, my insurance rates skyrocketed, causing me untold financial pain."

Susanna squirmed, remembering the weekend last fall she and Farida had driven down to Charlottesville to one of their favorite places, Thomas Jefferson's home at Monticello. Their idyllic girls' getaway ended on a sour note when they rear-ended another car heading home up the I-95. The front of Sanjay's fancy new Infiniti had crumpled.

"Are you bringing that up again?" Farida turned on Sanjay. "I told you that wasn't my fault."

"No, no, Sanjay," Susanna jumped in. "Nothing like that. I promise."

Farida busied herself putting together a lunch plate for him.

"Listen, I'm curious about something, Sanjay," Susanna said, trying to sound casual. "At work when you receive files from other agencies, are you able to open them? Are you all linked together nowadays?"

"Depends on the files," he said, throwing Susanna a quizzical look. "Each has its TFA, two factor authentication. In order to log into one of our systems, you first need to have a user name and password."

"So for instance, you could log into your system at work and be able to read a file from maybe the National Geospatial-Intelligence Agency?"

Sanjay looked over at Farida, and Farida threw Susanna a warning glance.

"Just as an example, I'm saying. Or the NSA, say, or the Military Sealift Command or the Department of Defense?" Susanna finished.

"Why the sudden interest?" Sanjay glanced from his wife to Susanna.

"Curiosity mostly." Susanna soothed his suspicions. "And I know you're very good at all that kind of stuff."

"Well, all the different agencies are better at sharing information now," he offered. "Our humint – human intelligence – and analytical capabilities have definitely increased over the last decade since 9/11." He grabbed a hot naan off the plate Farida was holding.

"But it's not easy coordinating a sprawling, multi-billion dollar intelligence community," he said, warming to his subject. "Mistakes do get made. And often."

He growled his approval when he bit into the fragrant, succulent Indian flatbread. "Speaking for the FBI myself, I can say the effort is certainly there. How much better have we gotten at it, though, is the real question that begs an answer."

"Indeed," Susanna said, encouraging him on.

"You know, I can tell you with certainty this." He cleared his throat. "No matter the agency, no matter the mission, we are all just busy being human. Very busy. No super powers involved. And that is the crux of the thing."

"My husband the philosopher king," Farida said as she pushed a plate of food into Sanjay's hands.

"But my fellow Americans can rest assured that somebody is always watching," he added with satisfaction. "Always. That I can tell you with confidence."

Susanna blinked. That was the scariest thing she had ever heard Sanjay say, and for a moment she thought he had been joking. Before he could say anything more, Farida steered him back outside with a cup of coffee and a stack of steaming naan on a plate.

"The rate you're going at, San, someone would think you had a lot of free time on your hands," she admonished him before he had a chance to protest. "Those pavers won't get done by themselves."

When she heard the door slam, she sat down at the table across from Susanna and stirred her coffee. "There's no way we can dig that stuff up today. So now," she commanded, "tell me everything. Out with it all."

Outside Susanna's bedroom window, the sun set, pulling a reluctant moon after it. The dogwood tree at the side of her house, covered in pink blooms like satin ribbons on a party dress, were drooping in the dusk.

Waiting for someone was not an easy business, especially when you tried to do everything possible to prove to yourself that you were, in fact, not waiting. It was hard to keep busy not waiting. Especially when you were not waiting for someone you really wanted to see. If they didn't matter to you much, it would have just been irritating and rude. Jade green? Periwinkle blue? Which dress should I wear for you? She laid the dresses out on her bed.

Seven o'clock came and went, as did eight and nine and ten after it. No sign of Robert. For a fleeting moment, she caught the whisper of her mother's voice. "Stupid, stupid, you." Susanna ignored her, but her mother insisted. "It's your own fault. Should I count the ways?"

Susanna had put so many years between them. So why did she carry her mother's voice around in her head as if she was a girl still, beating herself up all on her own when her mother wasn't there to do it for her? She went to the window and looked out, but all she saw was her neighbor Bill dragging a piece of heavy, rusted, black iron fencing up the driveway to the back of his house. The metal scraped along the asphalt like fingernails on a blackboard. He stopped, glanced up at her bedroom window. The look in his eyes made her step back. The aching she saw there was steaming and dark, and it frightened her. She jerked the curtain shut and tried to relax. Did that man have no kids or family or friends at all?

She thought of where she and Robert were going to go. St. Michaels was such a pretty little harbor on the Chesapeake, with its ramshackle waterfront eateries and lots of fresh, steamed crabs and the water lapping at your feet as you sat on the dock in the sunshine. She hadn't been out there in a while, and she was looking forward to it. But where was he?

At eleven o'clock Susanna went to her cell phone to find the number that he had called her from that morning, but the number was not there. There was no record of it. It had been blocked.

When midnight came and went, she unpacked her overnight bag and flung it aside. She was not even mystified or upset anymore. Thank God she hadn't opened her heart to that bastard. She knew she couldn't trust him. She yanked off her pretty blue dress and heard it tear as it went up over her head. Groaning, she threw the dress to the floor and kicked it aside. And fell asleep on her bed, still in her black lace corset, the one that hugged her hips so nicely and showed off her breasts.

CHAPTER:
TWELVE

THE CARELESS WIND WHISTLED AND BLEW, and the long, bony fingers of dawn stretched past the curtains into Susanna's bedroom and skimmed her body, making her shiver in her dreams. Robert stood at the foot of her bed, watching her sleep.

A nest of books feathered her bedside table, and the alarm clock read 5:10 a.m. The quiet inside the room enveloped him. His tie hung loosely around his neck, and his face was drawn, his eyes clouded with worry. He had no idea he would be this late. This wasn't fair to her. He knew how reluctantly she had agreed to see him again, and he didn't blame her. How could he even begin to explain? How much could he tell her? Not nearly enough. He had just wanted to come home and make love to her again. Home? He must be losing his mind.

She looked so good in that black lingerie thing. His body responded to her as he came closer to her sleeping form. His eyes drank in the curve of her belly, the fullness of her breasts, her mouth, and his dick ached with appreciation. Lord, if he ever needed someone, he needed her. Her rich auburn hair fanned out on the pillow around her, and he wanted to run his fingers through it. He wanted her to wake up and reach for him.

Her vulnerability that she tried so hard to hide moved him, and in her eyes he saw the promise of the man he could be. He wanted to know this woman, and he wanted to be known by her. He glimpsed possibilities and hope, and it was a powerful brew he felt. He could sense what he had been defending against his whole life. With his ex, their joining had been convenient, safe, minimal disclosure or involvement required, and he had thought that was enough. Adequate sex, "hey" in the morning, "See ya when I see ya, babe. I'm back in a week. You?" End of story. And when the occasional bumps came up, "Let's do stuff together, let's share more," they both would agree it was needed but then balk and jump back. Nobody felt the need to follow through.

Susanna Bailey had shifted the entire equation of his life, made him want things he never wanted before. A deep, soulful connection, a woman who saw beneath the surface, who wanted more than just his dick and his services even though she protested that she wanted nothing at all. This was a woman to get entangled with, messy and real. He wanted to be the one she called out for in the night. He wanted that feeling of belonging that beckoned when he was with her, that feeling of belonging so dangerous to a life like his. Had he ever felt anything close to this before? Definitely not.

What the hell was he thinking? Had he lost his fucking mind? This was exhaustion talking. Why hadn't he let her go after their night together? That's what he should have done. He turned off the bedside lamp and pulled some kind of blanket off the chair by the bed and covered her, careful not to wake her. He didn't want her to feel cold. He'd already crossed the line once there, and it had not been enough for him. That night was not supposed to happen at all, but now he needed it not to happen some more. He'd always survived on his instincts, so why stop now, he told himself. He wanted everything this woman had to offer, and he knew that was a lot. But could he offer her what she deserved in return? He stared at her. They might just create something meaningful that was their own, but first he had to disentangle himself from the sticky web that had become his life.

Robert picked up a blue dress from the floor. It was soft in his fingers, and the whisper of her scent on it teased his senses and aroused him again. He set it carefully onto an armchair as his dick strained against his zipper. Cursing under his breath, he turned away and tried to focus his thoughts. Could Susanna seriously have been involved in some way with Colin Nashta? That made no sense, but even so, being here now was sheer destructiveness. Unless he searched her home. He should have done it already. The leads that made no sense were the ones you followed first.

The rest of him argued that was faulty logic. He couldn't search her house without betraying her trust.

Even if she didn't know what he had done, he would know. And he wouldn't be able to look her in the eye. He didn't want Susanna a part of the investigation even though his gut was telling him that somehow she was involved. And that made his presence here untenable.

How had he gotten to this place? Was this what he had signed up for? The Department of Defense's head clean-up boy, so good at catching spooks that had turned, other countries' and his own, so good at making the government's assorted dirty secrets disappear with such professionalism and precision. To begin as a spy catcher and end as a clean-up service? Was this what he spent the years at the Naval Academy for? Is this what he had joined the Defense Intelligence Agency for willingly and with a sense of duty and a head clouded with bravery and patriotism, drunk on testosterone and his own invincibility?

He started walking around Susanna's bedroom, glancing about, running his hand along the dark surfaces. Just do it. Better yet, go search her study. He stopped himself at the door, set his hands on the doorjamb to stop himself, and inhaled. Get the job done, his thoughts urged, bring it in. And then you can stand before her a free man. Do it.

His team was still working the leads on the two men who were with Colin Nashta at the time of Nashta's death, but nothing had surfaced on the market yet, no intel for sale to the highest bidder. So their focus was widening to all the people present the day of Nashta's death, just as he had taught them. The Department of Justice lawyers were under the microscope, as was Nashta's lawyer. And there was a strong interest growing in the court reporter who found Nashta's body. Robert knew chances were high she could somehow have what Nashta had stolen. Even his team had come to the conclusion that Susanna had to be investigated further. He knew it was the only thing to do, and he also knew that he wasn't going to do it. Where was the honor in a mission like this? This was a point where he could be not as bad.

His footsteps led him back to Susanna's bedside, and he sat down wearily in the gray armchair next to her bed and studied her. Who was this fucking beautiful woman that he wanted to drown himself in? Was this how it happened, then, coming to the end of the road? Not expecting it, and yet there it was, and suddenly knowing it, seeing it jagged and bare. He was standing on the edge of the known world, and in that moment he could finally admit to himself that he wanted off. And he wondered if she would be there to break his fall.

He watched her as she stirred in her sleep until his eyelids started to droop and he could no longer fight off the clinging bands of fatigue. He wasn't a betting man.

Susanna stared at Robert, asleep in the plush, dove gray armchair next to her bed, his head slumped onto his shoulder, his pin-striped suit creased and furrowed. So he had bothered to show up. She looked down and saw that she was still in the black corset and winced. She had been going for sexy with that. Thank goodness she was covered with her chenille wrap, even though she didn't remember doing that.

She looked back at Robert, careful not to move and wake him, and conflicting emotions flooded her. He looked so uncared-for. Had no kindness ever been wasted on this man? Such a tenderness overwhelmed her that she could barely hold on to her anger.

His face was shadowed by a night's stubble, lines crossed his forehead like rivers on a map, and his short, brown hair stuck out at odd angles. Definitely not your smooth, male-model type, she thought wryly but had to admit to herself that she found his worse-for-wear solidity far sexier. This was not the chiseled vanity of lesser men. This was a man whose chest you could clamber up if the urge so took you. Her fingers reached out to touch him, but she pulled back. Let him sleep. She shifted without a sound and tried to slip out of the bed, but the movement must have alarmed him somehow.

His eyes shot open, and he was awake and alert instantly. He sat up in the chair. She watched him lower his guard as he realized where he was. They looked at one another for what seemed an eternity. Susanna broke the spell first, getting up from her bed wordlessly and going to the bathroom, slamming the door behind her. When she opened it again, she had a bathrobe covering her, there was toothpaste on her chin, and she threw a toothbrush at Robert. It crinkled in its plastic package as he caught it and set it down before looking back at her. She hadn't bothered washing her face or brushing her hair, and she wasn't smiling.

"Next time knock on my front door like anyone else. Got it?"

She went past him and down the stairs to her kitchen to make a pot of tea. White cupboards adorned the soft gray walls of her kitchen, and above her sink was a large window that overlooked her backyard. On the windowsill sat three small metal pots planted with basil, spearmint, and thyme. She reached out and crushed a spearmint leaf in her fingers and then rubbed them on a sprig of the thyme, breathing in the soothing green aroma.

When she turned from the stove, Robert was in her kitchen too. She watched him as he pulled off his suit jacket and threw it onto a kitchen chair. She was glad of the physical distance between them. It gave her a chance to gather her anger more defiantly around her. He caught her looking, and neither felt the need for the safety of words. He yanked his tie off over his head and tossed it onto the chair. The kettle started to whistle, and she turned to the stove.

She made tea, her movements slow and deliberate, and pulled two mugs out of the cupboard and set them down on the countertop and put the box of Red Rose teabags back into the cupboard. Robert kept his distance, but she could feel his eyes on her.

She finally forced herself to turn around. "I wondered whether you changed your mind, whether something had happened to you, where you were."

His eyes were stormy and unreadable, and he didn't respond.

"That's it?" she demanded. Surely his heart bled nails.

"What do you want? To parry and thrust and feint?"

"I want an apology."

He spread his arms out to either side, as if he was defenseless before her, as if he was saying, "Here I am. Do what you will." What he actually said was, "I am sorry."

"Good. Tea?" she asked, ignoring him.

"Never touch the stuff."

That got him a hint of a smile. "Well, there's a bottle of Aquavit in the fridge."

"What is that?"

"It's a liquor distilled from potatoes."

"Good thing you did the shopping."

"It was a gift." She smiled despite herself. "I thought we weren't going to parry and thrust and feint?" She could feel his eyes on her. "You can make something called a 'toddy' with it," she went on. "That's a liquor fermented from palm trees. I did a case on various distillates once."

He nodded and almost smiled.

"I've got strawberry yogurt in there. And a frozen pizza too. I did the groceries."

He went over to the fridge, brushing past her, and looked inside. "Maybe I should do the grocery shopping for you sometime," he said, turning to her. "I'm not sure you've quite gotten the hang of it."

And before she could move away, he pulled her to him. He lifted her chin, and his lips brushed hers, sending a shiver through her. Then he released her, and she could sense the effort of his restraint. He turned away from her and pulled a small bottle of orange mango juice out of the fridge and went to her cupboards looking for a glass. Susanna took the teapot over to the kitchen table and busied herself with a mug and milk and sweetener.

Emptying his glass in one long drink, Robert set it down on the smooth, granite surface, leaned back against the counter, rolling up his sleeves, and looked at her. She noticed the muscles and tendons of his forearms, took in his navy blue shirt, unbuttoned at the neck, the black leather of his belt, the trousers of the finest pin-striped cloth. She saw the outline of his erection straining against the fabric, and she absolutely needed to undo his belt and unzip those pants.

A slow eddy started its sensuous and hypnotic swirl around the charged space between them.

"What is it, Susanna?" he asked innocently.

The force of her desire scared her, threatened to over-whelm her. She had never felt such animal hunger before. It defied all reason, and she hated feeling so out of control.

He cleared his throat. "Listen, I can't always make the call to let you know when I won't make it, but yesterday I did. I tried. I couldn't get through. I'm sorry about that. I know it's not fair to you but — "

"I understand that, Robert." She didn't meet his eyes. "Well, not really. Actually, I don't understand. I don't understand anything that's going on here."

"Look, obviously St. Michaels is out, but I'm here now. I need to get over to Annapolis. Come with me. We can spend a night there."

She looked at him. He expected her to drop everything and just go.

"I know a place we can stay." He paused. "I can't think of anything I need more right now. Can you?"

She couldn't answer. That's exactly what she wanted too if she was being honest with herself, but she wasn't sure it was the smartest thing to do. Letting herself become so affected by him was definitely not good, but he had been so slow, gentle too, and that had been unexpected, and he seemed confident that she'd come to him eventually. But just because fate had come hammering on her door again, it didn't mean she was obliged to open it.

"I want more, but give me this." His eyes locked on hers, and sparks of tension flew across at him.

She didn't want to give him a chance, didn't want his smooth talking, his vague explanations. She wanted to shut him up, to hurt him for not showing up. She wanted him to feel as powerless as her need for him made her feel, as powerless as she'd felt the night before when he didn't appear.

"Take off your clothes," she said.

He didn't move.

"You heard me." Her voice was harsh, and she caught the

moment of hurt in his eyes before he had a chance to cover it with a rising anger. Good, she thought. Now you know how it feels. He pulled a kitchen chair over to him, scraping it hard against the floor. Then he sat down onto it, almost breaking it with the force of his action, and yanked off his socks. She could hear the blood start to pound in her ears. He unzipped his pants and got up, letting them fall to the floor.

He must have heard her quick intake of breath because he glanced at her as he shoved his underwear down over the muscles of his thighs, stepped out of them, and started unbuttoning the bottom buttons on his shirt. His erection got in his way, and he shoved it aside to get at the buttons.

She felt a violent heat surging through her body and pooling between her thighs. Oh, Sweet Jesus, she thought as she watched him, he had such a beautiful cock — and even better, he knows what to do with it. Her body shuddered at the memory. And his hands, his clever fingers, his mouth, oh the magical things they were capable of. It was enough to make a grown woman cry.

"Is this what you want?" he demanded hoarsely, and she could see he was fighting to control his anger.

The violence in his voice scared her. What am I doing? she thought. Her body started to tremble. This is not what I want.

"Making love to you is the easy part," he growled as he grabbed the heft of his penis to stop it straining against his clenched stomach muscles. "Fucking you is even easier," he spat out.

"Okay. Stop," she pleaded suddenly. "Please stop."

"What the hell are you playing at, Susanna?"

She could feel her heart breaking.

"Now you come over here to me," he commanded. "You think getting me naked is somehow making me vulnerable or something? You're trying to make a point? You don't need to."

She turned away as he stood across the room from her, solid and immovable, dark anger rolling off him. After a few moments, she whispered, "Please get out" and turned back to see his eyes turn from molten pewter to ice. He shoved his clothes back on and grabbed his jacket and headed for the door. Then he stopped, came back, grabbed her by the arm, making her wince, and pulled her to him. Her eyes shot daggers of pride at him, and still he squeezed her arm even harder. Didn't he understand about pride or didn't he understand about fear?

"Stop. That hurts," she protested, trying to shake free of him.

"Not as much as missing me is going to hurt, tiger."

And for a second she thought he was going to kiss her, but he released her arm roughly and stormed out of the house.

CHAPTER:
THIRTEEN

FOR FUCK'S SAKE, ROBERT THOUGHT as he jumped into a black, unmarked SUV parked in Susanna's driveway and pounded his fist into the steering wheel. He winced with pain and pounded the steering wheel again. What the fuck? He'd have been mad too if she stood him up. There he was thinking of getting into something with her, yet he couldn't even make room for her, accommodate her, indulge her, try to understand her? There he was telling himself he was falling in love with her, that he was up for it, that he sensed her hesitation and saw he had to coax her along and was fine with it. And this is how he did it? He pounded the steering wheel again.

Glaring out the windscreen, he stopped. Susanna's neighbor stood in his driveway, mouth gaping open, the early morning sun forming a soft halo around him as he watched

Robert. And it hit Robert that death was there in every single sunrise, clicking its nails patiently, waiting. Time was not his forever, and he knew what he wanted. So what the hell was he doing?

Methodically he willed himself to calm down, and realizing the neighbor was still watching him, he rolled down his window.

His voice was sharp, cold steel. "How's that security clearance coming along?"

Surprised, the neighbor mumbled something inaudible in response.

Robert fumbled in his jacket and pulled out a silver badge and swung it in the man's direction. "Stop unloading your empties into Susanna Bailey's trash. I'm on to you. Got it?"

The man's eyes widened, and he hurried into his car and backed out of his driveway as fast as he could without a word.

Robert got out of his SUV, slammed the door after him, and went back into Susanna's house. He found her on the kitchen floor, sitting with her arms wrapped around her knees. He bent down to her and pushed her hair aside and saw that she was in tears. His jaw clenched. Hurting her was the last damn thing he wanted to do. He was going to have to get a lot better at this shit and fast. He got down on the floor beside her and folded her into his arms as remorse gnawed through his gut.

"Shhh, don't cry," he whispered into her hair. "Please don't cry, baby. You're breaking my heart." And he stroked her and stroked her until her tears stopped.

"I'm not going anywhere," he muttered.

"Go. Don't you get it? Go." Her voice was muffled in his chest, and his shirt was wet from her tears. "Go for God's sake."

And he kept comforting her, whispering to her that he was as stupid as she was scared but they would work it out together. "It's going to be okay. No one's died of this before," he reassured her and himself at the same time. "We can be brave together."

"This wasn't supposed to happen to me at this point in my life. My heart was dead and buried with Michael. You weren't supposed to happen." She wiped her nose on his shirtfront. "What am I supposed to do with this? With you?"

And he said he knew not what else until her eyes fluttered open, and her gaze tangled with his. His fingers went to her face, and his thumb wiped away the traces of her tears. She climbed into his lap and clasped her arms around his neck and started to nuzzle her face into the muscles of his neck and feather kisses over his jaw and his beard and his ear and murmur things he couldn't make out into his hair. And he was hard as the Rock of Gibraltar again.

"I'm sorry, Susanna," he muttered thickly. "About last night. When I wrap this case up, it will be different. Promise."

She unclasped herself from his neck, her eyes dark and liquid heat, and without moving off his lap, she started to undo his pants.

"No, wait. Not like this."

Susanna stopped him with a sweet, wet kiss and slowly released his aching cock, drawing a moan from deep within him. She yanked his shirt off, tearing it in her urgency. And in that moment, he understood her, understood the emotional healing of a sensual touch. He did. And he wanted it too.

She shifted, and he hissed through clenched teeth as he watched her impatient fingers inch aside the corset's restricting black fabric between her legs, and he saw how slick and swollen with desire for him she was. She pulled up to her knees and shifted again.

"That's so beautiful," he groaned as his mouth took her again and she caressed his throbbing head.

"Christ. What are you doing to me, Susanna?" The reins of control were slipping out of his grasp. She impaled herself on him in one deep, brain-shattering, hot slide, moaning as she clasped her arms around the muscles of his neck again. And he was lost.

"Hold on for me," she whispered. "Hold on."

"Say my name." His voice was low, guttural.

"Just don't move."

"Say my name." He pushed back and looked into her eyes with a fierce intensity. "Do it."

"Robert," she murmured.

His mouth found hers, and he devoured her as he fought his trembling body to hold still, fought the primal need to thrust, their bodies fused together in a wet, pulsing heat, hearts beating hard against each other. And he wanted to stay imprisoned in this exquisite pain forever.

The morning sun slowly traced a path across the kitchen floor and over their entwined, spent bodies. But it had not been enough. Robert carried Susanna up to her bedroom. He kissed her temples, her eyes, the corners of her mouth and laid her down on the bed.

He'd left his phone down in the kitchen and didn't check his messages until much later. "O800 hours. Ft. Meade headquarters of the National Security Agency/Defense Intelligence Agency joint mission program. Urgent call for all members of the Special Mission Task Force to check in. No Nashta intel has surfaced on the international market in 64 hours, necessitating upgrade in domestic search and destroy."

The bedroom was bathed in that same soft morning light. Robert needed to see all of Susanna and tore her black lingerie thing in half with one efficient movement before she had a chance to protest. They were both naked at last, and he stood over her and feasted his eyes on her. Her own were glazed with pleasure, like a cat with a bellyful of cream, her defenses scattered, forgotten for the moment. He liked that. A lot. Her fear mystified him, left him more observant, left him wanting to know how such a luscious creature could be afraid of revealing herself, opening her heart, but he would deal with all of it. What was it that scared her? Losing control? Getting hurt again? Maybe something deeper, uglier, older?

But right now he was still hungry, and his dick throbbed greedily. It took all his restraint not to leap on her and bury himself to the hilt inside her like a caveman. But he needed more from her than that. He let his finger trace her swollen mouth, and her eyes fluttered shut. Then he parted her lips and forced his finger into her mouth. She ran her tongue around it as he pulled it out and then inserted it into her mouth again. He watched her nipples pearl, and his dick grew even harder.

He removed his wet finger from her mouth, and his fingers started a slow, gentle exploration of her body. She moaned softly, and her body arched in response. His tongue traced a delicious, warm trail up her leg, and he spread her thighs. Her breath caught. His tongue took her, taunted and teased her, making her cry out as his mouth possessed her, bruised her, until she writhed beneath him.

She tasted so good he couldn't get enough. His hands gripped her hips like a vice so that she was unable to move as his mouth mercilessly aroused her, brought her to the edge, until she begged him for release. He pulled back and looked at her, his eyes half-lidded, as aroused as she was, drunk with the scent and taste of her.

"Please, Robert," she whispered.

He gave her a half smile. "Not yet."

"Yes, now, now."

He didn't know how much longer he could hold on to his own self-control. Her hips tried to buck beneath his hands, but he showed her no mercy and held her tight. He would not give her what her body cried out for. And his mouth went back to the buried treasure between her thighs until his cock throbbed so painfully and desire pounded so forcefully through his body that he didn't have the strength to tease her any longer.

He pulled himself up, braced his arms on either side of her, and plunged into her with blinding need. He tore a gasp from somewhere deep inside her. His body shuddered as he felt the wet, luscious tightness of her, and his mouth took hers hungrily. He slowly withdrew, and she moaned as he entered her again, just an inch at a time now.

"You feel so good," she growled softly, fisting her hands in his hair.

He gritted his teeth. How long could he hang on? He gave her one more inch. And one more.

Susanna groaned as she wrapped a leg around his waist. "More. Give me more."

Another inch and another and another, and her hips thrust greedily up to take the rest of him. Robert felt her muscles tighten around him, and he withdrew one excruciating, tight, wet inch at a time. Her breath came out in ragged gasps. And he finally gave her what she needed, driving into her hard and deep, to the very core of her, until she started to buck beneath him. He felt her body go tense with release as she started to contract in hot, lush waves. Her teeth sank into the muscle of his shoulder as she muffled a cry. It was the last thing he was aware of as his own orgasm ripped through him.

Robert reached out a hand to her.

They lay in Susanna's bed facing each other. Susanna didn't move, but his simple gesture had a profound effect on her. A part of her understood that he had ventured further than anyone before, to places where her body stored memories of traumas long forgotten, and still he offered her his hand.

His hands were strong, his lips were sweet, but could she follow him deeper into that no-man's land of vulnerability, of revelation, of opening her heart again, fraught with unknown calamity and threat? And would she find him still beside her there? Amidst the gaping holes of his own tangled soul?

"Give me your hand," he insisted and pulled her to him and kissed her on the lips again.

CHAPTER:
FOURTEEN

THE BRICK-PAVED STREETS of old Annapolis wound up and around and back down to the Chesapeake Bay in a delightful maze, and cool spring air off the water gusted around Susanna as she walked. She enjoyed the breeze and pulled her hair back into a ponytail to stop it flying into her face. Good thing she'd brought some jeans and a sweater.

Seventeenth and eighteenth century, Federal-style buildings and clapboard houses lined the quaint little streets of the town all the way down to the harbor that fronted the United States Naval Academy.

Robert had promised her she would enjoy discovering the town when they parted earlier on King George Street at the gates of the Naval Academy. He had some work to take care of. They had reached Annapolis just before noon, and Robert had checked them into a small inn, The Royal Folly.

The owners greeted him as if they knew him, but Susanna didn't ask any questions. It was the loveliest inn she'd ever been to.

Now she strolled from the Naval Academy along Main Street, breathing in the crisp, fresh air off the bay. "From Knowledge, Sea Power," the motto of the Academy, went so well with him, she thought. Robert Crowell and power of any kind sat together easily as old friends. And when he focused, he was the most intensely focused man she had ever known. When he had checked in with his work earlier, his face had been a mask, his concentration impenetrable.

She walked the old brick sidewalks of Annapolis much as Thomas Jefferson must have done 350 years earlier when Annapolis had been the capitol of the United States. Were these the same streets he tread as he grappled with ideas that would help shape the Declaration of Independence? The pursuit of happiness? That thought alone thrilled Susanna down to her toes as she let the little town work its magic on her.

Her body felt so good as she walked, thrumming from the exercise and sated with Robert. Her thighs ached and her nipples were sore and tender, but she couldn't remember the last time she felt so damn magnificent. State Circle, Cornhill Street, Duke of Gloucester, School Street. She didn't worry about getting lost as long as she had the blue and white dome of the Old Treasury Building in sight.

Down at the waterfront, she studied the Alex Haley sculpture, the writer cast in bronze, telling the story of Roots to two small sculptures of children sprawled on the brick sidewalk before him. And a chill ran through her as she imagined the seaport of Annapolis in the 1700s when ships carrying their cargoes, alternately exotic or horrifying, from distant lands sailed into the bustling port.

When evening fell, Susanna found herself on Compromise Street, wandering in and out of little shops that caught her attention. The streams of people on the streets thinned, the sun started to set, and the gusting maritime wind picked up in intensity. Susanna wrapped her arms around herself as she read an events calendar tacked onto a storefront that offered a landowner money-saving workshop and spiritual mentoring from a woman called Barbara Sue.

Suddenly someone grabbed her from behind, and she let out a scream. She tried to fight them off until she realized it was Robert behind her.

"Whoa, tiger. It's me," he whispered in her ear as he turned her around.

"Oh my God, don't ever do that again." Susanna's voice quivered with anger.

"Didn't realize I'd scare you."

"Well, start realizing."

He scooped her up in his arms and kissed her. Warmth coursed through her body at his touch, his embrace soothing her, and her body relaxed. She saw that he had changed, and his suit was gone. He wore a black t-shirt, a black light-weight windbreaker, and jeans.

"How did you find me?"

"Annapolis is not a big place."

She frowned at him but then saw that he was happy, grinning happy, smiling-in-his-eyes happy. "We've got one more day here. All of tomorrow. We don't have to rush back to D.C. in the morning. What do you think?" He hesitated. "I mean, if that's okay with you."

"How did you manage that?" she asked, more pleased than she let on.

"I just got back from Fort Meade. Took care of a lot of work."

"I thought you were at the Naval Academy?"

"I was, only briefly. I had to get over to Fort Meade. It's just a couple miles down the road," he said. "I thought you'd be fine on your own."

"Of course I'd be fine on my own."

"So we can sleep in tomorrow morning and do whatever the hell we want the whole day."

"Really?" She liked the sound of that a lot.

He smiled down at her, noticed her hair, and with one hand eased it out of its ponytail, freeing it and running his hands through it, tugging it with obvious pleasure. Her body responded with a dart of heat directly to her belly. He nuzzled her warm neck and gave it a hard nip with his teeth.

"Ouch. That hurt," she swatted him away, fighting the smile that tugged at the corner of her mouth.

"Oh, but it hurt so good." He gave her a lazy grin. "Come on. Let's go get something to eat. I know a place."

He offered her his hand, and she took it grudgingly, but

her insides did an odd little two-step at the feel of her hand in his.

"What happened to your suit?" she asked him as they walked.

"You really like those, don't you?" he chuckled. "I picked up on that. Maybe I'll have to throw one on for you when we get back to our room."

"Stop it," she laughed and slid an arm under his windbreaker and around his waist. His body was warm and solid and fit perfectly around hers. They headed towards West Street, passing shops, coffee bars, and restaurants as they walked.

"Where to?" she asked.

"The Rams Head Tavern. One of the finest establishments in town."

"Can we eat there?"

"And how," he said, kissing the top of her head.

They heard someone call out and turned to see an older woman motioning to Robert from across the street.

"Why, is that you Robbie? Robbie Crowell?" The woman was dressed in a flowery visiting dress, matching sweater, and black sensible shoes, with a mauve feathered hat adorning her head.

Robert stopped in his tracks. After a momentary hesitation, he looked at Susanna, seemed to make a decision, and crossed the street toward the woman, Susanna's hand in his.

"Ms. Hortense, I thought that was you," he said with a slow grin, releasing Susanna's hand.

"Robbie, you recognized me? I wouldn't have imagined." The woman threw her arms around him in a fierce hug. The top of her hat barely reached to his shoulders. He embraced her gently and stepped back.

"Susanna, this is Ms. Hortense."

Ms. Hortense glanced from Susanna back to Robert.

"You haven't changed a bit," he said to her, bringing a blush to the older woman's face.

"Oh, don't fool. What's it been? At least 20 years. I'm aging, Robbie."

"I don't see that, Ms. Hortense," he said, patting her hand. "Not a bit. You're as lovely as I always remembered you."

Her head nodded with approval at that as she adjusted the hat on her head. "You've growed up well. I can see that, Robbie."

"And who do I have to thank for that, Ms. Hortense, if not you?"

She grabbed his hand again and patted it vigorously.

"Last I saw you you were graduating the Academy, with Honors. Though I did see your father a while back, bless his heart."

"Don't bother with the blessing, Ms. Hortense."

Susanna looked at him, surprised at the sudden sharpness in his tone.

"Oh, I don't know about that." Ms. Hortense screwed up her mouth in thought. "I know you didn't have it easy, Robbie, but there was many worse than him."

A laughing couple walked past them on the sidewalk and bumped into Ms. Hortense. Robert shot out a hand to steady her. As she regained her balance, she regarded Susanna as if only seeing her now.

"Why, this must be your wife," she smiled and held out a hand to Susanna. "I heard you'd gotten married, but your daddy didn't mention what a pretty thing she was. Good for you, Robbie. I can only hope her heart is as kind as the rest of her is lovely, praise the Lord."

Susanna smiled as she shook Ms. Hortense's hand. Robert shifted awkwardly from foot to foot.

"Ms. Hortense," he hesitated.

The woman looked at him.

"This is not my wife."

Ms. Hortense's mouth formed a silent O.

"My wife left me." He paused. "I was no good at being married, Ms. Hortense."

"Oh. Oh."

"This is my friend Susanna Bailey."

"I see." There was a silence as Ms. Hortense scrutinized Susanna a second time.

"So how is Mr. Carl doing?" Robert asked.

Ms. Hortense gave them a sly grin. "He's at home babysitting little Tariq so as I can get to my cooking club tonight. That's Janailla's little boy. He'll be four next month. Janailla's done well."

"The lovely Janailla," Robert said.

"She is teaching physics at Maryland State now."

Robert looked at Susanna. "Ms. Hortense was always worried about my being a bad influence on her daughter. And she was right to worry."

"Don't be silly, Robbie." Ms. Hortense looked from Robert to Susanna. "Janailla never had an eye for our Robbie. No matter how much he danced for her." And she broke out in a chuckle at the memory.

"Now, Ms. Hortense," Robert protested. "Wait a minute."

"What was that music? K.C. and the Sunshine Band? Over and over and over again. Near drove Carl and me out of our minds." And she hooted with amusement again. "But I must say she sure did take her good time finding a man to her satisfaction. Had me worried, she did."

She looked back at Robert. "That girl didn't get married 'til she was near 35. Caused me a lot of sleepless nights."

"Sounds like she grew up smart. Took her time," Robert said. "Knew who she was, what she wanted before getting married. Good for her. Janailla always was smarter than the rest of us."

Ms. Hortense paused and looked at Robert thoughtfully. "You don't go fussing yourself, Robbie. You are a good man, just like you were a good boy. Don't never forget."

She turned to Susanna, and her voice was fierce. "Did you know Officer Robert Crowell here graduated with Honors from the United States Naval Academy?" Her voice caught, and Susanna didn't understand her sudden upset.

"And he is a fine man, indeed. Fine and brave and strong.

Carl and I have always been very proud of him. As was his daddy. He just wasn't good at showing it much."

Robert shifted, clearly uncomfortable with the direction their conversation was taking. Susanna looked at him, her eyes full of questions, trying to take in everything she'd just learned. Naval officer?

"Don't bother yourself now, Robbie," Ms. Hortense said, addressing Robert's discomfort. "You will be all right. Your life still stretches before you. You are not done yet, son." She paused to catch her breath. "Now I've got to get over to St. Anne's basement before the club is done. We're doing calamari, Greek style, tonight. Are you home long?"

Robert hesitated. "No, Ms. Hortense, I am not."

"Well, I know better than to ask. But you come by and see us if you get a chance before you ship out again. I know Carl will be glad to see you."

"I'll do my best," Robert said.

They looked at each other, and then Robert drew her into his arms again. Susanna felt the surge of emotion between them and stepped back to give them some privacy. Ms. Hortense released him after a moment and patted his hand again. Then she turned and started down West Street, grabbing onto her hat as a gust of wind tried to steal it away.

Robert watched her go.

Susanna took a step toward him. "You okay?"

He nodded and held his hand out to her. "Come on."

Susanna could see Robbie in the grown man who stood before her now proffering his hand, and her heart constricted. Keeping her heart under lock and key was not going to be as easy as she'd envisioned.

CHAPTER:
FIFTEEN

THEY REACHED THE CROWDED ENTRANCE of the Rams Head Tavern, holding hands like a couple of teenagers, jostled by patrons overflowing the space, spilling out onto the sidewalk. Susanna slid her arm around Robert's waist and felt his protective arm around her shoulders, his voice in her ear. The air was redolent with the aroma of brewing beer and a hypnotic, heavy bass beat that vibrated through every vertebra of her spine — swirling, swampy Southern sounds of a band she could hear but not see. And through the archway, over the heads of the people crowded into the tavern, huge copper vats were visible where beers were brewing. The Rams Head was all exposed brick and dark wooden booths, music and boisterous laughter and people jostling for space.

Susanna drew Robert's head down to her mouth as she struggled to make herself heard, her tone rife with humor.

"Robert, I just want to say one thing. I would most definitely appreciate it if you were to dance for me. Any time. Any place."

He blinked as if he didn't hear her, and then a wicked grin spread across his face. It made her belly do a tiny somersault.

"I may be open to persuasion," he said.

She kissed him on the mouth.

"Let me think about that, but where would I dig up some old KC and The Sunshine Band?" he asked, and it was Susanna's turn to laugh. As they talked, everything else seemed to fade away, and she had no idea how long they stood there until they were interrupted by a bartender hollering over the din to catch Robert's attention.

Robert seemed to tense up when he saw the man, but that impression was gone so fast that Susanna thought maybe she'd imagined it. Robert nodded in his direction, and the bartender motioned him over. The two men shook hands, spoke briefly into each other's ear. The bartender looked over Robert's shoulder at Susanna. Cold eyes surveyed her with a reptilian slide, jolting her. He smiled, but only the required minimum.

What was that about, Susanna wondered.

"I told Robert to get his hide on down to the cellar, get yourselves a little peace and quiet," he yelled to her over the noise of the crowd. "And I'll rustle you up the first table I get available over in the dining room."

Robert slid his hand up under Susanna's sweater onto the small of her back and steered her through the crowd towards a doorway off to the side of the main room.

"Seems like a lot of people around here know you," she said.

He didn't answer as he pulled open the heavy door, and she followed him down a narrow, dimly lit set of stairs to the tiniest little cellar bar she had ever been in.

A small, glass-mirrored bar with half a dozen battered stools around it, all occupied, a couple of small tables and chairs, walls painted black, and an old jukebox from which B.B. King was wailing "The Thrill is Gone." The music wove a heady spell over the dark, subterranean cavern, worlds away from the lively rooms upstairs at the Rams Head.

Again, this bartender seemed to nod in recognition too. Robert returned the greeting as he led Susanna to the one remaining free table in a dark corner and pulled out a chair for her. A fat candle flickered on the table, spilling wax over the worn wood of the tabletop. Susanna was about to sit down, but he grabbed her by a loop on her jeans and pulled her into him, cupping her butt in his warm, strong hands. "I've been needing to do that since I saw you on the street," he growled into her hair.

She looked up at him. His eyes caught hers and refused to let her go, and that knowing half-smile of his had her breath hitching. What was it about the man? All he had to do was look at her a certain way, and desire started to flow through her as relentless and demanding as the B.B. King on the jukebox. She felt him hard and straining through his jeans against her belly, and she instinctively pressed even more tightly into him, making him groan. Their eyes stayed locked on each other, and she wanted to drown in the depths she saw there. The utter perfection of the moment settled around her, and she knew then that it would stay in her memory forever, the sheer beauty, the raw power of it. In that one exquisite moment, she felt fully alive.

And then Van Morrison started crooning about standing with the sisters of mercy, and she knew absolutely that she had stumbled into heaven. And she marveled at a God who had graced people with such amazing bodies and hearts and minds, made them capable of such incredible sensation, such powerful emotion.

And gratitude coursed through her for her own body, for Robert's, for men like Robert, for men like B.B. King and the gifts that he could share. And for the aching majesty of Van the Man, god among mortals, revealing the sublime longing of his own soul. And for all the other gods and goddesses among us. Such gratitude. All in that one complete moment in time.

Robert nudged her on the chin. "Are you all right, Susanna?"

"I don't know," she said with a shaky laugh, and she pushed him down into his chair. "Is this the best fuck music or what?"

He sat back with a look of surprise on his face, but when he spoke, his voice was low, teasing. "Well, don't be shy, Susanna. Tell me what you really want."

She bit her lip, not able to find the words.

He watched her. "We should talk," he said. "No more fooling around. I promise."

"Good." She nodded her head as he squeezed her by the hand.

"I owe you some explanation," he added, letting out a long breath.

"Let me take a crazy guess." She slid down into the chair beside him. "Annapolis is your home town?"

He helped take her sweater off. "I grew up around the corner from here." His fingers grazed the back of her neck, rested under her silk camisole, and then he hung her sweater across the back of the chair.

"Why didn't you tell me?" she asked.

He shrugged out of his windbreaker. "West Street used to be a real dump, where hookers trawled when I walked home from baseball practice at night. It wasn't the gentrified street you saw today. That's for sure." He glanced around the room and then back at Susanna. "And this basement is the original Rams Head Tavern. This is all there was when I was growing up. This was my old man's home away from home. I used to hate the sight of the place."

"And Ms. Hortense?" Susanna asked.

"When I was around ten or eleven, my mom disappeared. Never saw her again. The old man blamed me, said I had too many needs," he murmured." Said it was enough to drive anyone off. I believed him."

Susanna reached over to lay her hand on Robert's, but he moved back in his chair.

"I guess she got tired of the never-ending battles, the nightly black and blue. I was a kid. What did I know?"

His words broke her heart, but Susanna realized that he would see it as a sign of weakness to take any comfort from her. Boy, she had a couple things she needed to teach this man.

"Ms. Hortense raised me for a couple bucks an hour. And sometimes the old man wouldn't even pay her that, claimed he was broke, complained she was charging too much."

"I'm sorry," she said, "that's all." She'd spent her whole life pining for a father. Everything would have been different if only she had one. She had been so sure of it. So Robert's words were twice as upsetting to hear, and she could only imagine his pain, which he'd probably buried so deeply it didn't even register anymore. And she could sympathize with that.

"He was a pencil-pushing bureaucrat at the Naval Surface Warfare Center on Dinger Street. He was a civ but acted like a tough guy. I grew up thinking he was more important that the Commander in Chief. He worked with Ms. Hortense's husband Carl. So he unloaded me on her. His own family didn't want to know. There was no one else. He had no friends."

He looked at her. "My old man's two true companions were his bottle and his fist."

"That was one hell of a way to grow up."

"Like Ms. Hortense said, there was a lot worse than him."

"Same song, different refrain? You know what? That's bull. Knowing there's worse out there never lessens the blunt force of the punches or the ugliness of the grasping fingers."

"Maybe not," he said and leaned in and ran his knuckles down the side of her face. "But talking about it now isn't going to fix anything. We aren't defined by the sins of our fathers."

"Who said that?"

"I don't know. Somebody." He paused. "Being nothing like him is the only revenge I know."

"And are you doing that?"

He stopped, didn't answer, countered with a question of his own. "What about you?"

The bartender set down a bottle of Jamesons Irish Whiskey and a couple shot glasses on the table between them.

"Courtesy of the house, sir."

"No thanks, Nate. Take it away. I'll just have an Oyster Stout."

Sir? Susanna's eyes went from the bartender to Robert. Nate?

Robert caught her look. "Unless you're up for a shot of good Irish whiskey. After our heart-warming conversation, I wouldn't blame you."

"I'm not much of a drinker. Maybe a glass of wine."

"Okay, Nate. You heard her."

The bartender looked at Susanna. "I've got a nice Shiraz, if you're fine with that?"

When she nodded, the bartender retreated with the bottle of whiskey in his hand.

"Man, good thing he came over," Robert said. "This was turning into a bloody shrink session or something."

Susanna looked at him thoughtfully. "Let me guess. If we hadn't bumped into Ms. Hortense, you wouldn't have told me any of this, would you?"

He studied her. "Am I allowed to shrug my shoulders without coming off as callous?"

"Not even that Annapolis is where you grew up?"

"Is it important?"

"Yes, it is. I want to know you, Robert. I want to know all about you. More than what I know."

"No, you don't. I want to hear about you, my lovely, Canadian-made Susanna Bailey, and what is it that got you running all the way down here to big ole, bad ole America?"

"You're so smooth, but I'm on to you," she smiled, and watched the merriment dancing in his eyes. "And I'm not big on talking about myself, you know, all that personal stuff."

"I've noticed," he said. "And that is a rare quality indeed, unfortunately much underrated these days. I do appreciate it, but I also want to get to know you better. Come on. Tell me a little about yourself. Give it a try. It's good for you. You can start slow."

"No, Robert. It's good for you. Once again you get to divert the focus off yourself."

"That way you won't be able to steal my heart away."

The sincerity she saw in his eyes made her laugh out loud, and she looked at him with pure pleasure. "Ditto."

He cracked a grin. "Am I sensing something in common here? Isn't that supposed to be nice, when two people getting to know each other have something in common, something they can share," he joked. "Even when it's only an unhealthy neurosis or a fear of being known?"

"I want to ask you something about Ms. Hortense."

"First tell me who was it that spooked you."

"What do you mean?"

"I can have them killed, you know. It's a small world." His eyes danced with humor.

"Thank you," she said with a wry smile. "That's why I like you. You really care."

He was going to say something but stopped himself and studied her. "I remember something about the woman who gave birth to you? What was it you said?"

Susanna hated talking about her childhood almost as much as she disliked talking about herself. It was worse than going to the dentist. Robert sat solid as a rock, his focus on her quiet and complete, waiting. Oh, how she would have preferred to climb into his lap instead and rest her head against his neck where it curved to his shoulder and feel his warm and steady pulse. Shadows flickered, and the room hummed around them. She mumbled, not sure what she would say. But how else could she give him a chance if not by sharing at least the tiniest bit? A flush of heat suffused her face. She hoped he couldn't see it in the dark. With Michael it had been different, undemanding. He never asked much, and if she didn't volunteer, he didn't mind.

"I was a convenient inconvenience in my mother's life, and she made sure I never forgot it," Susanna said. "She was a woman who liked to express her disappointments in a very physical way." Her hand went to the little table, and her finger moved over it, feeling the grooves and gashes in the wood. "It made her feel better. And that was the only thing that ever mattered." She glanced up at Robert, then back down at the table. She shifted in her chair, unsettled. She knew that he understood her words and the spaces in between.

"And your father?"

"He may have been around for a bit when I was young. I can't remember. Big Dave, her fave drunk with the uppercut of a true heavyweight, that's what my mother called him."

She swallowed hard under his steady gaze. "And that's it, Robert. I grew up in a state of high alert, learning the fine art of worthlessness, the craft of invisibility, and thinking I had more uncles than anyone else in the world. End of story." The warmth of the room lay heavy on her, and the jukebox hiccupped and started to wail.

"And now you live with everything she taught you held close to your heart," Robert said softly.

"No, of course not," she protested.

"Good," he said, "because it's never about the shit that's happened. It's about the part that comes after."

"So they say." Susanna looked at him. "But I have wasted obscene stretches of my adult life buying clothing and shopping for the woman I desperately wanted to be, who of course was any woman but me — and accumulating cookbooks like amulets."

"Cookbooks?"

"Cookbooks. Hoping to somehow fall into the magical, lovely lives I saw in the photos there. Fabulous people laughing and cooking delicious things in beautiful kitchens. Any life but my own, no matter the cost, had to have more value, had to be better. Whatever they were selling, I was the first shopper in line."

"The fine art of worthlessness," Robert echoed her words. "I like that. That's a good one. Well, it does keep the wheels of consumerism greased. And it made a cook out of you." He hesitated. "Didn't it?"

She shook her head no, and they both started to laugh. "I hate to disappoint you."

Robert drank the glass of water in front of him and regarded her, and she realized that she'd never shared this much with anyone before, and she wondered if it was the same for him. But if she was planning to keep her heart safe, this was not the way to go about it.

"But I did finally grow up to understand that my mother's sorrows didn't belong to me," she added. "Her life was not my fault. And later I met Michael and moved on. In a way, he saved me."

Robert leaned over the table and kissed Susanna on the cheek. "For what it's worth, I think your kitchen is real pretty and nice," he whispered, and his breath caressed her ear.

CHAPTER:
SIXTEEN

THE BARTENDER APPEARED BEFORE THEM and cleared his throat as he set down Robert's beer and a bottle of Fat Bastard Shiraz, along with a single wine glass.

Susanna's eyes widened. "A glass would have been fine."

"Compliments of the house," the bartender said as he poured. Then he picked up the corkscrew, and with a slight incline of the head to Robert, he left.

What was the deal with these bartenders? Susanna looked at the label on the wine bottle and tried to pinpoint what exactly had just made her feel uneasy. It wasn't Robert. She was liking him more and more. But was this really just a getaway for the two of them, like he'd said, or was this trip somehow related to his work? Or Mr. Nashta? Or the stereograms?

"Robert, are you on the clock right now?"

He gave her a sharp look. "No. Why?"

She couldn't answer. She didn't want to spoil the mood. Here she was actually getting to know him, and she didn't want it to stop. "Not important." She sipped her wine. "I didn't know you were a Naval officer."

"Now you do." He took a swig of his beer, his eyes on her. "So your mom is who you were running from when you left Canada?"

"I wasn't running. Well, maybe just a slight jog."

"Then why leave?"

"Adventure. Change. It's a big, interesting world out there. Why not?" Susanna took another sip of her wine. "Oh, this is very nice."

"Do you ever see her now?"

She shrugged. "Only in my nightmares."

Robert chuckled. She liked that, knowing that she could make him laugh. "It wasn't just that. Michael was an American. He wanted to come home."

Robert nodded, and Susanna asked, "Why was Ms. Hortense upset when she talked about your graduation from the Naval Academy?"

He picked up his bottle and downed half the beer in one long pull and set the bottle down hard. Then he picked it up again, started to roll it around in his hands, set it down and tore off an edge of the label. "Because I went to the Academy with Stanton, their son."

"Their son?" That was the last thing Susanna expected.

"We grew up like brothers, thanks to that woman's

kindness. We were the same age, young and stupid as all hell. And we both graduated with Honors and became officers. I went into the Navy, Stanton into the Marines." An edge of bitterness crept into his voice. "And I never stopped him. That's how I thanked them all."

She set down her glass of wine. "But" —

"He was set on the Corps. Wanted the real deal, he said. And got killed in Iraq on his very first tour." His voice trailed off. "And I'm still here."

He shook his head. "I can only imagine how Ms. Hortense and Carl felt about that."

Susanna felt the guilt tear through him as though it had all just happened, sensed the wound, raw and festering still, and she couldn't think of anything comforting to say that wouldn't come out sounding trite or hollow. She wanted to tell him Stanton's death wasn't his fault, but she knew he wouldn't hear her.

"I was on the other side of the world when I got the news. Couldn't even get leave to come back for his funeral. I wasn't legally family."

The bartender came over to Robert and bent down and whispered something in his ear. Susanna let out a long breath as she watched them, and her brow furrowed. There was that unease again. She took a sip of her wine and tried to focus on the taste and sensation of it on her tongue and push aside the sense of foreboding that prickled her skin and sent a shiver through her despite the warmth of the room.

Was she imagining things that weren't there? She didn't

know, but it was definitely time to clarify the situation, to come clean, to find out from Robert what was on those stereograms and memory stick and clear up the murky waters that had brought them together. Then she could truly enjoy their time together. She forced herself to swallow the wine, and it went down rich and warm and soothing.

Robert glanced over at her, then back to the bartender crouched at his side. When the bartender left, Robert said, "Come on. Let me show you the fantastic jukebox in this place. I've got to take care of something real quick" and pulled her to her feet. Depositing a handful of coins into her hand, he added, "I'll be right back. Choose wisely."

Susanna's eyes widened as she saw all the songs, shimmering like jewels under the layer of dust that covered the old jukebox. She deposited a handful of coins and made her way back to their table, her body swaying ever so slowly to the music. She saw Robert at the bar, talking with the bartender and another man. Maybe he knew them from his Naval Academy days. She sipped her wine. But it didn't look like casual conversation. When he came back, he gave her a smile even though she saw that his fist was clenched.

"Is everything okay?"

He took a drink from his bottle. "Yup."

"Why do all the bartenders here know you?"

"Small town."

"Do they work with you?"

"Not now, Susanna." She heard the entreaty in his voice.

"If not now, when?"

He didn't answer. Yes, this too could wait. She wanted to stay in their own little world a little longer as much as he did.

"That's some jukebox," she said, and she could see him relax as he contemplated her.

"I thought you'd enjoy it."

"The only thing missing is a wee touch of The Clash or The Ramones to liven things up, and it's solid gold," she smiled.

"Shit," he said. "I can't even pretend to understand you on that. Sit tight a second." He dug in the pockets of his jeans and went over to the jukebox. When he came back, he pulled Susanna to her feet as a harmonica started keening.

"You Shook Me. Let's dance." He wrapped her into his arms and started to slow dance with her to an old Willie Dixon blues number.

"Now this is something I can understand," he murmured in her ear.

With Robert, slow dancing was more body grind than dance, but Susanna loved every minute of it. She couldn't remember the last time she had danced with anyone, and he sang along with Willie Dixon into her ear. "You move me pretty mama, just like a hurricane…"

She buried her face into his chest and gave herself up to him, let him move her slowly around. The cotton of his t-shirt felt soft and his body heat reassuring against her cheek, and he smelled so good. When the song finished, she stepped back, blinking, and looked around the dark little bar. Candlelight flickered on the tabletops. No one seemed to pay them any attention even though they were the only ones dancing.

Then a saxophone began to wail, and Robert winked at her. "This one is for you."

He swooped her into his arms again and began to twirl her around to a faster beat, and he grinned like a goofball as he swung her around. She couldn't stop laughing, and she loved him for it. And Van Morrison sang his heart out. "Hey, Mr. D.J., play something just for my baby and me, won't you make everything all right." The music cast its mesmerizing web around them, and it felt like they were the only people in the room until the bartender tapped Robert on the shoulder. "Table's available upstairs."

Susanna looked at the bartender as she fanned herself with her hand. "Goodness me. I'm breathless. I must be getting the vapors. Isn't that what fine Southern ladies here call it?"

"This is not technically the South," the bartender said, looking at her dismissively. "The State of Virginia is, technically, the dividing line."

She wasn't going to let this man spoil her fun. "Nevertheless, I need to go and splash some cold water on my face." She glanced over her shoulder at Robert. "You are the most surprising man I know."

He smiled. "I can live with that."

Susanna looked at herself in the bathroom mirror as she applied more foundation to the scar on her cheek, then matted it with a dab of powder. Robert obviously hadn't noticed it yet, or he wouldn't be looking at her the way she caught him doing. Her auburn hair curled around her in a messy rat's nest that had her cringing, but she was happy. Yes, siree. She smacked a touch of color onto her lips, pulled her phone out of her purse, and called Farida.

"Boy, am I glad I came to Annapolis, Farida."

"Boy, am I glad you called."

"I am happy. Really happy. I didn't realize how much I needed this break. And I'm coming home a day late."

Farida jumped in before Susanna went on, "Not so fast, Cowboy Bob. Hold on. There's something I want to tell you."

Whenever Farida called her that, something was amiss. "What is it?"

"I've finished editing the last day's transcript of Mr. Nashta's testimony."

"Great. Email it to Pat at the office."

"That Mr. Nashta, his demeanor changed very much that last day when your Robert Crowell showed up. Did you realize that?"

Susanna stood squeezed in with a half dozen other women, all touching up their make-up or hair in the mirror that covered the entire wall over the sinks. The bathroom was abuzz with their chatter, and Susanna had to put the phone closer to her ear.

Farida was saying, "Mr. Nashta became completely frightened or something, like he sensed a danger. I'm not sure how to better explain it. Please be careful over there in Annapolis with that spy fellow. That's all I have to say."

"I know, Farida. I sensed that too. I am being careful and vigilant. But Robert's lovely."

"I'll say no more."

"Thank you. I just want to have a nice little getaway."

"Well, maybe just one more thing. How do you know that this is any different from when you've bought an entire cream strawberry cake to eat by yourself because it was so good, or in my case an entire pot of buttery dal makhani cooked over a low flame for many hours?"

Susanna didn't reply.

"Were we not convinced of its goodness and necessity in our body at that greedy moment? Were we not? And only after the insanity settled, or in my case the pot was empty, were we willing to entertain the suspicion that perhaps our lusty appetites were not the best arbiters of goodness after all."

"Lusty appetites, Farida? I haven't been with anyone since Michael died. Give me a break. Strawberry cream cakes don't count."

"You have a point," Farida conceded. "But you have to be careful. I have a bad feeling..."

"This is my instinct talking. And I'm listening."

"So this fellow is cream cakes and dal makhani and Russell Robin Hood rolled into one?"

Susanna laughed. "Trust me. I think he's the real thing."

"You remember in the movie that scene where the lady takes off Robin Hood's chain mail?"

"Oh, yeah," Susanna said. "Hot."

"Oh dear, I remember that scene so well. Whatever happened to that actor anyway? " Farida took a deep, calming breath. "I should have insisted you join the Friends of Jefferson Debating Society with me. It would have been a safe outlet for your energies and passions."

"I love you too. Talk soon." Susanna disconnected and threw her phone into her purse and swept aside Farida's concerns. Tell me this. Tell me this. Tell me this. If you can't trust your gut instinct, then what have you got?

CHAPTER:
SEVENTEEN

THE MOUTHWATERING AROMAS of grilled shrimp and brewing beer wafted over the dining room, and Susanna's stomach growled in response. Music streamed over from the night-club part of the Rams Head Tavern and mingled with the diners overflowing the tables. Robert sat in a booth on a black leather banquette, engrossed in what seemed an intense conversation on his phone. When he glanced up and saw Susanna approaching, he ended his call and looked at her, his expression inscrutable. Susanna smiled as she slid into the booth across from him. The bottle of Fat Bastard Shiraz, still two-thirds full, sat on the table between them along.

"Work?" she asked, and when he didn't answer, she said, "I'm starving."

His eyes went to her mouth and lingered there.

"Stop that."

"What?"

"Looking at me like that."

"Where should I look?"

"Well, not at my mouth."

He considered her. "You're right. One of the first behaviors military personnel are taught is to look directly into the eyes of one's adversary."

She stopped, then laughed and raised her hands in question. "Is that what we are?"

He winked. "But be wary of using excessive hand movements. It will give you away every time. That's rule number two."

Her eyes grew large. Was there a shift in the atmosphere, or was she imagining it?

"It's so easy to tease you," Robert said.

The waiter came over, balancing a tray on one hand, set down glasses of water and another beer, and took their order.

"Here's to my little guardian of the record," Robert said as he clinked his beer bottle against her glass. "And here's to doing the right thing."

Susanna looked around the dining room, unsettled, and she felt Robert's eyes on her. Maybe Farida had spooked her. That was all. When she turned back, he held her gaze. The bass sounds from next door vibrated the floor beneath them in a steady beat, and the water glasses danced on the table. She picked up her glass and took a sip of wine. "To honorable men and women everywhere," she responded and glanced around the dining room again. Something seemed to have shifted just the tiniest bit between them, but she wasn't sure what it was.

"You know, honor and integrity do not come without a price," he said.

She looked at him. "But without them, what have you got?" She took a stab at lightening the mood. "Like the song says, you've got to be iron like a lion in Zion."

It seemed to work because Robert laughed. "Okay. To Bob Marley," he said, and they both raised their glasses but neither drank.

"I never would have guessed you for a Bob Marley fan."

"I'm not, especially. Stanton was," Robert said. "Bob was a little too righteous for me."

"Hey, I'm a fan."

"I know you are," he said. "I'm more of an Everlast kind of guy myself."

She was grateful that the earlier tension seemed to have passed. "I don't think I've ever talked so much with anyone besides Marie."

"Marie? French Canadian best friend from Toronto. I remember, " he said.

"Oui. I'm impressed," she said.

"Lives on an island in the middle of the city," he said. "I never knew Toronto had an island."

"Ward Island. It's on Lake Ontario. You can take a water taxi from downtown. Or a ferry. It's this green, little pastoral village, with unbelievable views of the city skyscrapers across the water. No cars allowed. And it's got a great restaurant too."

"Show me sometime."

"I'd love to." She smiled. "Marie's always wanting me to go back. I don't know."

"And I bet you speak French too?" His eyes twinkled. "That is sexy."

Susanna laughed. "Don't get too excited now, Robert. My French is pretty elementary. Turn to the left. Turn to the right. Zut alors!"

When he didn't respond, she explained. "That means darn it!"

He nodded. "I like listening to you. I think I'm beginning to understand you. You know what I mean?"

"I'm finding it all a little overwhelming."

"We're doing this warp speed, remember?"

She nodded. "Warp speed."

His gaze turned contemplative. "So the Navy was my ticket out, and Michael was yours."

"Don't say it like that. I loved him, and I missed him very much."

"Good for him. I was pretty fond of the Navy myself."

The waiter set down two plates of crab cakes and left with the pepper grinder under his arm.

"So tell me about Mr. Nashta," Susanna said as she dove into her food.

"Mr. Nashta?" She seemed to take Robert by surprise with her question. "Serious?"

"Yes." Maybe this wasn't the time, but she had this weight sitting on her, and maybe it was time to deal with it.

"I didn't realize how hungry I was," he said and started in on his own food.

"He brought us together, didn't he?" she said through a mouthful of crab cake.

"I guess you could look at it that way."

"Why would someone want to kill him?"

"I've been trying to find that out myself because they totally screwed up my job." He put down his fork and looked at her. "Experienced agents don't get caught often. Going gray, they can traverse the world and operate in all sorts of environments for a very long time."

"Agents? Like secret agent? Are you saying Mr. Nashta was a spy?" She almost giggled, and she wasn't sure if it was with fear or disbelief. She set her own fork down. When she thought of spies, James Bond was the image that popped into her mind, and she just couldn't picture Mr. Nashta in that category. It was laughable.

"A spy for whom?" she asked.

Robert rubbed his thumb and forefinger together.

"What does that mean?"

"For the highest bidder. For whoever paid him the most money for what he was selling."

"What was he selling?" And Susanna suddenly knew the answer to that question even as she asked it, and the knowledge sank like a rock to the pit of her stomach.

Robert didn't answer her.

"You don't know?" she asked.

"Do you?" he countered.

"No, of course not. What are you talking about?" But she knew exactly what he was talking about. Whatever was on that memory stick and stereograms now buried in a plastic bag under Farida's potting shed was what he was talking about. But she wasn't a complete liar, she consoled herself. She really didn't know what exactly was on them. Maybe this was the moment she'd been waiting for. Maybe it was time to tell him about it.

"We could have arrested him earlier," Robert said," but it was more productive to keep an eye on him to see who he talked to, figure out just what he knew, where he went, who he tried to sell to. Reel in the bigger prize." He paused. "We thought we were a step ahead of him."

"But he was killed before you got him?" He nodded.

And she understood the danger she was in as if for the first time. "Do you know who killed him?

"Yes." He went back to his food. "Now we do."

Her eyes darted around the room as if she might see his killers among the diners there. "Are you going to tell me?"

"Are you asking?"

"Yes, I am."

He speared another forkful, his eyes intent on his plate, but his body stilled. "Why?"

Her mouth went dry. "He was the witness. We were on the third day of depositions. So we had chatted and stuff. I had gotten to know Mr. Nashta a little."

He glanced up at her. "How? How did you get to know him?"

"Just small talk at the breaks, things like that." She gulped. "Was it the men on the bench who killed him?"

"Did you ever meet with him outside of work? Like that day in Franklin Park, was that an arranged meeting? Did he ever give you anything?"

"No, of course not." She almost flinched but managed to keep her eyes on his. "What do you mean?" That wasn't a complete lie. She had no idea that Mr. Nashta threw those classified documents into her bag that day. She waited for Robert to go on, her mind whirling. Maybe this was the moment to tell him. She could backpedal. Or maybe not. But she was afraid above all.

He shrugged. "It was just a question."

"The police already asked me all this stuff. So did you and your lady friend."

"She isn't my friend. She's a colleague. Listen, Susanna, if Colin Nashta hadn't been killed, he would have lived out his days in prison. I can promise you that."

"That's so hard to believe. Mr. Nashta was the most unassuming little man you can imagine. A little high-strung maybe, but still."

"Then he was good at his job. Real spies look like Colin Nashta, not like James Bond," he said, as if he had read her mind.

"He had a blue plastic comb, for goodness sake."

"He stole government secrets that he had gotten access to in his job. He would have gone down for treason. Do you understand?"

Her eyes widened. "But he seemed so harmless."

"Selling confidential U.S. government information to the highest bidder is not harmless. It's treason. It's a threat to national security, and it can endanger American lives."

Oh shit. She took a sip from her wine glass, her fingers shaky on the stem, and studied the botanical print design on the tablecloth. She was going to prison for treason. This was crazy. Robert watched her speculatively but didn't say anything.

"So did Mr. Nashta manage to complete the sale before he was killed?" she asked.

"No."

Oh, this was very bad. She needed space to think. Better to change the subject. "Back at the scene that day, why were you looking for his watch?"

"Routine. He may have hidden something in it."

"And the secret stuff he had stolen, how would it endanger American lives?"

"That's classified. I can't tell you that."

Susanna knew she was definitely in over her head. He would think she was involved in this whole thing if she told him now. What had she gotten herself into? Visions of being thrown into Guantanamo Bay clouded her mind. Was that place even open anymore? She picked up her fork, her eyes on her food, but her appetite had vanished.

"Do you want to ask me anything else?" he said.

"If you're going to tell me the truth," she mumbled.

"Like you've been doing?" he answered, sending a shiver through her.

"What do you mean?" she practically squeaked and quickly went to clear her throat.

Robert took a drink from his water glass and set it back down on the table. She looked at the beads of condensation forming on the glass and the marks left by his fingers. She had to divert his attention and figure out how she was going to get out of this mess.

"So you're not a Naval officer anymore?" she managed to ask.

"I work in Counter-Intelligence."

"For the Navy?"

"And other agencies, as needed."

She looked at him. "Does that mean you are a spy too, Robert?"

"No, Susanna, it does not. It means I am a spy catcher. I seek out and identify espionage activities. And I was a spy handler before that."

"So why were you throwing all these different agency names around before? It's all so confusing."

His gaze didn't stray from her face. "I'm stranded between the devil and the deep blue sea."

"Oh," she said. "What does that mean? Is that supposed to be confusing?"

"Obfuscatingly so."

"Will you ever be honest with me?"

"I haven't been honest with anyone in a very long time," he answered. "You'd be surprised how far that can take you."

"No, I wouldn't. The world is full of liars." She was one to talk, she thought sourly.

"But I am being completely honest with you right now," he said.

"Are you?"

"Yes. What about you?"

She ignored his question. "So what about that Sealift Command? And what about that Aerial Intelligence or whatever that was?"

"Excellent agencies, both of them."

"You don't work for them?"

He shrugged his shoulders.

"You never did start out in the Sealift Command?"

He said nothing.

"This is insane. No wonder your marriage didn't last. It's like trying to communicate with a mirage or something."

"That was below the belt."

"But it's true. How can you have a normal life? How can you live with someone in such a cloud of deception?"

He raised an eyebrow and took a sip of his beer. Susanna watched him drink and set the bottle down. "I'm thinking of retiring," he said matter-of-factly.

"I'm serious," she said.

"I'm serious too. It's not easy, but it's not impossible." His eyes traveled over her face lazily and rested on her mouth as he seemed to consider his answer.

"And then what?" she asked.

"Mow the lawn. Read a book." He looked away from her, his thoughts going with him. "Disappear."

"What does that mean?" She watched him watch a woman in a tight blue dress squeeze into a chair at the table across from them.

"Find my way back to the living. It's been a long time coming." He stopped, his eyes still on the woman. "Get into bed with you and not surface for days."

Susanna's heart did a crazy little somersault.

A waiter, wiping his hands on his long black apron, approached the lady in blue and her two male companions. She turned to him, a sheen of anticipation lighting up her face. Robert looked back at Susanna. "Maybe get a teaching post at some university. You know, political science, international affairs, something like that. That's what happens to the lucky boys. That's the reward," he said wryly.

"I find it hard to picture you as a professor," she whispered, but she could feel an irregular heartbeat start up in her chest. She liked the sound of that.

He watched her. "Then there are always the myriad consulting positions, you know, defense contracting, security, guns for hire — the kind of stuff that leaves a bad taste in your mouth. But let's keep it positive. A post at the Naval Academy does come up once a decade or so."

An unexpected silence settled between them, a fog of unspoken things — yearning, uncertainty, foolishness. It made both of them uneasy, and Susanna scrambled to fill the void, not daring to look at him, not wanting him to see what was in her eyes.

"You told the Department of Justice lawyers you were from Military Sealift Command."

"You tell them whatever you need to get the job done."

"Did they know who you really were?"

"Some of them may have guessed, but no one would be stupid enough to ask me questions. They knew I had clearance."

"What about the judge?"

"She was fully apprised of the situation."

"Oh." Susanna thought about that and about how clueless she had been as to what had been going on around her. But at least she was learning more about him at last.

"Though I may be in an intelligence unit, Susanna, I am still a Naval officer. The Sealift Command is comprised of civilian personnel, and they work with us on joint operations when needed."

"Okay. And what about the Department of Defense?"

"I do work for the Department of Defense, and I answer to the Secretary of Defense. I didn't lie to you even though I should have. I work for the DIA, the Defense Intelligence Agency, which integrates all the military intelligence of the vast DoD intelligence and counter-intelligence activities."

"So you work at the DIA?"

"At this time for a department within that organization. On secondment. I do what the political masters demand, without question."

She caught the subtle shift in his tone, the cynicism shading his words.

He paused and considered her for a very long time. "Now, what about you?"

"What about me? I've already told you about me."

He didn't say anything, and it made her nervous. "You remember how we met," she said. "You were wearing those fancy suits and pretending to be a lawyer or whoever it was you were pretending to be?"

He studied her as he pushed his plate aside. "And are you being completely honest with me?"

She hesitated, only a fraction of a second. "Of course I am."

How in the world was she supposed to tell him what she had done without implicating herself in some kind of espionage? Best to leave that stuff where it was and let it disintegrate into dust under Farida's old shed. It would be easier that way. What a hypocrite she was, with all that talk of honor and honesty and doing the right thing. She was torn with indecision. Why in the world did she think a weekend away with this man was ever a good idea?

He studied her some more and finally said, "Susanna, I believe you." But something had shifted in his eyes.

CHAPTER:
EIGHTEEN

SUSANNA SAT ACROSS FROM HIM, shifting the old Annapolis kaleidoscope, reconfiguring the rusty images, beckoning to him like a new dream, surrounded by people enjoying themselves, sweaty and loud, and the lady in the too-tight blue who can't stop laughing, her laughter tinkling high notes on a piano, all of it so far, far away from his old world. Yet Susanna fit into this scene, and he was glad of it. Robert sat back watching her, but his mind strayed to the old nightmares.

In his mind's eye, he was always running in the same baseball diamond, and it was always wet with rain. He liked to pretend his mom was sitting in the stands cheering him on, waving a Crackerjack box in her hand. His hair was dripping, his shirt stuck to his back, sneakers squishing around in the mud as the rain washed away the dust and make the blades of grass coruscate like emeralds. He ran bases with the fast wind off the Chesapeake that chased the storm clouds over to D.C. and made everything smell new and taste of promise. But when he sneaked another glance at the bleachers, they would be windswept and empty. Like a chewed-up, old cassette tape, the dream never moved past that point, and he'd wake up cursing, oblivious to why Annapolis or baseball was sticky on his mind like gum in his hair, not knowing what had dragged him from vital hours of sleep, and vowing to cut down on the coffee. It must be giving him heartburn.

Susanna's voice shook him out of his ruminations. "Actually, Robert, there's something I've been meaning to tell you."

He saw that she seemed to be struggling with her words. "I don't even know where to how to start. I'm sorry I didn't —"

"Wait. Stop, Susanna. I don't want to talk about this anymore." He grabbed her hand in his and forced it down onto the center of the table, making the forks bounce. He knew what she was going to say, and he didn't want to hear it. He'd already figured it out back at her place the other night, and right now he'd had enough talk of work. He'd figure out the best way to deal with it all soon enough.

"I don't want to talk. I don't want to play stupid games."

She looked surprised by the force of his grip, and he released his hold on her. It didn't even matter why she had lied. He knew she was probably frightened of what he would think, worried that suspicion would cloud what they had. Oh, how naïve she was.

"But there's something —" she started.

"I know, Susanna." He stood up abruptly, slid into her side of the booth, and took her face into his hands. She felt small, fragile, breakable under his fingers. His eyes went to her mouth, and he leaned in and brushed his lips over hers very, very slowly, needing this, needing to savor her and watch her eyes flutter shut. Then he kissed her more fully until her body shuddered and he felt his own responding.

Her little moan was audible only to his ears. Satisfied at last, he drew back, wrapping strands of her hair through his fingers. This is where he belonged. He understood that now like he understood breathing. Mowing a lawn with her, reading with her, listening to her, touching her. He'd never been so certain of anything in his life. Two dozen years of service. Coming up to a hundred missions. His duty was done. Wrap this one up and retire his stripes. He rubbed an auburn curl between his thumb and index finger. Her hair was silky soft to his touch, like the rest of her. Then the thought crossed his mind that he'd never owned a lawn or a lawnmower before. He'd adapt.

He felt the effect his kiss had on her. Good. He liked to feel her defenses melting away, and she amused him when she didn't want to give him the satisfaction of knowing it. A smile pulled at the corners of his mouth as he gave her hair a gentle tug.

"Wipe that smirk off your face," she muttered under her breath, her cheeks flushed, pretty as a rose, a faint scar accentuating her loveliness.

"I'm not smirking. That's my smile."

"No, it isn't, smartass." She shoved him in the chest, laughing, pushing him back, and his foot knocked over her purse on the floor. He leaned down, grabbed her purse, set it on the table beside him, and tried to regroup his position.

"We're in a crowded restaurant, Robert, and we're behaving like a couple of fools."

"No one's looking." He bent toward her again, and she couldn't escape him. She was already pressed up against the back of the booth.

"Oh, you're incorrigible." She tried to sound serious.

"Just one more kiss," he whispered and nipped her ear and went to her neck and started to drag his mouth slowly down.

"God, that feels so good," she murmured.

Suddenly Robert stopped dead still, sensing an intrusion before he even heard it. Instinctively he whirled around at the same time as his hand shot out, like a steel trap, and locked onto a man's arm as he passed their table. Susanna almost jumped out of the booth with shock. He hadn't meant to frighten her.

"Oh my God," she cried. "What the —"

"Don't move, or I break it," Robert growled at the man, his voice low and controlled, adrenaline pumping full blast. "Susanna, sit down."

"Whoa, dude," the young man stammered, shaking his streaked blond hair out of his eyes, wincing as Robert intensified the grip on his arm until his fingers released their hold on Susanna's purse.

"The lady's purse was falling. I just wanted to help, man." Fear flickered in his eyes. "Let go of my arm before you break it."

Robert eyed him with such ferocity that the young man blanched.

"I'm telling you, dude, take a chill pill. Lady's purse was falling." He tried to twist out of Robert's grip.

Robert's voice was steel. "Cut it, plebe."

He grabbed the man by his Tommy Hilfiger, striped shirt-front with his free hand and pulled him down to his eye level, popping a couple shirt buttons, smooth and fast. No need to draw the other diners' attention.

"Where's your ID?" Robert demanded quietly. "Place it on the table, nice and slow."

"Huh? What are you about, man?" The man started raising his voice, causing a slight ripple in the immediate vicinity of their booth. "Let go of my arm."

"Keep your voice down, troop. You know the scoop."

Before he could answer, Robert frisked him in one fast, smooth move.

"Holy shit, dude. What's your problemo?"

Robert kept his grip on the young man's arm, and at the same time his other hand dove for the man's calf. If you had blinked, you would have missed it. Bingo. He felt the gun in its Velcro strap-on holster.

"Okay, dude," Robert said softly, mocking him, as he pulled up the man's chino pant leg to give Susanna a quick glimpse and watched her eyes grow wide in confusion.

"This is a free country. I got a permit for that," the man hissed at Robert.

"If I find anything in that purse missing or, worse yet, something there that shouldn't be, I will personally find you and break every one of your fingers." Robert released him, keeping a tight control over his own voice. "You see me in the hallway, you better run. Got it, dude?"

The young man shook himself straight and marched off, head held high, keeping his torn shirt together with one hand, shaking his streaked blond head. Robert did a quick scan of the dining room, and assessing everything as under control, his eyes came back to rest on Susanna. She sat pale, silent, squeezed as far back into the booth as possible.

"Sorry." He said to Susanna before grabbing his beer and taking a long swig, giving the adrenaline a chance to slow down, furious with whichever agency had the nerve to sic a kid on him.

"Shit." The thought that it could be his own office drained the color from his face. He had told Nate, the basement bartender, that he was off the clock. He'd roast his balls for insubordination if it transpired that Nate had gone over his head. But Nate was a good kid. He'd taught him his Tradecraft 101. He knew this kid. It had to have been Jared Sleight, working the upstairs bar. He didn't even know which agency that purulent fucker worked for these days, but it wasn't Naval. Probably NSA, the secret-est of the secret, more affectionately known as No Such Agency or Never Say Anything. They slurped up agents like a fat man with a milkshake. Both operatives had surprised him by their presence at the tavern, as he had undoubtedly surprised them with his. Junior agents both, not under his command, but clearly on the job.

Susanna was still speechless. He pushed her purse over to her.

"Take a careful look through your purse and make sure there is nothing in there that is not yours."

"What just happened here? What was that?" she whispered.

"Just do it." His tone was sharper than he intended, and he modulated it with some effort. "Make sure he didn't take anything of yours or drop anything in there."

If they had sent someone to either plant a trace or transmitter in Susanna's bag or to search it, then they knew that he was with her. So why not leave him to do the job? Goddamn. Was this not his purview? It must have been those NSA pricks. Always gunning for the soft target. Man, he hated these joint missions.

Susanna emptied the contents of her purse onto the table and looked them over, then shook her head.

"What just happened?" she stammered, and her anger and fright peppered him like little hailstones. He picked up her empty purse, examined the lining expertly, felt the various pockets and compartments, then returned it to her.

He picked up his beer. "Give me a minute. Okay?"

But she couldn't. "What the hell is on that memory stick and those stereograms that are so damn important?" she blurted out.

His beer bottle froze in mid-air. Susanna's words reverberated through the booth around them and out and out further and spilled into West Street and beyond.

"Oh, shit," he said, the depth of his gaze holding hers, his jaw clenching. He had never told her it was a memory stick they were after. His eyes grew hard, intent. "Oh, shit."

Heat suffused her face in washes of red. She tried to cover her mistake, attempted a smile and fumbled, and it came out more like a grimace. He lowered his bottle and sat back in the booth. He could feel her effort not to look away, could see the pulse pounding in her throat, understood that she thought she couldn't break eye contact. Beads of sweat broke out over her top lip, and he knew she wouldn't dare swipe at them. He watched her. Breathe deeply. That's all she had to do.

She had sat across from him lying her brave little heart out, and she never flinched. Ah, the warm feeling. Shit. She was as clever as four monkeys and courageous to boot. Unwittingly embroiled in this against her will and circumspect enough to hold back that memory stick. He couldn't help but admire her for that. Microphone feedback from the band in the next room screeched into his thoughts, and the vibration of a bass guitar throbbed through the floorboards.

"My love," he murmured. Why couldn't she have kept up the charade? As long as she didn't tell him she had that classified memory stick, he could have gone on pretending he didn't know. He would not have to decide what to do about it just yet. Why did she have to go and force his hand?

Grabbing his beer, he pushed out of the booth and threw Susanna a glance. "I need some air."

He pushed through the civilian crowds mingling in the various rooms of the tavern, brushing past laughter and expectation and effortless being and burping and grins, and he did not feel as insulated from it all as he usually did, in fact felt a seductive pull towards it instead of away from it. He headed for the cool night air of the back patio. A muscle pulsated involuntarily in his bicep, and he consciously slowed and deepened his breathing.

It was the first lesson of tradecraft. Never let anyone catch you off guard, throw you off balance. How had he let himself get so entangled? Was he finally starting to lose his mind to his dick in his old age? He slowed down, forced himself to pause. That wasn't fair to Susanna. Nor was it the truth. The truth was she had given him the singular, ineffable gift of wanting to be a part of the world around him again. She had touched him like no woman before. It had been a long time coming.

Almost twenty years ago when the Secretary of Defense had set up the SSB, the Strategic Support Branch, that clandestine unit that not even Congress had been aware of, personnel were pulled from the various branches of the military, selected for their analytical abilities, personal intelligence, and strength under fire. Robert had been one of their first recruits. His service had been exemplary, and soon he trained others, put teams together, and ran missions, no questions asked. Even his ill-fated marriage didn't slow him down.

Until one day he walked into a D.C. elevator, closing in on a target, and everything changed. He was supposed to go in, do the job, and get the hell out. Strike, retrieve, destroy, retreat. One self gone. Mindless. Soulless. Unquestioning. Hello motherfucker. But he had dragged Susanna Bailey into his fucked up assignment, dragged her out of her safe, normal existence, and he owed her some clarity, if nothing else. So what the fuck was it that he really wanted?

He needed some space, had to think things through. This was nothing but a clean-up job no matter how you wrapped it, the latest in a long odorama of governmental nasty, and he had had a bad feeling about the job from the start. But not about Susanna. He'd never had any doubts about the rightness of her, if he was honest with himself.

CHAPTER:
NINETEEN

A BREEZE OFF THE BAY RUSTLED the deeply lobed, silvery leaves of the Wye oaks above Robert, raised the hairs on his arm, and stroked the back of his neck with a cool, soothing touch. Robert looked around and saw that he was already outside on the back patio of the tavern, and he didn't remember getting out there.

He scanned the area. A couple engaged in a quiet tete-a-tete at a table close by. A lone drinker in a slinky black dress with a leather jacket thrown over it, probably with the band, sitting at a table under a beige umbrella, engrossed in her cell phone. He relaxed.

Was this his point of no return then, beckoning like an intermittent glimmer — lighthouse red and indistinct through the fogbank? Is this not what he had wanted since the night he walked into Susanna's house, if he bothered to take the time to actually think about it? Hadn't he felt something similar and just as disorienting the other night in her bedroom as he watched her sleep? Or earlier at dinner as strands of her hair caressed his fingers and rendered his brain insensate? Did his heart already understand what he was afraid to recognize?

Why did he hesitate? Did he really want to end up a burned-out old shit, duty discharged, adrift in a limbo of Xanax or booze, feeling like he'd been royally had, a blinkered racehorse past its prime, put out to pasture and not a day too soon? A coward like his old man? Forty-seven years old, and slamming into sixty was how he felt.

A trio of musicians set up their instruments off to one side of the patio, next to a space heater. Their patter soothed his roiling mind, and he was relieved to notice that this band promised to be more laid back than the one playing inside.

He had suspected that somehow Susanna had come into possession of the stolen classified stuff — it was his gut talking. So he listened to her explain how she was not in any way involved with Colin Nashta and his blue fucking plastic comb. He had to laugh despite himself. The things that woman picked up on. If she only knew it didn't matter that she was lying to him about it. He was lying to her too about what was really on them. So they were pretty much equal on that score. Not that it made him feel any better.

He sat down at a patio table next to a nice-smelling bush with some purple flowers on it and plonked down his beer bottle. That was the good thing about spring on land, the way it smelled. At sea it was endless brine and plankton and gunmetal gray. He knew Susanna would come to him, wanting to confess it all. It was just a matter of time. She didn't have a false bone in that sweet body of hers, and he loved her for it. She couldn't even hang on a week in her attempts at skullduggery.

But could he do the right thing by letting her do the right thing? He knew how much that meant to her, how it helped her hang on to that tenuous hope that not everybody was bad, that darkness and blame were not the motor that powered us all, and that a moral compass was more than a vague fairytale prop.

He shifted in his chair and stared up at the tall canopy of oaks sheltering the patio. Their leaves were covered with a fine soft down that gave the trees a misty, frosted appearance. It was damn beautiful. Or he could just get the job done. Easier for him. Wrap it up, turn it in, mission accomplished, and it's Diego Garcia, home I go. Debrief, de-stress, forfeit and forget. Back to the dead coconut crabs and the endless waves that battered the coral reefs, crashed onto the burning sand, tore at the sand shrubs, and slowly decimated the atoll in a centuries-old advance to victory. Home sweet home. But then there was Susanna. A lifeline? A chance at something else? Or two high-speed trains passing in the night? What would happen to her if he let her go? The thought of her with another man had his stomach clenching, his fists balling up.

How bad could the fallout be? He was a senior intelligence officer, his record spotless. He was entitled to one fuck-up. He had leeway. He'd earned that much. What would happen? A slap on the wrist after an extensive debrief? Detention? One never knew. For every clean-up man, there was a clean-up man, from the bottom straight to the top. But in the end it didn't matter. He knew what decision to take. He knew what he had to do. He shoved away from the table and headed back to the crowded dining room, his mind made up. But before he even reached the booth where he had left her, he saw that it was empty.

Susanna stepped out onto the back patio, past a sign that read "Beer Garden," and was enchanted. Blooming blue wisteria draped over the brick walls. Old, wrought iron tables and chairs with umbrellas and heated lanterns to keep patrons warm in the spring evening, lilacs perfuming the cozy, walled-in space. A musical trio was playing something jazzy and soft, and couples were dancing. It was so perfect it broke her heart.

Obviously this was not the place for her. Her's was the world of fuck-ups and messes and lying like a fool. Why couldn't she have been upfront with Robert from the start? He must be disgusted with her. She was such an idiot. She glanced around the patio but didn't see him anywhere. She'd already been out front looking for him, had to pass that snake-eyes creep of a bartender at the main bar. She shivered and pulled her sweater on. He was probably so disappointed in her that he had left and gone back to the inn. Maybe he was packing his bag even now as she walked around looking for him.

The trio finished a number, and couples drifted to their tables. She turned as an older man and woman passed her with a polite "Excuse me," and that is when she saw Robert, standing in the doorway. Her heart skipped a beat. So he hadn't gone after all. She was unable to decipher the look in those stormy gray eyes, but she sighed with relief. He smiled at her, lazy and slow, and she found herself smiling back. Somehow everything was going to be okay. A couple long strides, and he was by her side, looking down at her.

"I thought you had left," she managed.

"I thought you'd gone too." He slid his arm around her waist.

"I wouldn't blame you if you had."

She pulled back. She didn't see how relieved he was to find her. "Listen, Robert, there's no two ways about it. I lied to you, and if you can't forgive me, I understand."

"Susanna" —

"I'll go back to the inn and get my things, save you the embarrassment of asking me to leave."

"Slow down" —

"I'm such an idiot. Always take the easy way out. I have the memory stick and the stereograms. I should have told you from the start. Mr. Nashta must have thrown them into my bag on that last day of depositions. I didn't even realize it until the next day, 'til after we'd found his body."

"Wait a minute."

But she hurried on, relieved to finally be getting it off her chest. "I don't know how it happened, Robert, and that part is the truth. Mr. Nashta must have gotten spooked. I freaked out when I found the things at home. I had no idea what they were, didn't know what to do with them. I didn't want to get blamed for taking them. I hid them" —

He glanced around and stopped her.

"— in —"

"No. Don't tell me. Don't say anything else."

"I'll give it all to you when we get back to D.C."

His voice was quiet, measured. "Susanna, I think we need to stop talking about this now, and I don't think you want to be telling me anything more."

"But I don't want them. I was just trying to figure out what they were and who the rightful owner was and if Mr. Nashta" —

"Jesus Christ, Susanna. Shut up. How many more times can I tell you? I won't warn you again. Don't tell me something unless you intend for me to act on it."

"But I've barely begun" —

"Good. Keep it that way."

She was baffled. "What? Am I going to prison for treason? Be honest with me."

"No." He shook his head in exasperation and looked down at her. "Can you just look at me for the next minute without saying another word?"

"Of course."

"Hmm. Good." His arms encircled her and drew her

closer, and his gaze stayed on her, steadying her. She saw no anger in his eyes, no accusation. She inhaled sweet, lilac-scented air and caught the distant salty tang of the ocean. She slowed her racing mind, her eyes resting on his until she felt calm again. She pulled up and grazed his chin with a kiss, wrapping her arms around his neck, and bumped her nose against his in an Eskimo kiss, making him smile.

She nudged aside his windbreaker and laid her head on his chest, against the soft black t-shirt. She could hear his heart beating.

He whispered into her hair. "Everything will be fine. Do you trust me, Susanna? Serious."

She looked up at him, considered the question, and realized that she did. Was not wisdom sensory? Her body knew. This man had kindness and strength woven into every fiber of his being.

"Serious, I do," she answered. She knew she could count on him.

"Good. Then let's not talk anymore right now. Okay?"

She nodded, and he drew her closer still and brushed a kiss across her temple, her nose, her cheek, and on her mouth, tentative at first and then again, and every cell in her body responded, sending heat unspooling like a fine red cloth.

"Come on. Let's go and dance one more time," he whispered.

"I love that about you, that you can dance."

"Part of every officer's training." He winked as he drew

her out to the middle of the patio, and they joined the other couples already dancing to a slow song.

Susanna looked up at the canopy of trees and watched the wind rustle the leaves as the saxophone wailed. Wrapped in Robert's arms, she knew that she was where she should be, and everything felt all right, and the rest of the night was theirs, and they could take all the time they needed to relearn the words "I love you." And she was sure that if any of the other dancing couples were to glance their way, they would say to themselves, "Look at that. Those two people are happy."

Susanna Bailey's neighbor Bill was a man of vast patience and deep roots in good Falls Church soil, but on this night, his magnanimity was fraying like an old coat. The antics over at Susanna's place would wear out the patience of any reasonable man. He seethed as he pushed aside the branch that jutted into his side and found a more comfortable vantage point through the bushes between their houses. Were there two men in there now? Good thing he was around, keeping an eye on the goings-on around here. He could have sworn he'd seen two men enter her house, come a'courting probably, sneaky, dark-skinned dogs. All that banging and crashing about. What was that woman up to in there with them? He'd heard those Canadians were a shifty lot, almost as crazy as the Australians, and everybody knew about that bunch.

And Susanna's choice in men, well that didn't even stand thinking about. That woman's standards were on the way down if she was consenting to be seeing the likes of those two, he thought, and this being the same Miss Susanna Bailey who wouldn't deign to give him the time of day, especially since the unfortunate fact of the recycling bin incidents. Who knew she'd be so touchy about it. It was not a good economy to be losing his job in. So if higher security clearance was the way to go, that was the way Bill Strong went. Always on the straight and narrow. A man does what needs doing is all.

He fumed and tossed about in his jumble of thoughts until he realized that Susanna wasn't even home, because he'd watched her leaving earlier, and so he had actually just watched two men break into her house. Pausing, he took a better look through the bushes that separated the sides of their two houses. Should he intercept this crime in progress or surveille and note? Or call the cops? He zipped up his sweater and decided to make a call to the local PD. His name wasn't Bill Strong for nothing.

But as he started for his house, he thought about how he really didn't appreciate that revolving door of men at Susanna Bailey's, like that raving guy banging on his steering wheel the other morning, so threatening and disrespectful. Actually, the more Bill thought about it, the more he realized what a woman of low morals Susanna was, taking on all comers these days. Except for him. Had his carnations counted for nothing? He should have reported her to Homeland Security ages ago. Why bother calling the cops now? So instead, he snuck back to his observation post in the bushes and positioned himself between the two largest shrubs just as the two same men departed her house via the front door. Interesting.

A low fog blurred his vision, but Bill squinted hard and tried to make out their facial features. It would be important if he had to file a police report at some time in the future. As they jumped into their car and pulled away, his attention was drawn by another car appearing at the top of the street. It slowed, dimming its lights as it drew nearer, and killed the engine as it slid up to the curb in front of Susanna's house. And two different men exited this vehicle and crept up Susanna's walkway in the dark. The two sets of men had barely missed each other.

Bill almost had a palpitation as he watched. What the hell was going on here? Better go in, make a coffee, and figure out the best course of action. Slowly backing out of the shrubbery, he turned quietly to sneak back into his house, and froze. There was a man standing in the darkness by Susanna's back door, looking straight at him. Barely visible in the gloom, his face was covered in a black mask. Bill froze as his eyes widened, but he managed to stay firm on his feet. Slowly the man raised a finger to the hole in the mask where his mouth was, warning Bill to not make a peep, as if he expected Bill to scream or shout like a girl.

Bill blinked as he regained his senses, and then he wordlessly spun on his heels and doubled back inside, bolting the door behind him. Whether this was a dating farrago or a series of break-ins, he didn't care anymore. He didn't need any trouble that could endanger his promotion, not when he'd been waiting on his security clearance so long.

CHAPTER:
TWENTY

ROBERT AND SUSANNA HEADED BACK to the Royal Folly Inn.
Their footfalls echoed along a street illuminated by the soft
glow of black, nineteenth century streetlamps. The sounds of
revelry faded into the distance. Robert stopped abruptly and
turned around. Far behind, a car with dimmed headlights
slowed down and pulled into a parking space.

"What is it?" Susanna followed his gaze.

"I don't know." Robert shook his head. "It's nothing.
Forget it. Let's go."

Susanna spotted the steeple of St. Anne's church rising
above the treetops, surrounded by more stars than she ever
imagined could fit in the night sky, and she thought of Ms.
Hortense, cooking up a storm at her Greek cooking lesson.

They came to Church Circle, and Robert unexpectedly
pulled Susanna to the right. "Let's go past the water. It's

beautiful at night." He glanced behind them. "It's one of the things I miss about this town."

She put her arm through his companionably. She could understand why he'd miss such a lovely little place. She was falling in love with it herself. They passed the harbor, and sounds of a party drifted over the water from a large yacht decked out in hundreds of twinkling lights. Susanna slowed down to listen to the music spilling out over the dark waves.

It was "Johnny B. Goode," a reverberating, slowed-down reggae version.

"I don't remember parties like that when I was here," Robert said, slowing down. He looked behind them again, and then his eyes came to rest on Susanna.

She sang softly with the song, her eyes on Robert, and her hips moved suggestively. "Go, go, Johnny. Johnny be good tonight." He responded with a low, husky laugh as he watched her, and it intensified her own awareness of him.

His body stilled as she raised her arms over her head and danced, hypnotizing him with her hips, moving oh so slowly against him then, and he was gone. She could feel every atom of his body melting into her, wanting her, and she pulled his head down so she could flick her tongue over his mouth, tempting but denying him until his eyes shut and he groaned.

When she finally gave him her mouth, he took her like a starved man, and when he couldn't get enough from her mouth, he shifted her around so that the curve of her rump was grinding into him, as sweet and slow as the heavy reggae rhythm. She wiggled around to look at him. Every lusty bit of him emanated confidence and ease.

"I'd give a million bucks for half the confidence you've got, Robert Crowell," she said, breathless with desire.

"I'll think about that, Susanna Bailey," he chortled as his hands pulled her hips into him again, and he pressed hard, denim against denim.

"Do you have any idea how sexy it makes you?" she murmured.

He paused, released his grip on her, stopped her. "Give me your heart instead," he said.

"You already have it," she whispered.

He lifted her chin and brushed the hair out of her face. "I want to do this with you forever."

"Me too." She met his gaze as he traced his thumb over her bottom lip. "Until I'm an old frump and so are you, until we're so old we can't do it anymore."

He fought a grin. "In that case we better put a rush on it. I'm starting to feel those creaking bones already."

"Wait a minute," she protested. "Yours or mine?"

He laughed, and she raised a hand to his face and ran her fingers along his jaw. He stopped her and kissed the palm of her hand. "I want to spend the rest of my life making you feel good. That turns me on big time."

"Aye, Sir," she murmured. "I think that can be arranged."

"I want to catch up on all the years I missed being with you. I want to protect you, hold you, take you six ways to Sunday and more. Susanna, I – I – damn" –

She watched Robert grapple with what he wanted to say, but she couldn't help him. Why did the thing she longed for scare her so? So instead, he brought his lips to hers again.

And wrapped in the night, their bodies moved just barely, close and slow. And the past lessened its grip ever so slightly, the lonely togetherness of lovers before, the missteps and mistakes, all of it so far away as they kissed and their souls touched in the knowing moonlight.

"Deep down in Jamaica close to Mandeville, back up in the woods on top of a hill, there stood an old hut made of earth and wood, where lived a country boy named Johnny B. Goode. Never learned to read and write so well, but he could play his guitar like ringing a bell. Go, go, Johnny. Johnny be good tonight."

Susanna could feel Robert as lost in their kiss as she was, drifting so far away that she thought perhaps they would never have to come back until she was so aroused she knew they had to get out of there.

"We need to get back to the inn," he muttered, echoing her thoughts, but his mouth could not stay away from hers. She held on to the hair at the nape of his neck, not wanting to let him go either yet, stumbling, stepping on his foot, clumsy with need. A sudden noise, a crack or a click, something close by Robert and Susanna, much closer than the yacht out on the bay, startled them and pushed them apart. A flash momentarily lit up the darkness. They looked around disoriented.

Sleeping boats rocked on the water, their masts softly

clanking. Onboard the big yacht, the party continued. Was that a camera flash or a flash of lightning from an approaching storm? Susanna glanced at the sky. The spell that held them in its thrall had been broken.

Robert muttered "Shit" under his breath and scanned the dockside and the road. A current of unease sparked around them as cold waves lapped against the cement moorings at the water's edge. Wordlessly, he took her by the arm and steered her away from the harbor, and disquiet whispered at their backs as they hurried along the sleeping streets. Unexpectedly, Susanna slowed down, wowed by the sight ahead of her, and Robert followed her gaze. She was staring at the Naval Academy Chapel, its copper dome looming on the skyline, lit up like a beacon in the night sky.

"Part of the Naval Academy," he said as he stopped beside her.

"It's beautiful."

He didn't seem to hear her, his thoughts somewhere else. Her eyes searched his face.

"Are you okay?"

"Reminds me of something is all."

Susanna squeezed his arm in question, feeling the bicep rock-solid under his skin.

"Something everyone had to memorize at the Academy. It's called the Honor Concept. I still remember it. 'Midshipmen are persons of integrity. They stand for that which is right. They tell the truth and ensure that the full truth is known.' We had to memorize those lines our very first year there." He looked at her. "Seems like a real long time ago."

Though he'd tossed them out lightly enough, she heard the disillusion in his words.

Robert did a quick scan of the road behind them before turning back to Susanna. "Penalties for violating the Honor Concept were severe. You could get expelled. It was the moral code by which we were supposed to live. Tell the truth and ensure that the full truth is known. Imagine that," he murmured sarcastically. He shook his head as he looked back at the Naval Academy. "Life was simple then. You were ruled by the code and the sextant and the sea."

She could see the emotions battling inside him.

"I can't remember the last time I had an honorable mission."

A chill ran through her at his words.

"This is not the man I wanted to be."

She instinctively held back the words of comfort she wanted to give him. He would take offence and freeze her out so fast she wouldn't have a chance to grab her coat. "Robert" –

"Don't do pity," he said dismissively as he started walking.

"That's not what I was offering."

She wanted nothing more at that moment than the warm room that awaited them at the Royal Folly Inn and this man in the bed with her where she could soothe him with her touch and kiss away the strife that etched his strong features.

She caught up to him, shoved her hands into the front pockets of her jeans, and kicked at a piece of disintegrating candy wrapper on the sidewalk.

"I'm really glad you pulled me out of the courtroom that day and kissed me," she said eventually, her words teasing. "Even though at the time, I wasn't at all convinced —"

He looked at her. "Pulled you? I thought you came willingly."

"I did come willingly, but that was later when you were in my bed. In the courtroom you were definitely taking a big chance."

An amused expression crossed his face. "And your point?"

"That's all." She shrugged. "I'm just glad you were brave enough to do it."

Robert took her face in his hands roughly. "I didn't know my life could ever be anything other than what it was," he said, "and then I walked into that law firm to nail Colin Nashta, and there you were. And you showed me that there was more. And I want it, if you'll have me."

Susanna shivered, and he unzipped his windbreaker, pulled it off, and wrapped it around her, over top her sweater. "Listen, what if I told you that what's on that memory stick is not what you think it is?"

"You mean not a threat to American lives or American security?

"No, not directly it's not."

"American lives are not at stake?"

He touched her hair when he saw the confusion on her face.

"So what is on there?" she asked.

"A nasty little embarrassment to the American government that I've been sent in to clean up before it falls into unfriendly hands. It's something I seem to be doing a lot of lately."

She studied him, couldn't understand what exactly he was saying. How could stereograms or aerial photos be embarrassing? What did that mean? A gust of wind whipped up the street, and she realized how cold he must be standing there in his t-shirt.

"Here, take your jacket back," she said, unwrapping herself and trying to put the windbreaker across his shoulders.

He watched her nipples harden through her sweater and stopped her. "Shit. I'm sorry. I could stay out here forever with you, Susanna, but we need to get back to the inn before you freeze to death and give me a heart attack in the process."

She blushed when she realized what he was looking at. "A little bracing wind won't kill me," she mumbled.

He pulled her into his arms, threw the jacket around her again, and hurried her down the street, trying to keep the worst of the wind off her with his body. "Maybe not, but being out here with you might kill me. My body can only take so much."

Never were two people happier to return to the Royal Folly Inn, into the embrace of its discreet, old world charm. No sooner had they closed the door to their room, grandly named the Queens Chambers, than they were pulling off their clothes, hungry for each other. Sweaters and shirts flew over their heads.

Robert's breath hitched as her top fell to the floor, revealing her lacy bra and the sweet, enticing curve of her breasts. Susanna took the few steps that separated them, and when she stood before him, she ran a trembling hand over the contours of his chest and felt him go still under her touch.

His eyes sought hers, and all the things he couldn't put into words were there, plain for her to see. The intensity of his gaze was more than she could bear, and she looked down to his hard stomach and the faint whorls of dark hair that formed a line, like a treasure map pointing the way down to the crown jewels hidden just out of reach. She started unzipping Robert's jeans and felt his erection straining for her.

He grabbed her by the arms, stopping her, and whispered in her ear to slow down. He threw his watch onto a writing table that stood up against a wall saturated a deep purple blue. His keys and wallet followed.

Susanna wiggled out of her own jeans and started to tug impatiently on his again.

"Slow down, tiger."

Her eyes went to his.

"Slow down and let me show you something," Robert

commanded in a voice that sent a dart of heat blooming between her thighs, and he hadn't even touched her.

She tried to pull him away from the table and towards the four-poster bed that dominated the room.

"Greedy, aren't you?" he laughed quietly, and before she knew what he was doing, he'd grabbed her, flipped her onto her stomach and pinned her beneath him, over the writing table. And before she had a chance to catch her breath, she heard his groan as he felt the wetness of her panties and shoved them down her legs with one hand. With a deft maneuver of his thigh behind her, he spread her legs, and his fingers went to her.

"God, you're so wet," he growled. And he slid a finger inside her, then two, forcing a gasp of pleasure out of her. She was trapped beneath him, and there was nowhere in the world she would rather be. He was infinitely stronger, he was in control, and it was utterly thrilling. She pushed hungrily against his fingers and felt his breath on her ear, murmuring something indiscernible at the same time as his thumb grazed her clit, teasing at first and then with more pressure until she thought she would lose her mind as a wild pleasure built up inside her.

A mewling sound escaped her lips as she turned her head to the side, looking for him, needing him, hungry for his kisses. She glimpsed the rough denim of his jeans down around his knees. She felt his hot breath caress her cheek, and then his mouth was on hers, feeding, knowing just what she wanted and when, as his fingers slid in and out, pressing against just the right spot inside her, until she felt delirious with abandon, thought her legs wouldn't hold up anymore.

Then he whispered hoarsely in her ear, "This is all for you, tiger" as he withdrew his slick fingers and pressed the glistening ridge of his erection hard against her wet opening but didn't enter her, teased her, forcing a moan out of her. Slowly he slid into her then until he filled her to the hilt, making her cry out, and she could feel her muscles clench around him as if they would never let him go. She was whimpering now, and he continued to whisper in her ear, driving her out of her mind as he took her from behind.

About to shatter, Susanna just needed that final push over the edge, and his knowing hand reached around and his fingers stroked her clit again just how she needed it as he drove into her harder and harder. She felt herself go faint, her mouth opened in a silent scream, and everything went gray and then black as her orgasm engulfed her.

After what seemed a long time, when the blackness finally ebbed and the violent pounding of her heart settled, she struggled to open her eyes. She felt a wetness on her cheek and Robert's warm body covering her still until he felt her begin to stir. He moved off her and gently helped her up. She was surprised at how weak and shaky she felt and was grateful for the writing table to lean against.

"This has never happened to me before," she stammered, fighting back tears. "Robert, I felt like – I felt – le petit mort. Now I know what they mean."

"Did I hurt you?" She saw the instant concern in his face.

"No. I – a great orgasm, it's, like the French say, a little death."

"You drive me crazy. I didn't mean to hurt you."

"No, you didn't. It's not that." She put a reassuring hand on his chest and felt his heart racing and saw relief wash over him. Her mind was not in a state to form any coherent thoughts.

Robert leaned over and rested his forehead against hers, and their fingers intertwined. A slow smile spread across her face. He licked a tear off her cheek and slowly ran his tongue around her swollen mouth and nipped at her bottom lip, and his penis pressed into her belly, demanding again and still slick with her juices.

"It's not what you do. It's how you do it," she whispered. "You are so" –

A chuckle of male satisfaction bubbled up from somewhere deep inside him.

"I love you, Susanna." He gathered her in his arms and kissed her deeply until she pushed him back to look at him.

"Are you going to run and hide now," he murmured, teasing her.

But her eyes were drawn down to his glistening erection. Oh, merciful heaven. He reached a hand behind her and unsnapped her bra, which she didn't realize she was still wearing, and released her breasts, and a soft hiss escaped him as he grew impossibly harder still.

"Come here." He took her hand and pulled her to the big four-poster bed that was the focal point of the beautiful purple blue room. "Now get in that bed, and let's do this properly."

And she gasped.

CHAPTER:
TWENTY-ONE

SUSANNA LAY ENFOLDED IN ROBERT'S ARMS, listening to his steady breathing and luxuriating in the feeling of safety that enveloped her. In this world of shifting illusion, it was a royal folly indeed. Around her everything was dark and warm and still. Outside the Chesapeake wind whispered at the windowpane, you do not have all the time in the world, but Susanna paid it no heed, and the moon shone through the curtain that covered the window.

Robert stirred, and she lifted her head and saw that he was awake, staring up at the ceiling. He looked at her, and she gave him a sleepy smile and kissed his cheek, her lips soft against the stubble.

"Tell me a story," he whispered.

She wasn't sure she had heard him.

He looked back up at the ceiling. "Fill it with heroes and glory."

She disentangled herself from his arms and from the sheets and pulled up onto his chest.

"And make it come out all right in the end," he murmured as he took a handful of her hair between his fingers.

She felt her heart overflowing. "I can't," she said quietly. "I'm no good at making stuff up."

Robert seemed to consider her answer for a while, and when he finally spoke, his voice was a low drawl, and he chewed the inside of his cheek to hide his smile. "Shit. No imagination and you snore too. I think I may be getting the short end of the stick here."

She poked him softly in the ribs, causing him to wince. "I do not snore. Stop saying that," she laughed, and when she looked at him, his eyes were so full of love and gentleness that she felt a surge of momentary panic in her chest.

Robert pulled on the hair that was twined between his fingers, and his eyes roamed over her face. "You know, Susanna, you don't have to be scared. I'm not Michael, and I'm not going to die."

Words caught in her throat. She understood how precious was that thing he was offering her. She drew away from him and moved down his body so she could lay her head onto his chest. She rubbed her cheek against the fine hair that speckled his stomach with some kind of animal instinct to comfort him, herself, not sure who needed it more just then. She buried her face in his armpit, breathing in the scent of him, until the panic surge subsided. Keep breathing. You will not drown, and he will not die. The wind rattled the windowpane.

Susanna sat back up, and their eyes met. "What about you? Will you ever be able to unburden your heart to me the way I know you want to? The mantle of secrecy weighs heavily."

In answer, he just looked at her as if pondering how to answer. Maybe she couldn't tell him a story, but she could comfort him in other ways. She leaned over and dragged her lips along his shoulder and took her time as she covered his entire body in lingering kisses. She savored his sharp intake of breath. She suckled at his nipple and tasted the saltiness of the ocean, and waves of love unfurled through her with his every soft moan.

He grabbed her hair again, in his fists this time, as he let her steal away his control, and the look he gave her was so unguarded, so defenseless. And she saw that her fingers were in just the right place where he needed them to be, just easy enough, just hard enough, just wet enough, just rough enough. Her eyes stayed on his face as she brought him to orgasm, wanting to burn the image of his surrender onto her memory forever. And his ragged panting afterward, trying to catch his breath, trying to gather his strength, that too. She wanted to remember all of it.

When his eyes opened, they were heavy-lidded and languid. He looked at her, and she met his gaze. He chuckled, and she grinned. Some more. Some more. Some more.

And this time when they made love, he forced her to keep her eyes open the entire time, and his eyes never left hers, and it was slow and sweet and everlasting and full of tenderness.

And the sweeter it grew between them, the darker the memories and nightmares that stalked her. As Robert slept at her side, Susanna gazed at the silver moon, fighting to keep her eyes open, trying to lure her ten-year-old self back to the deep sleep where she lived, in the dustbin of her childhood memories. But Susanna's eyelids grew heavier by the minute.

Falling down the stairs was a different experience for different people. For Susanna it had been because of her own dumbness.

"Only you, Susanna, are goddamn stupid enough to fall down the stairs," her mother had laughed, looking so pretty, like a mermaid in her green shiny dress.

But Susanna didn't think it was all completely her fault. It was the shoes from Uncle Joe that did it. They were too big, but her mother had made her wear them. The front of one caught on the top step, and down she hurtled. At the bottom, she sat up slowly, her lip trembling, swallowing her tears. She felt an awful hurting on her cheek and saw blood on her sweater, the one from Uncle Trev, who came before Uncle Joe, and knew that now she was in really big trouble. Because after her mother finished laughing, she would get mad. Every time.

That scared her more than the hurting. More than the

time Uncle Steve, who came before Uncle Joe or Uncle Trev, pulled out her tooth because it was really sore, but he pulled out the wrong one because he'd had too many cocktails at mom's party. But he was a dentist. He knew what he was doing, her mother yelled, and the anger bounced off the shimmering beads of her dress. It was Susanna's fault that he left, and she would have to pay.

"You always have to pay the price. That's the way it works. So get used to it." Her mother grabbed her by the hair, and Susanna choked a scream.

"One day you're going to thank me for this," her mother said. And as Susanna struggled to get up, her mother's fist flew down to greet her.

It's not easy when you're eight and everything is your fault. Some uncles stayed the night, some stayed for breakfast, some stayed for a whole summer or even into fall. And as time passed, she learned her lesson for sure. Never take presents from uncles.

And as Susanna forced her eyes open, fighting to keep those distant memories out of her dreams, Big Dave Bailey glanced down from heaven above and winked at his beloved girl. Yes, my lovely, you are brave enough. You are.

Susanna woke to find Robert looking down at her. The curve of his mouth made her smile as she shook the uncles from her sleepy brain. She wiggled her toes and stretched her body under the covers. The sheets were so soft around her that she thought she was wrapped in a white cloud. She shut her eyes and opened them again. It felt like a particularly excellent morning.

She drifted languorously into consciousness until she realized Robert was studying the scar on her cheek. Her hand flew to her face, and she was jolted awake.

"Wow," he said, moving back, surprised by her sudden movement. "It's okay."

"No, it's not. What are you doing?"

"I was just looking at you as you slept. It was nice."

"It's ugly," she said, her hand covering the scar. "I don't want you to see me like this." She sat up in the bed, moving away from him. "No makeup covering it or anything."

He studied her thoughtfully.

She looked at the window where the morning sun peeked around the edges of the curtain, tossing wisps of light onto the writing table that stood against the dark purple wall. Her overnight bag sat on the mahogany luggage stand under the window. Their shoes and clothing lay scattered across the old polished wooden floor. His gun lay nestled in its holster on the side table beside the bed.

Robert took her face in his hand and turned her to him. "Susanna."

She heard the ripple of reproach in his voice.

"What?"

"Don't say shit like that. Okay?" He pulled her hand away from her scar. "You are gorgeous, and life is too short. Don't you understand?"

"Easy for you to say," she muttered, trying to move her face away from him. He held her tight.

"You think so?" He looked down at the scars on his own chest and arm. She followed his gaze and shivered at the thought of the pain that had brought those. What had she been thinking?

"This is not who you are," he said, touching her scar lightly. "This is what? A hundredth of you? A beautiful hundredth of you maybe, but only just a hundredth." He wrapped the covers around her. "It isn't your perfection that makes you so lovely, Susanna. It's all the other stuff. Swear to God." He traced the edge of her scar slowly with his finger. "The expanse of your kindness, the content of your heart."

Embarrassment suffused her cheeks with color, and she looked at him, amazed by his generosity in the face of her self-absorption.

"My Susanna, your body is a temple," he crooned and pulled her closer and nuzzled her neck and brought a smile to her face. Their bodies fit together so perfectly.

"Wise guy. How come I've never met anyone as nice as you before?" she said. "Thank you for giving me the benefit of the doubt every time."

"Let's move to the Blue Mountains and make babies," he said as he pushed up off the bed, "while we still have a chance."

She knew he was joking, but an unwanted feeling snagged on her insides. "I think the baby clock has more or less stopped ticking a long time ago, Robert. I'm fifty-one years old."

"I know. I'm forty-seven, and I lost that dream ages ago too," he said as he pulled on his jeans. "But maybe I'm one of the lucky fuckers who actually gets a second chance at making something else good in my life." He threw her a wink.

"Why do I get the feeling this doesn't have much to do with me?" she teased as she tried to get out of the bed, but he pushed her back into the pillows and rolled on top of her, supporting himself on his elbows.

"That's where you're wrong. It has everything to do with you."

They looked at one another. "Let's give us a chance," he said. "Yes or yes?"

"Stop looking at me with such serious eyes," Susanna said. "It scares me. Where are the Blue Mountains anyway?"

"You're kidding me?" he laughed. "You, the Bob Marley fan, don't know the Blue Mountains?"

She looked at him expectantly and admitted to herself how much she had missed all this for so long, talking, laughing, being on the same wavelength with a man, instead of trying to fill her loneliness with challenges and accomplishments. Yeah, that was good, but so was this. And maybe there was room in her life for all of it.

"It's one of the most beautiful places on God's green earth, Susanna, the Blue Mountains of Jamaica. They cut through the center of the island, and they're lush and green and covered in sugarcane and coconut and mango and banana and papaya trees, one mountain peak after another mountain peak after another, hundreds of them. It's the closest place to heaven I've ever seen." He paused. "Too bad parts of it are overrun with gangsters."

Susanna burst out laughing. "Oh, yes, except for that. Well, I'm sure heaven has its problems too." After a minute's hesitation, she added, "Yes. My answer is yes."

"Yes?"

"Yes." He grinned, and she wanted to kiss him, but instead she pushed Robert off her and sat up, pulling some covers around her. "I'd like to know what's on those stereograms and memory stick."

Her abrupt change of direction didn't seem to throw him, but his voice grew serious. "Okay."

"Back to the real world," she said, brushing the hair out of her face.

"No," he said. "You and me, that is the real world. The last few days with you has been the real part. Everything else is quicksand. Don't forget it."

CHAPTER:
TWENTY-TWO

SUSANNA SAT BACK and fixed her gaze on Robert.

"Colin Nashta was killed by two very angry guys from another part of the world who came over here and spent a lot of time and patience looking for an opportunity such as the one he finally presented them."

"The men on the bench." She thought back to the day of Mr. Nashta's murder. "I think they had dark hair. And they were wearing suits. They blended in. I can't remember much about them."

Robert shrugged. "I don't think anyone's in a hurry to catch his killers. It's what Colin Nashta stole that we need back." He looked at her, and she met his steady gaze.

"So what exactly was it that Mr. Nashta stole?"

"Good old Colin realized that he had inadvertently hit the jackpot when he was able to match up the stereograms to the interpretation keys on that little memory stick that you now have in your possession. He was a good photogrammetrist. I'll give him that. He was able to figure out what he was looking at."

"And?" she prompted him. "What was he looking at?"

"Surveillance images of European military installations taken by U.S. Navy planes, under direct orders from the Pentagon."

"And how is that the jackpot?"

"Because that is illegal. It's in contravention of all sorts of international and foreign domestic laws. And it's a big no no under the Law of the Sea, the UNCLOS treaty under the United Nations Charter."

Susanna knitted her brow.

"That a greedy little contract employee like Colin Nashta stumbled across that and was smart enough to put it together became a major headache for Intelligence. So they sent my crew in to clean up the liability and make it disappear."

"So America was spying on its friends in Europe? Which friends?"

"Don't ask for anything other than what I tell you."

"Of course. And please don't tell me anything that could hurt you down the road. That's the only thing that matters to me at this point." She placed her hand over his.

He raised an eyebrow.

"What?" she asked.

"Be careful or you might actually tell me you love me next. And we couldn't have that, could we?"

"That's not fair," she protested.

"When Colin Nashta started shopping around his goodies, his two new Iranian buddies knew they had struck gold. They checked his bona fides, found out he worked in the Pentagon, and knew he was legit."

"So the lawsuit against the defense contractor had nothing to do with any of this," she said.

"That's right. Nashta just happened to work for a company that was being sued by the government for breach of contract."

She shook her head in disbelief as she thought about that. "So how did you pick up his trail?"

"The Iranians paid him a large chunk of cash, on behalf of their state, for what he had stolen, which said cash he conscientiously deposited into his bank account for me to find. And that's what led us to him." Robert paused. "Unfortunately for him, after having delivered installment number one, for whatever reason Colin failed to deliver the second and final set of aerial photos and the all important memory stick with the photo interpretation keys on it. So they met with him that day in the park to clear things up."

Susanna blanched. "They cleared things up by killing him?"

"When he didn't deliver, they probably thought he had double-crossed them."

"But how did you know he didn't deliver?"

"Because of ripples through the intelligence community in the 48-hour period after his death. If he had sold it to someone else, that intel would have surfaced, and we would have been onto it fast. As it stands, the Iranians now have detailed photos of more than half of Europe's military installations. The implications of a nuclear threat to that continent, thanks to us, are unimaginable."

Susanna stared at him, taking in what he was telling her. She had read in the papers that Iranians were building nuclear weapons.

"And if our European allies found out about a security breach of such magnitude and the resultant nuclear threat, you can imagine the fallout," Robert went on. "So the bosses at the Pentagon lit a fire under us to get the stuff back at any cost and try to avert a total catastrophe. We were ready to scoop Nashta up when he went and got himself killed."

Susanna shook her head as the enormity of what was on that memory stick and stereograms sunk in. "So you narrowed down the possibilities of who may have gotten that memory stick and stuff from Mr. Nashta, and that's how I showed up in your scope."

He looked at her, and she dreaded his answer to what she was about to ask him. "And that's the reason why you approached me. Isn't it?"

"No." His answer was brusque but unequivocal.

"Really?"

He laid his hand on his heart for a moment, then put it back down on the bed. She almost wanted to cry with relief.

"If nothing else, your friend Colin and his Iranian buddies appreciated perfectly the worth of the embarrassing and illegal behavior on the part of this country. Colloquially speaking, we were caught with our pants down, fucking our real friends, not oil acquaintances, up the ying yang."

"Oh, jeez," she protested, "no need for graphic details."

"Keep your voice down. Okay?"

"And I never said Mr. Nashta was my friend. I felt badly for him because nobody at all, not one person, seemed to care about his death. Everyone just cared about how it affected them."

"Tell it to Social Services." He got up and rummaged around in his duffel bag and threw on a white t-shirt.

"But why would this country do something as stupid as taking illegal aerial photos in the first place?"

"Because some of the guys running the show around here think we're above the law, invincible," he said.

"But that's juvenile."

"Wouldn't be the first time," he said. "America's like an overgrown teenager whose intentions are mostly good but whose brain is so flooded with testosterone that he messes up as many times as he gets it right."

He pulled on a checked flannel shirt over his t-shirt but didn't bother tucking it into his jeans. "Sometimes we can't control all that power coursing through our veins."

She considered his words. "So if America is an overgrown teenager, that makes Europe what? A bunch of pompous, old farts?"

He laughed as he strapped his gun holster above his ankle in one efficient, rapid movement and slipped the gun inside it. "The brass can't afford any kind of scandal in this political climate. So adding to this country's woes and embarrassments on the international stage in times like these is gold, at the least."

Susanna went quiet. "So the Iranians are probably still looking for the stuff." She heard the tremor in her voice. Of course they wouldn't give up the search. Great. This didn't bear thinking about.

"I won't let anything happen to you." He looked at her. "But I won't lie. That stuff is worth a lot of money to certain players."

"So we fuck up in the first place by doing something illegal and stupid," she managed to say.

He nodded.

"And then the government sends you in to avert a public relations disaster or worse" —

"Or worse," he said. "If all of it had fallen into Iranian hands, ensuing disaster would have been inevitable."

"And now you've got to sweep it all under the carpet and make it disappear."

He nodded again and sat back down on the bed beside her.

"But I thought you were a spy catcher."

"Colin Nashta fell under my purview," he said. "He stole highly classified information. That, Susanna, is called espionage."

They sat looking at each other.

"Thank you for telling me."

"Yup." He looked away. "Thing is somewhere along

the way the line started blurring between doing my job and catching these guys so they can't hurt our country, and doing something I never would have signed up for — cleaning up our own wrongdoing."

Susanna understood where his disillusionment came from, and her heart went out to him. "I can't even begin to imagine" —

"That's the part that makes it hard going. Try that on for a year or three."

There was a soft knock on the door, and Susanna almost jumped.

Robert put a hand onto her arm. "Take it easy."

He got up and went over to the door. Susanna wrapped the sheet more tightly around her.

The innkeeper popped his head in the doorway, but Robert didn't let him further into the room, "Hello. Sorry to disturb, but I've got an urgent message for you, sir."

"Urgent enough to bother me here?"

"Unfortunately, sir." The little man stole a look at Susanna, and Robert followed his eyes.

"I was given the strictest instructions to pass on the message," the innkeeper said, his voice low. "Your assistant called."

Robert glanced over at Susanna again. She didn't know he had an assistant, but she knew better than to ask. With a smile, she headed for the bathroom, trailing the sheet behind her. As she closed the door after her, she caught the innkeeper's words.

"He said your devices were not working for he's had a heck of a time trying to reach you."

She leaned against the bathroom door. How did his work know he was here? Were they keeping tabs on him, or were they on to her now? Her toes dug into the thick little rug under her feet as she looked around. The bathroom was all soft white luxury. A gas fire flickered in the fireplace on the wall opposite the claw foot tub, and French doors led out to a small, private deck and bathed everything in a gentle morning light. This was a room for relaxation, not worry.

Susanna sunk into the tub and surrendered herself to the hot water. She inhaled deeply and wondered if it was always that way for Robert, if his work always reached its tentacles into the most private corners of his life. Her mind went over what he had told her. Averting a disaster by stopping the classified stuff falling into Iranian hands was his job, but did it always include covering up America's own underhanded affairs? Was that his honorable duty? Obey at all costs, no questions asked. Those were the rules, and she understood that. It was important if you were a soldier in combat. But at some point somebody had to be asking questions some of the time. It only made sense.

Yet here was Robert having to fulfill a questionable duty without a second's hesitation and with a trouble-free mind. Was that not too much to ask of any man or woman? Or were such considerations of no relevance, the frivolous meander-ings of a love-struck woman's heart? Closing her eyes, she submerged herself beneath the fragrant bubbles. She didn't feel so bad anymore about not turning that memory stick and stereograms over to somebody sooner. Why should she help the Department of Defense in a cover-up? Was the cloak of secrecy truly intended to hide all nature of malfeasance?

But what would happen to Robert if he didn't get his job done, if he didn't turn the stuff over to the Pentagon? The soft fragrance of verbena trailed her as she stepped out of the bathtub and pulled a thick towel off the heated towel rack. Exactly whose tab was this little getaway of theirs being charged to anyway? The thought made her pause. Wrapped in a white bathrobe and drying her hair with the towel, she went back into the bedroom. The doors to the antique armoire were open, and Robert's duffel bag was gone. Her eyes went from the unmade bed to her overnight bag still on the luggage rack under the window. She called Robert's name and walked to the window and pushed back the curtain. The window looked out onto an enclosed back garden which at that time of morning was empty save for a lone man eating toast at one of the teak tables set out on the patio. A riot of rhododendrons and azaleas in various tints of purple softened the edges of the flagstone patio, and a newspaper lay open before the man, next to a half-empty glass of orange juice. Susanna let the curtain fall back in place.

Her mind kicked around the quiet in the room. She'd never realized just how many degrees there actually were to silence, how many textures. With slow movements she took a vintage, flower-print, rayon dress and a dusky rose sweater out of her overnight bag and carried them to the bed. As she pulled the dress over her head, a soft noise froze her to the spot. Was that the turn of a lock? She heard a soft click and shimmied into the dress as fast as she could as Robert walked into the room. Her sigh of relief was almost audible. Why was she getting so jumpy?

"Wow. You look great." He closed the door behind him as his eyes drank her in. "Listen, I have to go to Fort Meade again. Some things need to be squared away. Sorry."

She tried to hide her disappointment.

"Shouldn't take more than an hour, two max. Then we can grab lunch down at the yacht yard. An old buddy of mine runs the place. Used to play ball together when we were kids. You'll like him. He organizes the annual Annapolis sock-burning ceremony."

"Say that again. Sock burning?"

Even though he smiled, Susanna saw that Robert's face was drawn, anxious, his mind on other things. "It's how Annapolis sailors mark the beginning of spring."

She went over to him and slid her arms around him. "You go do what you have to do. I could use a little down time," she said. "I love this place."

He kissed the top of her head. "Ummm. Your hair smells good."

She put a hand onto his arm, "Robert, thank you for fighting for this, for us getting away."

He chuckled, "Ah, I had faith in you."

"But I want to ask you something before you go. It's about everything you told me earlier."

He stopped and looked at her. Was it something she'd said? He seemed to study her as though she were some indecipherable archaic text. "Yeah, okay," he finally said, as if coming to a decision. "But not here. Let's go for a quick bike ride."

"Why can't we talk here?"

"Remember those bikes outside the front door? They're for the guests' use."

"All right. Are you sure you've got the time?" she asked. "Never mind. It sounds like fun. Maybe we'll find somewhere to grab a coffee and toast or something," she added. "I'm famished. Aren't you?"

CHAPTER:
TWENTY-THREE

SUSANNA BALANCED PRECARIOUSLY as she sat sideways in front of Robert, on the crossbar of their black bicycle, with one hand gripping the handlebars, as he pedaled. The sunshine that kissed her cheeks was soft and sweet, and her gaze was drawn to the blue and white cupola of the Old Treasury Building peeking out from the tree canopy, surrounded by a drift of puffy clouds.

Robert surprised her by insisting that they share the one bike even though there had been three of them in the stand outside the Royal Folly Inn. Now he sat on the bicycle seat behind her, his breath warm on her ear, his arms encircling her tightly as he pedaled them in the direction of North Street.

"Can you hear me all right?" he murmured in her ear as he cycled.

"Hear you? Sure. This town is wonderful, Robert."

They passed colonial homes lining one side of the street and rows of trees on the other that partially obscured the red brick buildings of St. John's College. Everything around her smelled fresh and earthy, the soil and grass and trees recently wakened from their winter slumbers.

"I'm so glad you brought me here."

"Me too," he said, but he sounded distracted, and Susanna caught him glancing around and behind him at regular intervals.

"So is Fort Meade where you work?"

"It's just home base for this job."

She glanced at him. "So where do you normally work?"

He kept his eyes on the road. "Unfortunately, I am not stationed here."

"Well, good thing I've got a decent long-distance plan. I'm always calling Canada."

When he didn't answer, she tried again. "So where are you stationed?"

He didn't seem to hear her as he pedaled the bike down North Street and around State Circle, past the Maryland State House, maneuvering around parked cars and a smattering of traffic. The sidewalks here were already bustling with tourists, sailors, and families. Crisp sea air blew up from the harbor, carrying with it the aroma of fresh ground coffee and something sugary.

Susanna almost swooned as she gripped the handlebars more tightly. "Are you based somewhere in Europe?" she asked, images of romantic getaways to Paris or London flitting across her mind, distracting her from the growling of her stomach.

He stole a glance behind him before answering. "No, I'm not."

She watched the Old Treasury Building go past as they turned onto Francis Street and coasted down the hill past the baskets of pink annuals that hung from the black lampposts. She hoped they might be headed down to the City Dock. There surely were places to eat down there.

"Susanna, listen to me. I've got an overly eager NSA crew on my hands, and there's no telling what they might do — no, keep looking straight ahead like you're enjoying the ride."

"I am enjoying the ride."

"Good. I've got to get that memory stick and the stereograms from you as soon as possible. The NSA's worried about the Iranians, that they're still after the stuff and beating us to it."

She looked at him in alarm, and he nudged her head forward with his cheek. And now she understood that sharing the bike, which she at first mistook for a wildly romantic impulse on his part, was no such thing. It was born of simple expediency. He needed to speak with her where there was no chance of being overheard.

"Are you in any danger?" Susanna asked, her mouth going dry. The thought of losing him when she'd only just found him sent her pulse racing and her heartbeat into overdrive.

"Don't worry about me," Robert said. "It's you I'm worried about, Susanna. It's a high-risk game. Intelligence operations go wrong. Civilian casualties occur. You just don't hear about it."

He swerved around a turning car. Susanna's grasp slipped, and she struggled to keep her balance on the bicycle's crossbar.

"And there's no fucking way I'm going to let anything happen to you," he muttered.

They rode past people sitting at an outdoor café, drinking and eating. Susanna smelled bacon and then syrupy waffles, and her stomach protested as their bicycle whizzed past without slowing. She shook her head. It was just wrong. Why couldn't they grab something to eat?

"You want the memory stick and stereograms even though returning them to the Department of Defense means covering up what they were doing," she said irritably.

She could feel him bristle. "No, I don't, but where do you think my paychecks come from?"

"Well, what kind of a job is that?"

"Grow up. Don't you get what I've been telling you?"

"No wonder you're ready to move to Jamaica and disappear."

"No." He nipped her ear as he pedaled. "That part is because of you. I thought we cleared that up."

"But not all because of me."

"Maybe not all."

He veered off to the left and away from the City Dock

and the sailboats dotting the waters of the Chesapeake Bay.

"Wait. Stop," Susanna called, spotting a bakery across the street. "Stop right now."

Robert braked, and Susanna jumped off the bicycle before Robert could say anything and hurried across the street. When she came out of the bakery a few minutes later with a paper bag in her hand, she saw that he was smiling.

As he helped her back onto the bicycle, he said, "Sorry. I'm not used to such domesticity yet."

"Start learning." She opened the bag and inhaled deeply, took out a warm croissant, and bit into it. Her eyes closed with pleasure as the buttery flakes melted on her tongue. She held it out for Robert. He kissed her first and then took a bite of the croissant. They stayed at the curbside until it was finished, and then he pushed away from the curb, and they set off again. Susanna pulled out a second croissant and fed both of them while Robert pedaled.

"Do you have to go to work tomorrow?" he asked.

"Probably." She tried to swipe at the crumbs on her mouth.

"So I'll see you after you're done, and we can take care of business, get it over with."

His words made her tense again. Why did it have to ruffle her so? People did things they knew were wrong all the time. A little wrong, a lot wrong. No biggie; right? Covered up, looked the other way, pretended they didn't understand, lied to themselves for convenience sake or greed or other things. But it did bother her. It always had.

She saw that they were on Prince George Street, and they seemed to be headed back up to the inn. "Why don't you just quit, Robert? Retire? Whatever," she said. "Your job sounds like bullshit." Before the words were even out, she knew they were a mistake. "That's not what I meant exactly. I'm sorry. Sometimes I don't think before I speak."

Robert said, "You think?"

"What I mean this kind of job you have to do here is sort of questionable. Let's be honest." "Right now quitting is not an option. Do you understand me, Susanna?"

"But earlier you said" –

"What I want and what I have to do are two different things."

"But does your conscience play no part in this job of yours?"

"Once you start questioning things, you're a goner."

"That's what happens to people, isn't it?" she said.

"What the hell is that supposed to mean?"

She didn't answer him, and she heard more curses under his breath. "I think we're having our first fight."

"I don't have the luxury of doing what you think is right all the time." Anger clipped his words. "I will not quit or walk away. Right now my unit depends on me. I will not compromise any of my operatives. These things are always relative."

"I see," she said sarcastically.

"Good." He echoed her tone. "We're not having a fight. We're expressing our points on the matter."

Susanna looked at the Colonial and Federal-style buildings they passed, recognizing some of them from her previous day's wandering.

"But I can do the right thing, Robert."

He said nothing for a while as he pedaled. "Yes, Susanna, you can."

They sailed past the Royal Folly Inn and into the grounds of St. John's College. She glanced back at the inn, surprised, but before she could protest, Robert said, "We need to finish this conversation."

"Can't we finish it in our room?"

"Not anymore. Not when someone's listening."

"Who's listening?" she asked. "Why didn't you do this kind of thing at my house?"

"I wasn't telling you the truth then."

She considered his words before she spoke again. "I want to make sure I've got this straight. If you were to find the evidence Mr. Nashta was selling, you would complete your mission?"

"It would help."

They cycled onto a brick path and through an allee of trees, and Susanna was momentarily distracted by the beauty around her. She turned back to Robert, raised a free hand to his face, and pecked him on the cheek.

"You're not making this any easier," he rumbled and tried not to smile as he glanced around him.

"Since when have you liked things easy?" she teased.

"Let's focus on the task at hand, shall we?" he said as they sailed through the park-like grounds.

"Yes, sir," she said and nibbled on his earlobe.

Robert tried to move his head away, but the bicycle wobbled, and he lost control of it. They veered off course and toppled onto a green verge lining the sides of the brick path. He broke her fall, and she tumbled yelling and laughing on top of him, onto the ungiving Kevlar beneath his clothing. Kevlar, that faithful shield against all evils. He must have put it on when she was in the bath. But why?

She tried to catch her breath as she looked down into his handsome, laughing face. "Absolutely beautiful," she said and looked around the grand front lawn and at the college buildings, and she meant every word.

"It's one of the oldest schools in the country," he said as they struggled into a sitting position and he pushed the bicycle aside. "You okay?"

She nodded as she straightened her dress and sat back on the grass, stretching her legs out in front of her and resting her weight on her arms behind her. Before her a majestic English Yew towered off to one side. She could feel Robert studying her profile.

"I know I'm being evasive with you, Susanna, but I just can't tell you anything else until the mission is discharged. That closes out the last chapter, and then we can slam that book shut and move on with our life."

She gazed at wisps of white cloud traversing the blue expanse of the sky. "So discharge it," she murmured. "Please."

"To do that, I have to find and return the memory stick and stereograms to the Pentagon." He did a quick scan of the grounds before bringing his attention back to her. "That's the easiest way out."

"So do it," she cried. "Fuck it. I'll give it all back to you."

She shut her eyes, and he leaned in close to her and whispered in her ear, "Even if doing the right thing means not returning them to the Pentagon?"

She looked at him, and her shoes dug into the grass.

"I know you don't mean that," he said. "And you know what? I understand why that's important to you."

"Don't kid yourself. It's important to you too, Robert."

"Is it?" He rubbed his hand over his face and looked at her cherry red leather purse lying in the new, spring grass. "That's a good color."

"You're not fooling me," she said. "Beneath that cynicism, you believe in second chances. And you know what? You're starting to convince me."

Robert got to his feet and extended a hand to Susanna. "Let's hike down to the creek. And then I've really got to get over to the NSA for a couple hours."

CHAPTER:
TWENTY-FOUR

THEY HEADED TOWARD COLLEGE CREEK with Robert wheeling the bicycle at his side. A couple young rabbits chased one another cross their path, startling them and making Susanna laugh. The occasional car passed by on nearby streets, but other than that only birdsong punctuated the peace.

"So how does a Naval officer end up in the spy-catching business?"

"You get sucked in while you're still full of patriotism and good intentions. You think you're doing something really useful, important. And at first you are," he said with a wry laugh. "Gathering intelligence, running agents, running down enemy operatives." He threw his free arm around her shoulder and nuzzled her neck as they walked. "And as you get better at it, you're required for more sensitive missions. That was how they sold it. Of course, once you understand what it is you're being tasked with, it's too late to back out. So you execute the mission as best you can and forget it."

"Sounds like a one-way road to burnout."

"Does it?" He smiled, but Susanna saw no warmth there. He pecked her on the nose, and she was surprised by all the physicality until she realized he was doing it as a cover, and his eyes were constantly surveying the terrain as he nuzzled her. She looked around, past a stand of towering sycamore trees, and saw a woman's soccer team at practice in one of the distant playing fields.

There seemed to be nobody else around, but then she had no idea how one would go about spying or eavesdropping on them. Wiretaps? Satellites? People hiding in the bushes with long-range microphones or binoculars? The whole thing felt surreal to her.

"Over time you figure out that it's your own side who are fucking things up half the time," Robert said as they walked. "And the day you realize that is a pretty damn sad day. And you finally understand that you're nothing but a garbage man. A vital job, yeah, but not heroic. You're just cleaning up the garbage."

Her heart went out to him. She reached up to kiss him, but his eyes stayed averted.

"The better you get at tradecraft, the harder it becomes to transfer out of Strategic Support Branch and back to a Naval posting. So you just keep on doing it."

She could understand that. One job after the other, staying busy, not having to think about the rest of your life.

"Can't someone else on your team finish up this mission?"

"Believe me, they will, sooner than you or I imagine if I don't bring it in soon. As a matter of fact, I'm sure the devolution has already begun. Ultimately I'm as expendable as anybody else."

She didn't understand. "But I thought you were the boss?"

"Just a very little one."

"So who's the big one?"

"Ah," he chuckled, "that would be the devil himself."

Susanna looked at him, saw the glint in his eye. "And who is that?"

"A nasty little man from Texas with glasses and a black void in the place where his soul should be."

"Who are you talking about?"

"It doesn't matter. Even he is disposable." Robert said.

They reached the banks of College Creek in time to see a Naval Academy crew team rowing by, their metallic blue oars slicing the water at regular intervals with a smooth whoosh. Robert wheeled the bike around as he watched them row. Susanna joined him.

"Think about this, Susanna," he said. "How much does the midshipman earn or the able seaman, the soldier or the marine, even with their hazard pay, when they are sent into combat zones compared to the old fucker who sits behind the desk, the political master who sends them into that war for his own profit and that of his friends and not always necessarily for the good of the country?"

"That's a depressing thought," she said. "How do they sleep at night? Doesn't their conscience bug them?"

"They sleep with the money tucked snug under their pillows. Life is cheap, morality relative. What you don't acknowledge does not exist. They do it because they know they'll get away with it."

Susanna looked at the marsh edging the shoreline of the creek.

"No honour, no justice," he muttered, and she knew he was thinking of his friend Stanton, Miss Hortense's son, who'd been killed in Iraq. Her gaze focused on the far bank of the creek, and for a moment she thought she saw a red fox watching them through the trees. She squinted to get a better look, but the animal vanished. How could someone not burn out after a while, she thought. Better to close your eyes and question nothing, distract yourself with life's trivialities, app yourself into oblivion. A vulture circled above and swooped down and disappeared into the brush.

"Wow. Did you see that?" Susanna turned to Robert, but his attention was focused on a car crawling along King George Street. "Hello, sunshine," he murmured. "There you are."

Susanna followed his gaze and watched the dark-colored sedan as it pulled over to the curb by the bridge that spanned the creek. It was partially obscured by the trees and the boathouse at the end of the college grounds.

"Is that car following us?"

"Don't worry about it. Either the National Security

Agency or my own crew put a tail on me. I was summoned early this morning and have yet to show up. They get anxious. I would have done the same."

Robert laid the bicycle on the grass, and they sat down on the bank. He took Susanna's hand, but she hesitated. "Shouldn't you be going then?"

"It can wait a little longer."

"Are you sure?"

He pushed a strand of hair out of her face and tucked it behind her ear, and her lips brushed his palm as he removed his hand.

"What were you saying?" he asked, distracted.

"I saw a vulture over there above those trees. That was all." She looked out at the creek.

"Yeah, me too."

They sat side by side gazing at the marsh grasses, but for Susanna all color had drained from the morning. She looked at the boathouse a couple hundred yards away and at the car partially hidden beyond, and her fingers started picking at the young blades of grass until dirt rimmed her nails.

"I know someone at the Washington Post," Robert said. "She'd run with the story if I brought it to her."

Susanna looked at him. "You would do that?"

"If I give her the stereograms and memory stick, she'll break the story wide open."

"Really? Who is she?"

"Her name is Barb Newman. She's on the International Affairs desk, but she'll know how to deal with it." He considered Susanna for a moment. "Second floor. She'll take it and run with it."

Susanna had no doubt that it was the only thing to do, and relief washed over her. "Robert, if you were to do that, what would happen to you? What danger does it put you in?"

"We've been over this. Are you changing your mind?" he asked and held her gaze. And she knew that he was a good man, and his steadfastness filled her heart with more love than she ever imagined possible.

"Maybe your bosses will assume Mr. Nashta took the stuff to the press himself before his death, and that's why you couldn't find it," she said.

"Maybe. Maybe not. But after today I never want you to mention a word about that memory stick or stereograms to me or to anyone else again. Do you understand? Ever. You don't even know what they are. Got it?"

She nodded.

"Certain quarters in D.C. have a way of turning lies into the truth and the truth into hysterical fabrications. Don't let it throw you."

"But what happens to you?" she asked him again as a large crow alighted on the bank in a ruffle of feathers and stalked along the edge of the marsh, tailed by its somber shadow. Its black claws sunk into the earth with each determined step.

"Depends how it plays out. Not everyone gets a chance at a do-over."

Susanna turned to Robert. "And then your job will be done?"

"And then we will have done the right thing." He gave her a wink.

Perversely the thought did nothing to calm her unease, and she felt herself wavering. "Your bravery warms my heart."

"Don't be sarcastic." Robert squeezed her hand, and his smile was slow and genuine. "Thanks for giving me the benefit of the doubt every time."

Those were her words, and he had remembered them. Swallowing hard, she trying to recall the Naval Academy oath Robert had recited to her the other day. "Midshipmen are persons of integrity," she started. Maybe all this would somehow help him do right by Stanton's memory in some small way too.

"They stand for that which is right." Robert picked up the words, saying them under his breath. "They tell the truth and ensure" —

"That the full truth is known." Susanna finished the oath for him. Her hand snuck back into his, and they sat on the bank in silence. She watched the wind ripple the surface of the water. "Robert, please tell me, if you fail in this mission, will you be in any kind of trouble?"

"Should it matter?"

"No, it shouldn't, but" —

"So there's your answer. Are you a person of integrity at all times or only when it's convenient?"

His question stopped Susanna in mid-sentence because he was right. "I didn't know him, but I think Stanton would approve, wouldn't he?"

"Come here." Robert pulled her by the hand, and she moved into his lap. He wrapped his arms around her, and for the moment she felt safe even though there was nothing to feel safe about.

"I've told you everything that I can," he whispered in her ear. "Actually, much more than I ever should have. But I wanted you to know me, Susanna. This was the truth."

"What do you mean 'was'?" she asked, pulling back and looking into his face.

He lifted her chin. "You made me want to be known. You did that."

Something dark rippled through her. "Are you trying to tell me something?"

"No," he said.

"And what about us?" she asked.

"I want us. What about you?"

She nodded her head. "Will you ever be truly free?"

"I will make it happen. You should know that about me."

"And then we'll have all the time in the world to get to know one another properly?"

"Absolutely." His eyes filled with tenderness. "But we made a good start, didn't we?"

Susanna slid her hands around the back of his head and pulled him close until he gently loosened her grip and eased her away, and she could feel his subtle shift of energy.

"But right now I need to go have a quick word." He nodded in the direction of the car still partly hidden out of sight behind the boathouse. "I'll be back in a minute, and then I'm going to Fort Meade. The sooner I deal with that, the sooner we can go have a nice lunch. I know a place."

"No. Wait," she said, suddenly unable to let him go. "Tell me about the sock-burning festival."

He looked at her, amusement in his eyes.

"It's important," she said. "Please."

"Okay. There's a whole bunch of people down here who work all winter long on people's boats to get them in shape for the summer ahead. But doing maintenance work during the cold winter months can get pretty bleak and depressing. So one year back in the '80s at the first sign of spring, Louie built a bonfire and set his socks on fire in celebration of the coming warmer days."

Susanna smiled. "Louie is the friend you told me about?"

"He always was a celebration kind of guy."

"He sounds wonderful."

"Things just took off from there. I think the Maritime Museum has actually taken over the ceremony. But every spring hundreds of people get together, build a bonfire, torch their socks, pop a beer, eat oysters, drink wine, and generally look forward to working on boat decks without the need to wear socks." Robert eased Susanna off his lap and got to his feet.

"Thank you," she said, grabbing his hand and looking up at him.

"For what?"

"For bringing me to Annapolis." She remembered his words after their first night together, and now she understood what he had meant. "For trusting me. For everything."

He threw her a smile, stepped over the bicycle, and headed over to the car parked behind the boathouse on King George Street.

Susanna watched the big, black crow scavenging in the marsh. There was so much more to life than setting up the reporting office in Maryland or getting her security clearance. She had been running so long from challenge to challenge, breathlessly trying to feel a part of the world again, and now she didn't want to run anymore, and that was absolutely fine. She was reaching for something far more complex and beautiful, opening her heart again. And she had never felt more alive.

CHAPTER:
TWENTY-FIVE

THE RAISED VOICES REACHED SUSANNA almost at the same time as the caw-cawing of the crow made her start. As she scrambled to her feet, she saw the bird's powerful beak tug at something hidden in the tall grasses, and it began to struggle with its prey. She picked up the bike and grabbed her purse, but in her rush the purse slipped out of her grasp, spilling its contents onto the grass. A man's voices grew even louder as she rushed to gather everything up without letting go of the bike. She spotted her makeup compact, reached over for it, and the bicycle toppled against her. Its chain dug into her calf, and she yelped as pinpricks of pain shot up her leg.

She struggled to right the bicycle and kicked it in frustration when she saw the black grease marks along her leg and the bottom of her dress. An angry red welt throbbed on her calf, and the chain hung useless on the bike. Susanna swore out loud, shoved her purse over her shoulder and hurried toward the street, half dragging the bicycle along beside her.

Rounding the corner of the boathouse, she saw Robert standing by the car with a big, thickset, red-haired man with tiny dark eyes like watermelon seeds. He was smirking at Robert.

"You SSB guys think you run the show around here, but you don't. Murder ain't your purview, man."

Robert took a step toward him, and his voice was low. Susanna didn't hear what he said, but the energy it took to control his anger was sparking like a force field around him.

"Frickin' powerless and don't know it yet. Fuck you," the man spat out.

Both men caught sight of Susanna at the same time. "Don't blame you, though," he sneered, his eyes swiveling from Susanna back to Robert. "Yeah, might be distracting. A guy could veer off track a day or two for a piece of ass like that."

Robert's fist connected with the man's face so fast that Susanna barely registered it. The impact sent him sprawling to the sidewalk with a loud grunt, and spittle flew from his mouth, a spray of blood, and little flecks of white. He tried to say something but only managed to gurgle angrily. The power in Robert's fists left her shocked. These were the same hands that could tease almost damn mystical experiences out of her.

She let the bike fall and ran toward the two men. Fear and disbelief choked her. As she drew closer, she realized that what she mistook for flying white flecks were a couple of the man's teeth scattered over the sidewalk. Robert yanked him back to his feet, readying to hit him again. Susanna jumped in. "Robert, what are you doing?"

Robert spun around.

"Have you lost your mind?" she managed, feeling faint at the sight of his bloody knuckles.

The look he shot her was like a slap in the face, and she stepped back, stunned. He'd never looked at her that way before.

The big man's tiny seed eyes leered at Susanna as he pulled free of Robert's grip. "I'd fuck that myself," he spat out.

As Robert turned, the man crashed into him like a Mack truck, sending him hard into the side of the car with a dull thud. Susanna screamed. Robert doubled over, and the man rammed his fist into Robert's face, snapping his head to the side, into the passenger-side window. Susanna inhaled the copper scent of blood and started gagging. She had to do something fast. She yelled as loud as she could, but the men ignored her, drunk with fury as they were. She knew that place from dark long-agos. She had to stop them.

The big man glanced at her as Robert pushed away from the car, looking dazed, and lunged at him. The two grappled until, with a couple of swift left upper hooks, Robert started to topple him again. The big man screamed and fought for balance as he threw a blind punch at Robert.

"You are not a team player, man," he wheezed. "You're gonna pay for this."

Robert punched him in the gut so hard that the man started to retch.

"Wear your vest next time, asshole," Robert grunted.

The man howled and smashed Robert's knee, sideswiping him, and Robert threw an upper cut that sent him reeling. The man crashed against his car so hard that he dented it. The brutality swallowing up the two men blurred Susanna's eyes, and panic sucked the breath out of her.

"Stop. Stop," she yelled, horrified.

The big man was hunched over the car, his shoulders rising and falling, and when he swiveled around, there was a gun in his hand, pointed straight at Robert. "You take a step closer, and I'll do it." The man gulped fast, shallow breaths and tried to steady his shaking arm.

Susanna's mouth dropped open.

"You're pulling a weapon on me? Your commanding officer?" Robert exploded. In the split second it took Susanna to catch her breath, Robert swung around hard and kicked the gun out of man's hand. It hit the pavement and flew under the car. The big man yelped, and as both of them lunged forward after the gun, Susanna leapt onto the man's back and tried to knock him over. Grunting, he elbowed her to the ground. She ran at him again and hit him with her purse and her fists, but he swatted her aside like a fly and lunged after Robert, caught him in a headlock, and slammed his head down onto the hood of the car. No. Susanna tasted Robert's blood in her mouth and felt the blackness oozing over his vision as if it were her own. She heard screaming and realized it was her voice. She looked up and down the street frantically. Not a car to be seen, not a person, not a dog even.

Casting about in desperation, she saw a rock almost the size of a football in the grass near the bike. When she tried to lift it, it fell heavily, just missing her toes. Something screamed inside her head and broke through the system shutdown creeping over her. Blindly she grabbed for the rock again and managed to lift it and prop it against her body.

As she drew closer to the two men again, the reek of sweat and testosterone backhanded her. The big man towered over Robert, and his body was shaking with exertion. He still had Robert pinned to the hood of the car, and Susanna could see his meaty fingers wrapped around Robert's neck, choking him. The guy was going to kill him. Susanna heaved the rock with all her strength at the man's head, but it crashed off the hood of the car, inches from Robert's face. Susanna almost fainted. It missed the man completely and fell to the ground.

She grabbed the rock again, tearing her skin on the pavement. Wincing, she summoned all her strength and hurled the rock at the man again. This time it connected with the side of his head, glanced off his ear, slammed into his shoulder, and crashed down onto his foot, sending him whirling around, roaring in pain. Blood ran in rivulets down the side of his face, pooling around his bloody mouth. Robert pushed off the car hood, sucking air.

He took a couple shaky steps, and as the big man started to turn, Robert slammed his knee under his chin so hard the man crashed against the side of the car face first. Susanna heard metal crumple and saw his blood spray.

Collapsing to the sidewalk, he shrieked, "My nose, my nose. You broke my fucking nose."

Robert tried to catch his breath as he watched him on the ground. "I'll see you court-martialed for this."

"You can't," the man sputtered, spitting more blood. "I'm SIS, asshole."

"Watch me," Robert said, flexing his bloody knuckles, "you fat-ass, bullshitting desk jockey."

"Desk jockey? I'll have you arrested for assault and battery, you sonofabitch."

Robert lunged for the man and pulled him to his feet by the front of his ripped, stained jacket.

"Stop it, Robert," Susanna yelled, terrified they would start fighting again. When he ignored her, she started to pummel his back with her fists. Robert twisted the man's arms behind his back and turned his head to Susanna.

"Get the fuck off me, Susanna. It's okay." He pulled the big man's belt off with a fast jerk, tearing the belt loops on his pants. The man started to struggle again, but Robert managed to bind his hands behind his back with his leather belt.

"Ow, you bastard. You're cutting off my circulation," the man grunted. "You don't know what shit you're in."

"Hasn't anyone told you never to speak to a senior officer like that?" Robert said through gritted teeth.

The man tried to spit, but the spittle ran down his chin. Robert pulled and dragged him toward the back door of the car. He threw open the door with so much force he nearly ripped it off its hinges, and jamming the man's head down, he shoved him, kicking and struggling, into the back seat and slammed the door shut. Then he hurried around to the driver's side, wiping the blood off his face as he went, flung the car door open, bent in, and found the keys still in the ignition. Pulling them out, he went to the trunk and popped it open.

Susanna watched him search the trunk and find some rope. He glanced at her without a word, opened the car door again and, over kicks and loud growls of protest, managed to hog-tie the big man's feet together to his hands behind his back with the length of rope. Then he got out and slammed the door shut after him and strode over to Susanna as they heard faint howls from the back seat. She stood under a stand of oaks by the sidewalk, her arms wrapped tightly around herself, trying to control her trembling. The sun that slanted through the trees did little to warm her. It had been decades since she'd seen such rage.

Robert placed his hands onto her arms to steady her. "You're not hurt, are you?" He seemed to take in her shock and raised a bloodied hand to her face. "Let me look at you."

She flinched at the sight of his raw knuckles, and he cursed as he tried to wipe his hand on his jeans. "I'm sorry you had to see that. Didn't I tell you to wait for me by the creek?" He took a long breath, let it go, and then he saw the red welt on her calf. "Did he do that to you?"

They both turned at the sound of thumps coming from the back seat of the car as the big man tried to hurtle his body around inside, tried to kick the back door open. Susanna shook her head, unable to speak.

Robert bristled. "Does it hurt? What happened?"

"The bike."

He looked at her, uncomprehending. When he figured out what she was saying, he almost laughed, but she saw that his own body was still shaking from a surfeit of adrenaline. "Hey tiger, you were good," he said softly. Susanna saw his effort, his distress, and before she knew it, she was in his arms, shoulders heaving, fighting back her tears. It felt so good to be in his arms.

"You saved my ass back there," he chuckled into her hair. "Thanks."

"What the heck happened, Robert? Who is that guy?"

"Keith Collacutt, apparently." He took a deep breath and looked at her. "Same old power jockeying you see with the cops and the Feds. Shit happens sometimes when agencies have to work together. Nothing I can't handle."

Susanna looked at the dents that cratered the car and the blood all over him. "Yes, I can see you've got it all under control."

He didn't laugh. They were interrupted by more thumping and kicking from the car.

"Idiot," he said. "I've got to go."

"Right now?"

"He'll kick out one of the windows soon. I've got to take that bastard back. Everyone's got a minder, and mine just sent this guy to get me. If I get held up, I'll give you a call."

"Can't we go back to the hotel first so I can clean up your face a bit? And your hands?"

"I don't have time, Susanna. But you remember what I told you. Okay? You have to be careful, especially back in D.C."

"I'm not stupid."

"No, you're beautiful." His gaze swung back to the car. "But you can't take this lightly."

"Do I look like I'm doing that?"

"Calm down."

"I am calm," she hissed, feeling anything but calm. "Is all this trouble because of me?"

"No," he said. "Listen to me. Sometimes operatives have to go gray, but they don't always have to stay that way."

She looked at him blankly, no idea what he was talking about, and she didn't have the strength just now to try and figure it out. "Clear as mud."

His reply was short. "Let's finish this over lunch."

"Why the hell are we fighting?" she said, growing angrier by the minute.

"We're not fighting. I told you we had to deal with this fast. Right?"

She looked at his bloody knuckles and wanted to cry.

Robert took her by the shoulders and made her look into his face. "I'll see you for lunch. Okay? And how about if tomorrow night we go to that Vietnamese restaurant you keep telling me about, the one in Falls Church, near your place. Yeah? You want to do that? Spring rolls and all that good stuff?"

"The one at Seven Corners?" she asked incredulously.

"That's the one."

She hesitated, more confused than ever. "Sure."

"Good."

"Okay."

"Let's say 7:30?"

She stared at him, convinced one of them had lost their mind. "Why are you talking about dinner at this specific point in time?"

"I'm talking about dinner so that you will calm down, Susanna."

"I'm not a child."

He gripped her by the arm, making her wince, and she shrugged out of his grip. "Let go of me."

"Listen, I can't let you hold onto that classified stuff anymore. Every other agency on the case and the thwarted buyers will be descending on your home, ripping it to shreds, searching for those stereograms. Panic will make them ruthless. It's just a matter of time before you get hurt." He stopped himself from adding anything more.

"Well, that sure is calming me down." She thought of Farida and her family. She would never forgive herself if anything happened to them.

"I'm sorry to put you through this." Robert gave her a rueful smile full of things she did not understand.

"It was all my doing," she muttered. "Do you know where Seven Corners is?"

"I know where Seven Corners is, but don't bring anything

with you. You'll take me to get the stuff myself afterwards. Do you understand?"

She nodded, angry and frustrated with him, with herself, with the big, bloodied ginger in the back seat of the car, with that damned venal Mr. Nashta, and anyone else she could think of. If that mercenary fool hadn't dumped the memory stick and stereograms on her in the first place, none of this would be happening now. And Robert and she would have the chance to get to know one another in relative peace and safety like normal people. Then she remembered Mr. Nashta that last day in the deposition, how nervous he was as he combed his hair with a plastic comb. He must have felt like a cornered animal, his instincts screaming danger, just as hers were now. And she felt a pang of pity for him.

Robert took her chin in his hand gently. "I've got to go."

She looked into his eyes, those beautiful, stormy gray eyes that had captivated her from the day she first saw him, and nodded. She didn't trust herself to speak without bursting into tears.

"I'll see you back at the inn in an hour or so," he said.

She nodded. "Promise?"

Robert kissed her in answer and headed for the agency car, started it up, swung it around, and took off down King George Street with Big Red hog-tied and slurring complaints in the back seat.

And like that, he was gone.

CHAPTER:
TWENTY-SIX

SUSANNA WHEELED THE BICYCLE over to the Royal Folly Inn and headed for the back garden cafe, where she fell into a chair at a table farthest away from other guests and ordered a pot of tea. It seemed a calming, peaceful place to wait for Robert. The welt on her calf throbbed, tremors shook her body, the abrasions on her hands stung, and what was worse, fear coursed through her. How could their getaway have come to such an awful end?

As the lunch hour came and went and Robert didn't appear and the pot of Darjeeling in front of her grew cold, she sat and let more time pass. An hour. Two. Three. Hunger pangs gnawed at her belly, and still there was no sign of Robert. She should go on a harbor cruise or visit the Maritime Museum before he got back, make use of whatever time she had left here in Annapolis, but as she toyed with the options, she realized she was too drained for any of them. She doubted that she'd gotten more than four hours sleep the night before, and together with this morning's misadventure, she was weak with exhaustion. Long gone were the days of her youth when she could get by on next to no sleep. Not that she was complaining about the last night part.

Warmth spread through her at the memory until the image of Robert's bloodied fists broke into her reverie. She shifted in the chair, wincing, and stretched her aching legs. Everything felt stiff and sore. Her eyes took in the blooming azalea bush by her table with its profusion of purple flowers, and she realized it was time for her to leave. At this moment she wanted nothing more than the comfort of her home and her familiar world with its everyday certainties and inconsequential dramas.

Back in the plush Queen's Chambers room, Susanna swept her makeup and toothbrush into her overnight bag and zipped it shut resolutely. If Robert got caught up at the NSA, it wasn't surprising. She knew he'd call her when he could, and he'd have to understand why she chose to leave without him. They were supposed to have vacated the room hours ago anyway.

Out on Interstate 50, Susanna ground the gears of her compact rental as she headed back to Northern Virginia, battling with the gear stick the entire journey. But there had been no automatics available at the car rental place, and she just wanted to get home. She would never make that mistake again. As she neared the Beltway that ringed Washington,

D.C., she hit a solid wall of commuter traffic, but it didn't bother her as it normally would have. Her life had been turned upside down in the last week, and she had so much to think about. And people complained that nothing ever changed.

Back in the Queens Chambers at the Royal Folly Inn, the room phone rang, echoing through the emptiness. Sometime later, the innkeeper knocked on the door with an urgent message for Ms. Bailey, but there was no response. Crumpling up the paper on which he'd written the note, he stuffed it into his pocket while out on the banks of College Creek twilight fell. Two yellow-crowned night herons shuffled among the grasses in the muddy shallows, a row of baby ducks swam for shore, the river birches rustled, the birdsong quieted, the whisper of muskrats and other small inhabitants of the marsh stilled, and next to a decomposing sparrow tangled in the blades of grass on the bank, Susanna's cell phone vibrated and buzzed.

It was late when Susanna reached Falls Church. Stepping out of the rental car, she was accosted by such a deep longing for Annapolis that her heart ached. And she still hadn't heard from Robert. In front of her house, the red and pink azaleas were blooming as profusely as the ones at the Royal Folly Inn, and her dogwoods still shimmered in their colorful finery. It only felt like she'd been gone a long time.

She slid her key into the front door lock. It turned easily. Too easily. She stepped inside and paused. Something was wrong. Quickly she stepped back out and pulled the door shut and counted to ten and slowly opened the door again and poked her head back in and glanced around and listened. What was that noise, soft and indistinct? She listened harder and waited but heard nothing more than the hammering of her heart and the blood racing through her veins and pounding in her ears. Had she been robbed? The only things of any real value were her Doisneau and Davidson black-and-white photographs, but a quick glance reassured her they were still in place.

She stepped into the house and gently shut the door. The door handle was slippery in her hand, and she rubbed her palm on her sweater as she stood in the hallway looking around. Reassured that everything was as it should be, she dumped her overnight bag on the floor with an extra loud thump and went to her kitchen, switching on all the lights as she went. She turned on the old transistor radio that sat on top of her stainless steel refrigerator to dispel her heebie-jee-bies. She only got one station on the ancient radio since all the knobs were broken and the reception was iffy at best, but she refused to part with it. It was the sole thing in her life that had belonged to her father, Big Dave Bailey, the only proof that he ever existed. Then she stopped, perplexed, as something caught on the edge of her conscious and wouldn't let go.

She looked around her, but everything seemed to be in its place. When she walked into her study, the hairs on the back of her neck rose, and she gasped. Her computer was turned on. Her desk drawers were flung open. Others were upturned on the floor. The closet door was ajar. That was where she kept all the notes and information from her cases stacked numerically by date. As she drew closer, she saw files strewn over the floor in disarray. A soft thud from somewhere else in the house made her start. Somebody was in here with her.

A cold sweat slid down her back, fear sank its pincers into her spine. She needed a weapon. A stapler? Scissors? Focus, focus. A can of mace. Why didn't she have a can of mace in her desk drawer? She really had to get more organized. Damn it. She lived in America now. Why hadn't she bought some kind of gun yet?

She grabbed a letter opener off her desk and inched toward the door. As she fought her rising panic, the noises stopped. She froze, forced herself to breathe, in and out and in and out, as she listened. Nothing. She tiptoed toward the front of the house and stopped. The front door was ajar, and a chilly breeze was whistling in. Susanna slammed the door shut and fell against it. Whoever was in here was gone. After a moment's indecision, she headed upstairs, pulling herself along the banister for support, and hurried through every bedroom and bathroom. When she came back down, she was out of breath. Should she call the police? This was no ordinary break-in. She knew what they had been looking for, whoever it was, just as Robert had told her. Someone had been in her home, her sanctuary, and she felt physically violated.

And then she worried that Farida may be in danger. She dug frantically in her purse, searching for her cell phone, and when she didn't find it, she flung the purse down in frustration, and kicked it across the floor a couple times. Where the hell was her phone? As she searched her memory, she realized that she must have lost it in Annapolis. That's why she hadn't heard from Robert. But how to reach Farida? Get back in the rental car and drive over to Farida's. She didn't want to stay in her home alone tonight either. But what if whoever had been in her house was still outside, watching her, waiting? Was it the two Iranians Robert had told her about? Or someone from one of a myriad of spy outfits probably on her tail now? The last thing she wanted to do was lead anybody to Farida and her family.

She doubled-locked the front door and slid the brass security chain into place with a sharp bang and went to her study and had a look at her computer, wondering if they had been able to get around her password. The only thing she had that may have been of interest to anybody wasn't even in her house. Unless they wanted to search through all of Mr. Nashta's deposition transcripts, hoping to find clues in his testimony as to the whereabouts of the memory stick and stereograms. No wonder Robert was so adamant they deal with everything right away.

Her smile was grim as she sat down at her desk and started to check her email, deleting as she scrolled through the messages in her inbox. The office had booked her for a two-day hearing at the World Bank tomorrow. Oh, just what her wobbly nerves needed right now. Speakers from a hundred different countries pontificating in indecipherable English, most of them confident that they did not require the services of a translator.

She looked out her window as she drew the curtains and studied the cars parked along the road. There was a man sitting inside one. She stepped back from the window. Was he watching her? She dug out Michael's old bird-watching binoculars. Good thing they hadn't gone to the Goodwill. She aimed them through the edge of the curtain out onto the street. Now she could see two men in that same parked car. She sat down and thought about how to get past them without being noticed. Maybe she was overreacting, and they were nothing more than furtive lovers snatching a moment's privacy.

She didn't know what to think. How long were they planning to stay there? She started going over the different options open to her until exhaustion got the better of her and she dozed off. And awoke the following morning unmolested and unharmed and got to her hearing at the World Bank in plenty of time.

CHAPTER:
TWENTY-SEVEN

WHEN THE WORLD BANK SESSION broke at noon, Susanna agreed to lunch with the Congolese interpreter, but first she found a private phone cubicle and called her office.

"How's the job?" Pat Halliwell asked. "Remind me which country it is."

"Democratic Republic of Congo. We should be done tomorrow morning sometime."

"That's good because I need to put you on a deposition over at the Patent and Trademark Office Wednesday. Can you cover it?"

Susanna hesitated. She was still shaken up over the intruder in her house the night before and the events in Annapolis.

"By the way, Susanna, how was your getaway? You don't sound all that rested."

"Oh, you know," Susanna said, "it's never as long as you want it to be."

What got Susanna through the rest of the day was the thought of meeting Robert at the Vietnamese Place at Seven Corners for dinner. 7:30 couldn't come soon enough. She knew how worried he would be that she hadn't been answering her phone, and she was worried about him too, but she had no way to reach him. When the hearing wrapped for the day, she hurried back to one of the phone cubicles and called Farida.

"Why aren't you answering your phone?" Farida said. 'I was getting worried."

"I lost it."

"Definitely a misfortune. I've lost two this year. I feel your hurting."

"Farida, I found out what's on that memory stick and those stereograms."

"Shush. Not on the phone. Someone may be listening."

"I'm in a World Bank phone cubicle. You won't guess the half of it. It's seriously big."

"How was Robin Hood in Annapolis?"

"I had a beautiful time," Susanna said. "Well, most of it."

"Tell me when we see each other."

"He's wonderful. I know you'll like him. So will Sanjay. They're sort of in the same field."

"Well, all I know is he must be extravagantly handsome and gifted in the tactile skills too," Farida chuckled, "because you are sounding like a girl with her head in the skies."

Susanna almost smiled.

"As you should be. Why not? These things are important," Farida said. "Nothing to be coy about."

"It's so much more." Susanna tried to put her thoughts into words. "It's like this man truly sees me, you know? The real me. And he likes what he sees. Sometimes I catch him looking at me, and it's like – I don't know. No one has looked at me like that before, not even Michael."

"Well, as I always say, fate does whatever she wants whenever she wants. You just have to be willing to open the door when she comes knocking. And such a blessing you do deserve. It is time, I must admit. Michael would approve."

"You know something, Farida. Even with Michael, he never saw all of me, just the parts I thought were suitable for consumption. You know what I mean?"

"Sister, half the women on this planet know what you mean. Listen, let's get together tomorrow."

"I think it's better if I pop by tonight. I need to get 'you know what' from the garden. Robert will be with me."

"Surely this is not the way to introduce him to your friends."

"I know, but we really need to get 'you know what.'"

"That's impossible. Sanjay's home tonight. I don't want him to know what we've been up to. He'll go bananas."

"Let me think of a plan. I'll call you later."

Susanna got to the Pho restaurant at 7:30 that evening and asked for a table closer to the windows and shrugged out of her jacket. Vietnamese music tinkled over hidden speakers, and the smell of fresh ginger wafted over the dining room. It place was adorned with bamboo screens and colorful paper lanterns. She sipped her glass of water and glanced at the diners hunched over their bowls of steaming pho, slurping the soup unselfconsciously from a spoon as their chopsticks working furiously in their other hand.

She could hardly wait to see Robert, to feel his arms around her again. She had been disappointed when he didn't make it back to the inn yesterday, but she wasn't too surprised considering what had happened at the creek. It didn't matter anyhow. There would be time for all the lunches her heart desired. She would take him to her favorite places around Falls Church and Alexandria. They'd get together for dinner with Farida and Sanjay. The thought made her smile.

She hadn't even told Marie about him yet. She'd have to call her. She was dying to share her excitement, her joy. She had never felt this way about anybody in her life, and she wanted Marie to know, to be happy for her, to stop worrying so. Robert was strong, warm, tender, and she was wild about him. No, she was absolutely falling crazy in love with him, like some lovestruck teenager, not a grown woman in her fifties. He challenged her, and how rare was that? She could definitely make room in her world for him, readjust her priorities a little. Life was good, and she was glad to be feeling it again. Where was he anyway?

By ten of 8:00, as the waiter set down a plate of spring rolls stuffed with slivers of pork and fresh mint leaves wrapped in rice paper, a speck of worry appeared in the back of her mind. She motioned to the waiter. "There haven't been any phone calls, any messages for me?"

"No message for nobody."

She pushed a spring roll around the dipping sauce with her chopsticks. It was going on 8:00 o'clock. He'd been the one to stress the urgency of dealing with things as soon as possible. She tried to stop her thoughts spiraling, but she had been so sure she'd see him here tonight. Had she misread him and his intentions? She gripped a chopstick so hard it snapped in her hand. Maybe something had happened to him. No, she wasn't going to go there, borrowing suffering, worrying unnecessarily over dramas concocted by her imagination, she told herself and pushed away the plate. She had to pick up a new phone even though it wouldn't help her tonight as Robert wouldn't know her new number, and she certainly had no way of contacting him.

The spring roll caught in her throat. Maybe Robert had never intended to show up. Maybe he had been playing her all along. He was skilled at deception, was he not, at lying and sneaking around and hiding and all those other ugly things? That was his job, for God's sake. It probably didn't give him a moment's pause. But that was ridiculous. There was something good between them, and he'd been just as blown away by it as she was. She had not imagined that.

Robert's job was getting in the way, of course. She kept glancing at the wall clock that hung over the entrance of the restaurant, and her heart sank with every passing moment. He'd said he knew where Seven Corners was, but this was the real world. She looked down at her hands, pale and balled up into fists. It was time to leave.

Susanna stood in front of the Vietnamese Pho watching cars drive in and out of the parking lot as the setting sun, heavy and big and red, bled into the sky behind the Food Barn grocery store. She tried to decide what to do next until her dark thoughts were distracted by a familiar face. Her neighbor Bill Strong came shuffling out of the Food Barn, a grocery bag in one hand and a six-pack of beer in the other, trailing such an aura of loneliness that she winced. Was this the fate that stalked her too? When he spotted her, he seemed to momentarily start. Susanna gave him a polite, half-hearted wave, but he looked away furtively. Could it have been Bill who broke into her house last night?

As the sun disappeared behind the Food Barn, a strange foreboding prickled her skin, and she hurried across the parking lot to the cell phone store to escape it. There was a little death in every beautiful sunset and every sunrise too, clicking its nails impatiently. Waiting.

On the final day of the World Bank hearing, Susanna's fingers flew over the keys of her steno machine as she tried to focus on labor-intensive works in the Katanga Province, addressing sexual, gender-based violence in South Kivu, growth with governance in the mineral sector, and polio control. A realtime live feed went out from her computer to all the World Bank panel members.

The hearing sat almost three hours without a break, and at the end of it Susanna was ready to fall off her chair with exhaustion. But though she was loathe to admit it, the challenge and stress of this kind of work was her salvation at times when life threw her curves that felt too big. Being forced to focus on every single word spoken by everyone around her, oftentimes at speeds over 200 words a minute, having to figure out what exactly what they were trying to say, deciphering the different intonations, different accents every second of every hour and getting every one of those words down in shorthand on the steno machine was more than enough to melt her dura mater, obliterate her mind, and wipe it free of any other pain or distress that may have been troubling her. Hallelujah. Amen.

It was an old and noble profession, court reporting, but it definitely tested your limits of comprehension and speed. And to think that there were bureaucrats in the court system who thought that tape recorders could ever do as good or accurate a job was laughable. When the hearing wrapped at noon, Susanna called her office and was relieved to hear the office manager's voice on the other end and not Randolph Bush's.

After giving Pat her new cell number, Susanna said, "I hate to do this to you, but is there any way I can beg off tomorrow's patent and trademark case? Sorry to be so last minute. Have you got anyone else to cover it?" She realized she'd have to give Marie and everyone else her new number too.

"Last-minute indeed, Susanna, but I'll see what I can do. What's going on with you?"

Susanna hesitated. "Something's come up. I need to find someone. Just don't tell the boss, would you? I don't want to stress him."

"What do you mean you need to find someone?" Pat's voice grew stern. "Should I be worried?"

Despite Farida's warnings, Susanna needed to find Robert even if she didn't even know where to start looking. The only thing she did know was that she had to get ahold of him.

"Talk to me. Susanna? Are you still there?"

"I have to go, Pat. I've got another call coming in. Listen, don't worry. Everything's fine. I'll fill you in soon as I get the chance." She ended the call, and Farida's voice came in on the other line.

"Hey, what are you doing? Are you finished work?"

"I just wrapped up a hearing at the World Bank."

"Sanjay and I had lunch over at Eastern Market, and I've dropped him back at his office."

"Where are you now?"

"Literally? Well, I'm on 14th Street, about to turn onto Independence. I'm heading home. You want to come over?"

Susanna thought quickly. "Have you passed the Lincoln Memorial?"

"No. It's coming up on my right."

"Pull in, and I'll meet you there in a couple minutes. That will be safer, I think."

Susanna spotted Farida by Abraham Lincoln's massive, marble foot. Dwarfed by the nineteen-foot-high statue, her peach-colored sari shimmered softly around her as she paced impatiently to and fro. "What's wrong?" Farida asked her as Susanna approached. "I can always tell."

They hugged, and Susanna handed her the files for the Congo job and looked around the memorial. Its majesty never failed to overwhelm her, and it was relatively empty of tourists today, which was always a welcome relief. They walked out through the gigantic fluted columns and sat down on one of the seventy-eight steps in front of the memorial.

"I thought you were coming over last night," Farida said.

"I got stood up."

"By Mr. Magic Fingers?" Farida screwed up her face in disapproval. "I knew it."

"That's what I especially love about you, Farida, your compelling use of the English language," Susanna murmured sarcastically.

"Remnants of my British Colonialist schooling in India," Farida shot back.

"Someone broke into my house the night I got back from Annapolis. They were actually in the house when I went in."

Farida's eyes widened.

"They took off before I actually got a look at them. Or him. And then Robert didn't show up last night. We were supposed to meet at the Pho. And now I'm just worried about everything."

"Of course he didn't show up. Didn't I warn you about

that guy?" Farida started to shake her head. "Many, many times, if memory serves."

"Warn me what? I thought you said he sounded great and I deserved a break? You don't know him. Something has obviously held him up."

"Yes," Farida hissed in an undertone, "in a slippery, dark alley, I'm sure, with a knife in his back."

"Thanks for the positivity and support. I have to find him."

"No, you absolutely do not. Why didn't you tell me all this?"

"I'm telling you now." Susanna looked out over Constitution Gardens and the long, shimmering rectangle of the Reflecting Pool over to the Washington Monument at the other end. "I had to get a new phone last night. I lost mine in Annapolis."

Farida looked at her. "So what exactly is on those stereograms anyway?"

"You're not going to believe it."

The Lincoln Memorial loomed over them as they sat huddled and whispering, glancing around occasionally as Susanna talked, stopping whenever people climbed the white granite steps too near them. "If these guys killed Mr. Nashta for not handing over that stuff, they must be desperate," Farida said. "Maybe that's who was in your house the other night."

Their eyes locked. "I'm so sorry I got you involved in all this, Farida. I'll come get that stuff from your shed myself. When?"

"We may be giving these people too much credit, you

know. Agents do not always equal intelligence. We've got to stop scaring ourselves. "

Susanna's mouth was dry, but she went on, and when she finished, Farida sat back and gazed out at the Reflecting Pool. "The Washington Post, huh?"

"Should the government get away with sweeping this kind of stuff under the rug?" Susanna looked at her.

"Of course not. I am siding with you on that. It's a dangerous and dirty business they've cooked up. But what if Robert doesn't show up?"

"I have to find him. That's all. Maybe I should try calling the NSA and just asking for him outright."

"Are you out of your mind? What the heck does the NSA have to do with this, anyway?"

"That's the last place he was headed. Fort Meade."

"Oh, no, no, you want nothing to do with those people. Are you crazy? You stay off their radar if you know what's good for you. Listen, we can do this together if Robert doesn't materialize soon. He gave you the contact name at the paper; right?" Farida asked.

Susanna nodded, not convinced.

"I'll give you the all-clear when Sanjay isn't around, and then we'll do what needs doing. Together." Farida laughed grimly and put her arm around Susanna. "Look on the positive side. That spy brought back your zest for living, and at your age, not a minute too soon."

"Mr. Nashta brought back my zest for living?"

"No, my friend, that Robert guy did."

CHAPTER:
TWENTY-EIGHT

WHAT WERE FRIENDS FOR if you couldn't ignore their advice once in a while. Not that it did Susanna any good, she thought as she threw her cell phone into her purse with frustration. The NSA had denied any knowledge of Robert Crowell or his whereabouts. But then what had she expected? Farida had warned her that searching for him would be both futile and dangerous, but she hadn't listened. She had called three different departments, was put on hold for innumerable minutes, and was rewarded with a wall of indifference. What joint operations? What Defense Intelligence Agency? No, this was not the Navy. This is the National Security Agency, Ma'am. Now, do you mind spelling your name for me, please? Yes, this was Fort Meade, but if she was looking for a Naval officer, she ought to try calling the Navy.

Susanna wanted to scream into the phone. What was she supposed to tell them, that Robert was transporting a big man with eyes like watermelon seeds to Fort Meade the last time she had seen him and she was calling to follow up? Would that have helped trace him? She doubted it. But this wouldn't deter her, and her resolve remained strong. She spent the rest of the day criss-crossing the city, driving from agency to agency, looking for him. The hours followed one upon the other in a blur of questions and growing confusion. She had driven across the Anacostia River to the U.S. Naval Station and back over again to the Military Sealift Command at the Washington Navy Yard. She even called the Department of Justice, hoping one of the lawyers from Mr. Nashta's deposition would have some contact information for Robert Crowell. No such luck.

She had gone to the Military Sealift Command even though she had a sinking feeling that would be useless too. And it was. But she thought she had a better chance there than trying to get in at the Pentagon to see someone at the Defense Intelligence Agency. Plus, that one felt too dangerous, and she didn't want to get Robert into any trouble.

At the U.S. Naval Station, she got no further than the security booth, but at least they were kind enough to put a call through to both the Intel Department and to someone they said was in Human Resources. When one of the security officers handed her the telephone, she was told in words both unequivocal and firm that no one by the name of Robert Crowell does or ever has worked there. Nor did his name come up in any other department at the U.S. Naval Station in Washington.

The guards looked at her with sympathy as she thanked them, and one of them escorted her back to her car. She thought that was nice of them, but when she glanced back, she saw the other one speaking on the phone again as he studied the back of her car, probably getting her license plate number. And her heart sank when she saw a black SUV with tinted windows on her tail as she headed out of the Naval station and back into D.C. Her efforts had proven futile at every turn, and now, to add to her worries, she was being followed.

She pulled over on K Street in front of Franklin Park and double-parked, wondering what to do next. Resolving to follow every possible lead, she had ended up here hoping to speak to one of Mr. Nashta's lawyers. But in the lobby of the law firm, she was told that neither lawyer was in the office that day.

Not knowing where else to go, her eyes were drawn to the park, and after a second's hesitation, she put on her emergency blinkers, got out of her car and made a beeline for the bench where she had found Mr. Nashta's body. Was this not where everything began, and the first tenuous seeds of attraction sprouted up in the midst of death?

The police tape and all other evidence of a murder scene had been cleared away. She sat down on the bench and felt the hard wood beneath her, reassuring in its solidity. She ran her fingers over its scarred and weather-beaten surface. At least she could be sure of this. As the day wore on, an impenetrable veil of uncertainty had settled over her, throwing her sense of reality into disarray. She looked around the park as if it could offer up some of Robert's secrets to her. People were denying his very existence. But why should any of this surprise her? She met him over a dead body, for God's sake. Hadn't she been deluding herself all along?

Would she ever see him again, or had it all been but a carefully sewn tapestry of lies and deception? Her thoughts were bitter on the tongue. Except he still didn't have his hands on the classified government secrets he had been after all along. Out of the corner of her eye, she saw the black SUV that had been on her tail since the Naval Station pulling up behind a mail truck farther down the block. She swallowed hard and looked away.

Robert Crowell had come charging into her life just when she was resigning herself to a comfortable solitude. Her life had been fine. She had never minded her own company, and then he had to show up. Whenever he set his gaze on her or pulled her close, her insides had filled with a heat unlike any she'd ever known. Her body shivered at the memory. And her heart – oh, she'd didn't want to think about it anymore. "Let's give us a chance," he had said, and now he'd vanished into thin air, leaving her bewildered and her resolve faltering.

What else should she do? Drive out to Annapolis and be faced with more expressions of ignorance and hostile stares, more dead ends in some bureaucratic labyrinth of deceit? He hadn't even told her the name of his ship or where he was based. She would probably never find out what had happened to him. But he did exist, despite what people were trying to tell her today. She knew that. Just like Ms. Hortense knew. Robert was real, so very real. And he had given her more than he would ever know. His gift was priceless. She took a deep breath and looked at her hands resting on her lap, and her feet kicked at the dead grass. It was hard to believe that eleven days ago a venal little man's life had ended in this very spot.

When she looked up, her attention was drawn by two guys that sat on a bench across the way, and she remembered the two men sitting with Mr. Nashta on the very bench where she now sat. She shifted her weight uncomfortably. Anywhere else, two men sitting on a bench were just that. In D.C., they could be anything but. A soft fear wrapped around her. This place was really starting to get to her. When she looked at the men again, they were getting up.

They looked at her and started walking in her direction, and her heart started to beat faster as they drew nearer. Jumping off the bench, she shot a look at her car, but it was too far away. The coffee shop was closer. She hurried toward it as fast as her legs could carry her without actually breaking into a run. She glanced back and saw that they were now bearing down on her. Panic surged through her, and she ran. She couldn't move fast enough.

As she flung herself through the door of the coffee shop, a few patrons glanced up at her in surprise. She twisted around and looked back out. The two men stopped at the curb, watching her while they spoke to each other.

She hurried over to the barista. "There are two men outside and" –

The barista followed her gaze.

"They – they — " Susanna turned to get a better description of them, but they were crossing the street away from the coffee shop.

"Yeah?" the barista prompted, adjusting the scarf around his neck.

Susanna reddened as she turned back to him. Beginning to question her sanity, she sucked air and scrambled for words. "I was going to get them a coffee, but they decided not to wait."

"Oh, yeah?" he said. "So what can I do you for?"

"A decaf to go, please." She looked out the window, but they had disappeared. Further down the street, she saw a traffic cop placing a ticket on the windshield of her car. The barista set down her coffee on the counter and raked the hair out of his eyes.

"Do you by any chance remember that murder that happened over there in the park the other week?" she asked him.

"How can I forget? That dead guy had a lot of people who cared about him."

"What? Why do you say that?"

"All sorts been in here, asking after him. Not just the cops. He was a lucky man," the barista said. "People don't seem to wanna forget him. I get it. Sometimes it's hard to let go."

All sorts? She stared at him, at a loss for words. One lucky guy, that was Colin Nashta. Too bad he was dead.

Her new phone buzzed just as Susanna was pulling into her driveway. She parked and dug around in her purse, pulled it out and put it to her ear.

"So when are you coming home, sweetie?"

"Bonjour, Marie." Susanna smiled despite herself as she took the key out of the ignition. Even when they drove you crazy, there was nothing in the world like a best friend's voice to put a smile back on your face and soothe your jangled nerves.

"Hey, you got a new phone. Good for you. So are you moving home? I miss you all the time," Marie said in her heavily accented French Canadian.

Susanna gazed out the car windshield at her house and yard. "You know, you could start a conversation with a simple hello once in a while, just to mix things up. Why do you insist on starting every call the same way?"

"Because I'm in Toronto and you're there." Marie sighed theatrically through the phone. "Bon, d'accord. Hello, sweetie."

"It's good to hear your voice, Marie. Seriously."

"Are you drunk, cherie? You sound different."

"No," Susanna muttered, wondering how to even begin filling her in on everything, where to start. Was Marie right? Was it time to wrap up the precious memories, put them in a box and move back to Canada? If not now, when? But Marie didn't know about Robert Crowell yet, and maybe there was nothing to tell. But she knew one thing. Once she thought she was dead inside. Now she knew she most definitely wasn't.

"Well, I miss you. We all do," Marie said. "Michael's been gone awhile, you know. There's nothing keeping you down there."

"Ever heard the expression 'bloom where you're planted'?"

Marie snorted. "Sweetie, if you think you're blooming, I've got a nice used car, only a little rust. You want to buy?"

"I'm not moving back. You know that."

"Your friends and family are all up here. You belong here," Marie answered.

"Quelle famille? What family?"

"Me and Daniel and the kids. We're your family, Susanna. Who was it that said if you aren't lucky enough to be born into a half-decent one, you made your own? Remember? You did, and that's me, and don't forget it."

"But I've got the house here, the job. I'm settled. And I'm setting up the Maryland court reporting office too. It's more or less a done deal."

"You hate it there."

"I do not," Susanna said. "Adults adapt."

"Adapt? Ah, the first step on the slippery slope to giving up."

Susanna chuckled. "So cynical. That's what I love about

you. Why don't you fly down for a visit? Bring the kids. Spring is beautiful here."

"Oh, Sacre Dieu. Tu n'ecoute pas rien. You're not listening. By the way, I bumped into your sainted mother on Front Street the other day. She's old, harmless now. She can't hurt you anymore."

"So are we."

"Ouch," Marie laughed. "Mais, non. I disagree. They say fifty is the new fabulous."

"Did she ask about me?"

"Your mother? It was raining like you wouldn't believe. We didn't talk long."

"Of course not. Well, I had five persimmons on my persimmon tree last fall. How can you beat that?" They were interrupted by another call coming in. Robert? Quickly Susanna said, "Listen Marie, I've got so much to tell you, but I've got to run now."

"Are you sure you're okay, sweetie?"

"I promise to call later. Love you."

"A toute a l'heure, cherie. Bisous."

As Susanna got out of the car with her phone to her ear, her eye was drawn by a movement in the backyard. Was someone moving around in the bamboo along the edge of her property? *No, stop it.* She was not going to let her imagination get the better of her again. "Hello?" she said into the phone, hope in her voice.

"Come over tonight," Farida said. "Sanjay will be out."

Susanna swallowed her disappointment. "Farida, have

you noticed any suspicious activity around your place, anything at all out of place, anything like that?"

"No, I don't think so." Farida paused. "Why? What's happened now?"

"Nothing's happened. But I've made a decision about you know what. I'm going to take the"—

"Wait a minute. Stop. Not on the phone. Come over."

"I'm really wiped out. What about tomorrow? Plus, I think I'm being followed right now, and I don't want to lead anyone to you."

"Followed? Oh, great. You went to the NSA, didn't you?" Farida said. "Now they're probably tapping your line. Pegasus, anyone?"

"Did not." Susanna hesitated. "I called them."

"Oh, My, God!"

"Let's just dig up that bloody" —

"Shh, not on the phone. Somebody's already on your tail. And no emails either. Remember, electronic footprints."

"I just want all this to stop already." Susanna spotted her neighbor Bill Strong watching her through a slit in his kitchen blinds. When she caught his eye, his blinds snapped shut.

Farida whispered through the phone, "The most innocent things can hurt you."

"What? What innocent things?"

"Comments. Words." Farida's voice was so low Susanna could barely hear her. "We must consider every word, every nuance before speaking on the phone."

"Now who's getting carried away?" Susanna sighed, feeling Farida's ire.

"I cannot afford to get on their radar screens, thank you very much," Farida said. "Do I want to end up at Gitmo, never to be heard from again? No, no, and no."

"Gitmo? Oh, I get it. Okay. Keep your voice down. My head hurts." Susanna locked her car and headed for the front door. "I think they've finally shut Gitmo down anyway, haven't they?"

"For the love of Krishna, I can't be expected to remember everything."

"Okay, so let's meet tomorrow morning. Our favorite spot?"

Farida paused. "You mean the J?"

"That's a good one. Uh-huh, at the J."

"All right. Breakfast time?"

"Uh-huh. Sounds good. See you." Susanna disconnected, unlocked her door, and stepped into her house, closing the front door behind her. Her hand searched along the wall for the light switch.

She heard him before she saw him, a footfall of warning on a protesting floorboard. Strong hands gripped her around the throat like a vice, choking the breath out of her, and knocked her off her feet. She fell back into him hard, tried to scream, but he kept choking her as he dragged her further into her dark house. The stench of his sweat overpowered her as she fought him.

"This is my house. No, no." She tried to beg as panic blinded her. "What — do — you — want?"

"Don't struggle," he hissed and tightened his grip on her throat.

Her legs flailed wildly, and she knew she was going to pass out. Her instincts screamed to fight harder or she would die. Just like that, right here in her own house. As she fought him off, her teeth pierced her tongue, and she swallowed blood. Her arm swung out in the darkness. Help me. Help me. She jabbed her elbow behind her hard against the man and tried to grab his hair. He hissed something loud, sibilant, and kneed her in the back. The pain was fire. Tears burned her cheek, and her heart roared in her ears like an approaching avalanche. What was he saying? She couldn't hear. Fear swamped her, paralyzed her. The metal of his serrated blade flashed in the dim glow from a streetlamp. Terror howled in her brain. And everything felt like it was happening in slow motion.

Her mind was screaming at her that she could not give up. Her keys. She had her keys in her hand. Making a fist, she jabbed a key straight up and back and back and back with all her strength and felt it hit soft like jelly. Right into his eye? He screeched and released his grip, and she gulped air.

"Stupid bitch," he yelped.

The sweetest words she'd ever heard. In that split second, they spelled salvation. She had to run. He grunted as she struggled with him. Everything hurt, but she had to move. Her feet kicked, and her nails gouged. His hand flew from his eye, and he grasped for her and howled in protest. He managed to grab the hoop of her earring and held tight as she broke free, ripping her earlobe apart. Blood splattered them as pain tore through her. For a moment, Susanna thought she had fainted, but she could hear her own screams as though from afar.

"Screw you," she stammered and heaved and broke free at last. And took off. It felt as though she'd left her body and was looking down from a distance as she ran, fumbled with the front door, managed to pull it open, and tore out of the house blindly. For the tiniest moment in her space time continuum, she was sure that she was dead. But there was no tunnel, there was no light. No angel's wings caressed her. She could feel her legs pumping as they propelled her to the street in a panic and breathless, with blood streaking her face. And she understood that she was still in Falls Church, not in the vicinity of heaven, because she could hear the pounding of her feet as they raced up the street.

CHAPTER:
TWENTY-NINE

PANTING HARD, SUSANNA TORE past the house with the big magnolia tree and saw an Audi parked in the driveway, backtracked and ran up to the house and banged on the door, glancing desperately out to the street, hoping her attacker wasn't on her tail yet. After what seemed an eternity but probably wasn't more than a couple dozen heartbeats, a woman with a frizzy perm, wearing an aubergine-colored, velour tracksuit opened the door.

"Hell – o. I need your help," Susanna stuttered, shoulders heaving.

The woman stared at her.

"I'm your neighbor." Susanna's breathing was ragged and fast. "From a couple doors down. Can I use your phone? I need to call the police."

"Oh, yes. I know who you are." The woman's look was dubious, appraising. "What happened to you?"

"I — I — someone broke into my house."

The woman's eyes widened, and she stuck her head out, pushing Susanna aside as she looked down the street in the direction of her house.

Susanna tried to catch her breath as she repeated, "I have to call the cops."

The woman let her in, slammed the door shut, and eyed her warily. "You got asthma?"

Susanna looked at her in disbelief. "No. I was running."

The woman studied the blood drying over Susanna's face and neck and ear, and Susanna brought her hand to her cheek, trying to wipe it off, imagining what she must look like.

"Come on in the kitchen. I'll fix us a drink." The woman headed down the hall.

"I just need to use your phone if you don't mind."

"My name's Tanya, by the way. Tanya Leopold. We been neighbors a long time; right?" she called over her shoulder, not giving Susanna a chance to answer. "You're living all by yourself now, aren't you? Ever think of selling your house? I sold about five or six in the neighborhood just in the last year. I got my pulse on things around here. I do well over in Sleepy Hollow too. Hey, what landscaping service do you use?"

Huh? Susanna stood rooted to the spot, not sure what to do, her ear throbbing in pain. Had she stumbled into some surreal, alternate reality? Someone had just tried to kill her, and she needed to call the cops right away. What was wrong with this woman? Too many meds or booze maybe? Realizing she didn't have a lot of options in the moment, she followed Tanya into her kitchen. At least she would be safe here, and she could use a glass of water to wash the taste of blood out of her mouth. The kitchen was all gleaming dark wood and marble, and it smelled newly renovated. Susanna swayed and almost toppled onto the kitchen island. Her legs were like plasticine, and her body still shook.

"So what's your name, honey?" Tanya Leopold asked, her back to Susanna as she busied herself mixing drinks for them.

"Susanna Bailey," Susanna managed to gasp, not believing this was happening. The woman was acting as if this was some kind of social get-together. "Listen, I just need to use your phone, and I'll be gone. Are you feeling okay?"

"Who me? Hell, yeah. Better than you." Tanya shook her head, her back still to Susanna. . "I'll be even better after this here baby. So who was it broke in? Probably kids."

"No, it was a man. He grabbed me as I stepped into my hall. Can I use your phone?" Susanna asked yet again.

"Maybe it was friggin' Bill, Bill Strong, your neighbor. He probably finally went crackers."

"It wasn't him." Susanna looked around the room for a telephone. "But that guy is a bit off, isn't he?"

"He used to be okay back in the day, before the wife and kids went and got – oh, forget it."

That stopped Susanna. "Bill was married?"

"Yep, 'til his wife went and got herself and those two kiddoes smashed up on the 495. Remember that one?"

Tanya turned around and looked at Susanna. "They used to come to all our pool parties. They were a lot of fun. Handy with a shaker, Bill was. He's never been the same Bill since."

"That is sad, but it wasn't him," Susanna said. She hadn't known that about Bill. It helped explain the craziness. "I don't know if I can go back into my house."

"Sure you can. I'll bet they're gone by now. Here you go. This'll help." Tanya handed Susanna a tall glass with ice cubes and red liquid inside. "Vodka and cranberry juice. Liquid courage. A couple of these, and you'll be good as new."

This woman didn't seem to be taking Susanna's situation seriously at all. Susanna took the drink from her and glanced around the kitchen.

Tanya studied her. "You must have caught your earring on something. Looks like you ripped half your ear off. You want to go freshen up or something? There's some – oh, never mind. You can do it at home. Let's go sit. I got a couple tablets that might help."

"I need to call the cops," Susanna protested.

"I'm a real-estate agent. Did I tell you?" Tanya headed out of the kitchen. "I specialize in the Falls Church market."

Susanna stared at her back and wanted to sob, but she followed Tanya into a den done up in French Country and sat down where Tanya motioned and took a sip of her drink. When the alcohol hit the wound on her tongue, she almost screamed, and fresh tears sprung to her eyes. Gingerly she tilted her head to one side and tried to sip it that way. It worked. The drink was like a cool balm as it trickled down her burning throat. Relieved, she brought the glass to her mouth again, tilted her head to the side again and downed the drink in one long, icy slide. Her body relaxed a little into the plush comfort of the armchair.

"Boy, you know how to put 'em away, don't you?" Tanya said as she sat down across from Susanna, pulling her shoulders back and straightening out her legs in front of her. "I just got back from yoga. I go almost every night."

Susanna glanced around the room but didn't see a telephone in this room either.

Tanya took a sip of her drink. "Let me tell you there is absolutely nothing sadder in this world than too much exercise and not enough sex, don't you think?"

"What?" Maybe this was hell and she was dead after all. Susanna struggled back to her feet. "I really need to call the police."

"What good will that do? Have another drink instead." Tanya looked at Susanna. "Relax, honey. I'll get my phone. Come on. It's in my bag. You can talk to the cops while I mix us another one. You know, I've been selling houses for over twenty years." Tanya downed her drink and got to her feet and led Susanna back to the kitchen.

"Yes, you said," Susanna mumbled as she followed Tanya back to the kitchen. Sell her house? Maybe there was something to that. Sell her house that wasn't hers anymore. Michael was gone. Robert was – she couldn't bear to think about Robert. Sell her house and go back to Toronto. Maybe that wasn't a bad idea. It would sure make her friend Marie happy.

Tanya finally pulled a phone in a pink glittery case out of her bag, handed it to Susanna, and mixed another couple drinks for them. Susanna looked at it, disbelieving for a second that it was actually in her hand at last.

"Nothing like liquid rescue, I always say," Tanya drawled. "Works better than the cops far as I'm concerned."

Susanna called 9-1-1, reported the break-in, and spoke with them until Tanya set two fresh drinks down, sloshing in their glasses, ice cubes clinking, and took the phone from Susanna and handed her a couple wet napkins instead. Susanna attempted to clean her cheek and neck, wincing with pain. "I've been thinking, Tanya, I may be interested in selling my house," she said. "Why not? How fast can you do it?"

Tanya stopped, the glass halfway to her mouth, and blinked. "Serious?"

"But right now I've got to get back to my place. The cops should be there any minute."

"Well, that's great, Sue. Really." Tanya's smile was wide as avarice, and her eyes glittered with renewed life. "May I call you Sue?"

"Sure, Tanya," Susanna said as she headed for the front door. What did it matter?

Tanya grabbed a jacket, picked up the glasses, and followed Susanna out. "Well, I'll go with you. Don't want you wandering around out there on your own. Don't worry. I've got our drinks."

As they stepped out, they could see a police cruiser parked outside Susanna's house, and they hurried toward it.

"So you really want to sell?" Tanya asked her again.

"Yes, I think so. Thanks, Tanya."

"Well, the market is definitely hot. But then it's always hot in these parts, isn't it?"

"How soon can you get the process started?"

"Oh, tomorrow, yeah. Definitely." Tanya proffered her a second drink, but Susanna refused it.

Two officers stepped out of the cruiser as the women approached.

"By the way," Susanna turned to Tanya Leopold, who was now drinking alternately from her own glass and then from Susanna's. "A while back there was a guy that came to my door, asking all kinds of questions about your husband and you. I thought you should know."

Tanya's lips froze on the rim of her glass.

Calling the cops had been a waste of time, just as crazy realtor Tanya Leopold had predicted. Rote questions, a cursory look around the house, filing of a report, and a promise to get back to her with developments. But then what had Susanna expected? She stood before her bathroom mirror and tried to bandage her earlobe with some gauze. Exhaustion tugged at her as she cleaned her face and neck and hair. The cops had offered her a lift to the hospital, thought her ear could use a stitch or two, but she had declined. They asked if there was someone she could stay with. Yes, stay with a friend, good idea. She brushed her teeth and watched the spit swirl down the drain pink and faintly bloody. Her tongue throbbed, her ear ached, her whole body hurt, and her house hummed with a dangerous silence. No way was she staying here tonight.

She grabbed a couple aspirin and stared hard at her reflection in the mirror. As she was turning away, something stopped her. She looked back and winced. Her mother stood behind her, that old and ugly wavering ghost that refused to let her go. Susanna squinted and rubbed her eyes. No way, not now. She was way too tired for this.

"Look at you, look," her mother's ghost hissed softly in her ear. "Of course Robert's disappeared. He wouldn't stick around for you. Just like your old dad, buh-bye. Even Michael moved on in his own way, left you behind."

Slowly a hysterical laughter started to bubble up somewhere deep inside Susanna. Exhaustion spread through her aching body as she started to laugh, and she had to forcibly shake it off. She shoved the palm of her hand into the mirror, and her mother's spell splintered and disappeared. *I don't need you to beat me up. I'm pretty good at it myself.*

Susanna turned away and pulled off her torn and blood-stained shirt, unsnapped her bra, and threw everything into the hamper. In her bedroom she found a sweater, and as she pulled it over her head, her hand grazed her breast. She stilled. And thought of Robert's hand, hard and calloused, caressing her breast, pearling her nipple.

And she longed for him, for the safety of his arms, his touch, for his mouth that curved when he whispered in her ear, for his heart beating hard against hers. She looked at herself in the full-length mirror. But her hand was not his, and he was not here. And she hated him. She hated him more than she'd ever hated anyone in her life. "That too is a piece of the truth," she mumbled and turned away from the mirror. To steal away what he had only just given — she hated him. She'd almost been killed tonight, and he wasn't here to protect her, and she would probably never see him again.

She banged down the stairs, turning on all the lights as she went. She wasn't taking any chances with shadows. How right she'd been all along not to trust him, not to trust life again. She popped a CD into the stereo, and Whitey Ford started to moan some blues. Susanna needed more alcohol. But had she really just agreed to sell her house?

Going into her kitchen, she flung open the refrigerator, but it was disappointingly empty. She threw open the kitchen cupboards. Half a loaf of bread and chickpeas in a can. But next to that surely the devil's own creation, a huge bag of potato chips. Now, that there promised a fine and crinkling oblivion. Fueled by the anger that surfed atop her fear, she ripped open the bag and started in on the chips until her tongue burned and pulsated and her stomach churned. But still that precious oblivion eluded her. Maybe a drink would help. That Tanya was definitely on to something there. *What has happened to my life?* She was way too old and wise for this madness.

Getting as far as the hallway, Susanna froze, and her body protested at the remembered violence. Her limbs started to shake, and she had to turn away. Everything needed to be fixed and put back to the way it all was before in her life. She would turn the memory stick over to the National Security Agency or the Department of Defense or whoever the hell else wanted it so badly. That was the easiest thing to do, and she'd had enough. This is not my business, she thought.

She picked up her phone and tried to call Marie in Toronto, her eternal refuge in a storm, but it went straight to her messages. Damn it. Wasn't there a bottle of alcohol somewhere in this house? Susanna went back to the refrigerator. Oh, why had she thrown out that bottle of Aquavit? It had sat unopened in her refrigerator for so long, not bothering a soul. She opened her kitchen cupboards again, one by one, banging them hard, until at the back of one she spied a bottle of cooking sherry that Michael brought home years ago. He had always been the real cook in the family no matter how many cookbooks she picked up. She peered at the dusty bottle. Surely cooking sherry was not just for cooking? Susanna grabbed the bottle, swiped at the dust with the palm of her hand, unscrewed the lid, tilted her head to one side to bypass the wound on her tongue, took a swig, and almost gagged.

She sputtered as tears rolled down her cheek. *Screw you, Michael. This is all your fault.* She sank to the floor, tears of laughter running down her face and forced herself to down some more of the cooking sherry. It was helping numb the pain coursing through her body. *You're the one who dragged me here to this godforsaken town in the first place. None of this would have happened if it hadn't been for you.* But then she would not have met Robert either, and that was a sobering thought. She needed another drink or maybe five, or let's just make it an even baker's dozen. Mired in liquor and self-pity, she was starting to feel better. She downed the last of the sherry through gritted teeth and felt a Tennessee Williams moment coming on. All she wanted to do was emote, preferably at the top of her lungs, "Stella! Stella!" She turned the thought around and examined it from different angles.

With effort, she pulled herself to her feet and aimed her body for the front door. Steadying herself on the doorjamb, she marshaled her spinning senses. You can do this. Life was too short for sanity to be her only driver. Flinging open her front door, she was momentarily distracted by the lovely, gleaming, navy blue paint that covered the door and the intricate nature of her brass pineapple doorknocker. She stepped out, missed the step, and the cool night air slapped her hard as her ankle twisted and she started to go down.

She teetered and flailed until she grabbed a hold of the railing and managed to stop her fall. Her body hurt with the strain, but she attempted to straighten up. "Robert! Robert!" she yelled as loud as she could. "Robert, you bastard!" She heard the yelping of a dog and paused to catch her breath.

"Is everything okay?" a man's voice called out from the dark.

Susanna peered out at the street and saw a couple walking their little dog. The dog barked excitedly. Susanna managed to shove the hair out of her face and straighten up as every inch of her protested in pain and gave the couple a haughty stare.

"Are you all right?" the man asked again as the woman picked the little dog up into her arms with alarm.

Susanna wasn't sure what they wanted from her. "You bet. No worries."

They stared at her, so she gave them a small wave. "I was just calling the cat."

The man and woman glanced at each other and back at Susanna.

"He's getting old, hard of hearing." Susanna reached frantically behind her for the door handle. "You know how it goes."

Finally she managed to grab the doorknob, turned and stepped back into her house and slammed the door behind her as everything came up in one mighty gastric revolution, all over her clothes. And she slid to the ground gracefully and waltzed into a blessed blackness.

CHAPTER:
THIRTY

CURLICUES OF SUNLIGHT DRIFTED OVER SUSANNA and settled on her hands and arms as she forced her eyes open. Dried blood glued stray hairs to her face and made her wince as she tried to turn her head. A van rumbled loudly outside as it drove up her street, and her hand went to her ear and over the bandage still in place. Her eyes moved to the puddle of sun pooling at her feet. She tried to get up but failed. As she looked around her, everything from the previous day came back. She sniffed and groaned at the vomit on her clothes, screwed up her eyes tightly, and hoped things would be different when she opened them again. But no, awful covered everything, and her safe harbor was gone forever.

Shifting her aching body, a cry escaped her lips. Scariest of all was not knowing where Robert was. Her heart squeezed so tightly at the thought of him that it hurt, and her thoughts went to government secrets again. If Robert wasn't here to take those stereograms and memory stick to the press, then she would forget about all of the stuff and let it rot and turn to dust. Her head banged like a steel drum. Except everything was in Farida's backyard under her potting shed, and the danger that Farida and her family were now in because of her was more than Susanna could bear. She knew it was just a matter of time before somebody else got hurt or worse. She would never forgive herself if anything happened to them. *My life may have gone to hell, but I'm not taking Farida there with me.*

Susanna sucked air and pulled herself to her feet. She had to get that secret stuff out of there and to the newspaper where it belonged. She would do it for Robert. Maybe happily-ever-afters were meant for others and not for her, but it didn't matter. He had given her so much, she could do this for him. Gathering up her courage piece by piece, a steely resolve started to trickle through her. Every moment was a chance to be who she wanted to be. Those men who operated in the shadows would not make her cower. *You will not frighten me again. If I survived my mother, bastards, I can survive you.*

The ringing of the phone startled her. Robert? She cast about wildly until she spotted it on the kitchen counter. "Where are you?" Farida's voice sizzled through the line. "I've been here for half an hour already, visiting with Thomas."

"What?" Oh, crap. Susanna had completely forgotten about their meeting this morning. "I'll be right there. The J, yes. I'm just jumping into the shower."

She could do this. The Iranians would not beat her to it, and the agencies would not cover it up. She would not recoil when bastards bigger than she held her in their grip. And when life screeched and bellowed and raised the hairs on the back of her neck, she would run hollering and jumping and kicking straight at it. She would yell boo and laugh in its bully face.

And then she was getting the hell out of here and back to Toronto.

Just over the Roosevelt Bridge into Washington, D.C., Susanna realized she was being followed. She had first noticed the green station wagon as she left Falls Church but didn't give it much thought. Now it was pulling into the parking lot of the Jefferson Memorial a couple cars behind her, sending her pulse into overdrive. Her mind started to race. Who was it this time? Did it matter?

She had thought this would be a safe place for Farida and her to meet and talk freely, but she was wrong. The important thing now was that she not lead them to Farida. She got out of her car and headed for the marble circular memorial that housed the massive bronze sculpture of Thomas Jefferson. She was relieved to see tourists milling around and three or four tour buses idling at the curb. Safety in numbers.

Glancing over her shoulder as she took the memorial steps two at a time, she saw a couple men climb out of the station wagon. She spotted Farida sitting on their usual bench and rushed over to her, maneuvering through a group of tourists admiring the nineteen-foot Jefferson that towered over them in the middle of the rotunda. She slid onto the bench beside Farida. Her shirt was drenched in sweat, and she was practically panting. Farida did not look happy, and Susanna knew this development wasn't going to make things better. "Some men followed me here, and they'll get up here any second now. We don't have much time."

Farida blanched. Susanna jumped in before she could utter a word. "Let's just walk around and look at stuff as if we don't know each other. Mingle with a group. And then you get the heck out of here, and I'll hang around. Hopefully they'll stay with me, think I'm waiting to meet someone."

Susanna saw the fear in Farida's eyes as she got to her feet. "Or just go now. Get out of here. I'll be in touch."

Farida shot her a sharp look. "You don't look so good. What happened to your ear?"

"Listen, Farida, I'm going to take the stuff to the paper myself as soon as I can get it from your place. I've already put you in danger's way. I'm sorry for it, but it ends here. I'll take care of this."

"No, you won't," Farida said. "I'm going with you."

"I can't endanger you or your family any more than I already have. When can I get —"

The words froze on Susanna's lips as the two men entered the rotunda. "Start moving, Farida. Those men just walked in."

"Come over tomorrow morning around nine," Farida whispered, "after I've gotten the girls off to school. We'll take care of it then." Farida pulled a pair of sunglasses out of her purse and slid them on as she drifted off to study some inscriptions on the wall with a group of tourists armed with cameras and sunhats. Susanna got up and started circling the marble rotunda from the opposite direction, an eye on the men. They hadn't spotted her yet. As she neared Farida again, she stopped next to her and looked up at Thomas Jefferson and said, "I'm moving back to Toronto."

"What?" Farida turned to her in disbelief.

"No, don't look this way. They've spotted me now. You've got to go. Get out of here."

"I'll be waiting for you in the morning."

"No, you won't. I'm doing this alone." They glanced at one another.

"We're going to do this thing, sister, and we're going to do it together," Farida hissed at her before moving away with a group of women. Susanna kept her eyes averted and prayed that Farida would get out safely. A commotion erupted, and Susanna turned just as Farida hit one of the men with her purse. Susanna froze.

"Get away from me," Farida yelled at the man. The people around her drew closer.

"Help. Call the bus driver. This guy was grabbing my purse."

Farida was swept out of the rotunda in a little wave of concerned tourists and down the steps to the parking lot and the tour buses and safety. Susanna watched the group from the top of the rotunda stairs. From the side of her eye, she saw both men still inside. So they hadn't followed Farida. A Park Police car pulled up in front of the memorial, Susanna let out a long breath of relief, and as they came up into the rotunda, the two men slipped out.

She turned and stilled, her eye caught by her favorite Jefferson quote inscribed high up on the wall of the rotunda, the one about the pursuit of happiness. How beautiful was that? It never failed to touch her even when sometimes it seemed the country had lost its way, was stumbling, had gotten the words mixed up. She looked down at the marble bench beneath the inscription and sighed. How many hot, humid summer evenings had Farida and she spent on this same bench, sipping cool cans of lemonade, discussing Thomas Jefferson and his brave dreams and his clay feet as they swiped with lazy palms at the sweat that beaded their foreheads. And now it was all coming to an end. Susanna walked out to the white marble steps that overlooked the Tidal Basin. The Japanese cherries were blooming pink and white along the water's edge, and their soft fragrance filled the air. This was her favorite spot in D.C., and she would miss it.

She glanced behind her but didn't see the two men who had tailed her anywhere, and as long as the Park Police were still around, she knew she was safe. A thought tugged at her. It was okay to change plans, adjust course, but if she had turned everything over to Robert earlier, would things have turned out differently? Would he be standing here beside her now? Perhaps he would, but not as the man he wanted to be.

Heading down the marble steps of the memorial, her attention was drawn by a large family at the foot of the stairs. A handful of grownups gesticulating, laughing, and talking loudly in a foreign tongue, and at least as many children, tangled around their parents' legs and playing. Then one of the men dropped to the ground suddenly as if he was going to do push-ups, making Susanna jump involuntarily. But instead of pushups, he started to kiss the pavement, once, twice, and three times, much to the family's mirth and amusement.

"America!" he yelled out amidst their laughter. "I grab it! I love it! I kiss it!"

CHAPTER:
THIRTY-ONE

BEFORE DAWN HAD SET FOOT OVER THE HORIZON, Susanna was awake and dressing. Her sleep had been fitful, and she couldn't stay in her bed another minute. She made a pot of coffee, needing the caffeine, hot and strong. She had spied a dark SUV with tinted windows parked a couple doors down with somebody inside it, watching her house the whole night. And earlier a woman she'd never seen before had walked her dog up and down the street past Susanna's house at least a half dozen times. The only thing missing was the green station wagon, and they could have all gotten together and had a spook party, she thought bitterly. No. The only thing missing was Robert Crowell.

She tossed a heaping tablespoon of sugar into her second coffee and filled the mug to the brim with milk. When she had gotten home from the Jefferson Memorial yesterday, that crazy Tanya Leopold was waiting for her. Susanna studied her warily, but the woman seemed to be in possession of her faculties and gave Susanna a rundown on how things would proceed with the sale of her house. When she saw that Susanna did not seem interested in the details, she dropped the niceties and got on with the business at hand. And for that, Susanna had been thankful. She had given Tanya free run of the house and a spare key, and Tanya had spent the day with photographers and stylists, prepping the place for sale. Susanna wanted no part of it. She spent most of the day on the phone with Marie, who was overjoyed at her imminent return.

Now she went to the window and pushed the curtain aside. The SUV was still there, and people were moving inside. The dark glass shielded them from her, and she couldn't count how many of them there were. How was she supposed to get over to Farida's house without being tailed? There was no way she could take her own car or call for a taxi. They would see her leaving and follow. She went back into the kitchen and made toast and spent the hours to daybreak going over her options.

A soft rattling at her back door made her jump, and her coffee mug crashed to the floor, scattering shards of ceramic around her feet. Grabbing the closest thing to hand, a butter knife, she inched over to the door one nervous step after another. Then she counted to three and flicked the blind open. The wind blew her neighbor's garbage cans around, and the bamboo at the back of her yard swayed, but there was no one there.

Susanna's hand moved to her throat as she scanned the yard carefully. Then her eyes went to Bill Strong's house, and as she studied it, an idea started forming in the back of her mind. Didn't Bill Strong work somewhere in Alexandria or Crystal City? If she snuck over to his house, she could ask him for a lift. That way her car would stay in the driveway and she would have a chance of evading her watchers. It was her best plan for getting away undetected. It was her only plan.

Looking at the mess of broken ceramic on the floor and deciding that Tanya would have to deal with it, she grabbed her purse and keys and hurried out the back door, leaning against the door frame until it shut quietly behind her. Carefully, she snuck over to her neighbor's house, nudged along by a brisk wind that pushed her on and pinched her cheeks. She spied Bill through the window in his kitchen door, standing motionless in front of his refrigerator as if in a daze. She was about to tap softly when something stopped her.

His head was tilted up and to one side like he was looking at a spot on the ceiling. The faint sunlight slanting through the blinds pierced his body with shafts of light and illuminated him like a modern-day Saint Sebastian in thrall to the agony of arrows piercing his flesh. His horrible loneliness shimmered and rustled audibly like slivers of sunlight on bamboo. The moment was somehow too intimate, too unbearable to witness, and Susanna stepped back aghast.

At that same moment, Bill turned and saw her. His shock at seeing her at his kitchen door left him gawping. She had the strongest urge to run, but his eyes pinned her like a feral animal. She motioned for him to open the door. He glanced around his kitchen and then came over.

"I seem to be having a bit of car trouble this morning," Susanna said as she stepped into his kitchen while his eyes bore into her. "I was wondering…you don't happen to work over Crystal City or Alexandria way by any chance?"

His focus came to rest on her mouth.

"Thing is —"

He said, "Need a lift, right?" He shut the door behind her, pushing her into his kitchen. "I'm gonna get my jacket. I was just leaving anyhow."

"I really appreciate this, Bill." She turned, and he was right there, inches from her face, and she fought the urge to jump back.

"Where do you want to go?" he said.

"Alexandria." What was that smell that accosted her?

"Yep. Give me a minute," Bill said as he backed out of the room. "What happened to your ear?" he asked but didn't wait to hear her response.

Glancing around his kitchen, she was appalled by what she saw. Dirty dishes and pots covered every available inch of counter and filled the sink. Garbage tumbled out of an overflowing bin onto the floor, and the kitchen table was covered in a mess of newspapers three inches deep or more. The poor man, she thought, he needs a good cleaning service. Then she took another look at the table. What was that glinting from under those papers? She stopped and listened, and when she didn't hear Bill's footsteps, she tiptoed over to the table and lifted an edge of a newspaper pile, and her breath caught.

A black, snub-nosed handgun nestled amidst the garbage scattered over his table like a dead blackbird in its nest. She nudged another stack of newspapers aside and froze. There was a veritable armory of firearms under all the papers on his kitchen table, at least eight or nine guns of different calibers and sizes. Oh My God. Bill Strong was some kind of a lunatic. She started backing out of the kitchen as quietly as she could when he appeared in the doorway. He must have noticed the pallor on her face or the panic in her steps because his eyes narrowed.

She floundered. "I think I may just call in sick today and not go in after all."

His look was guarded. "What's the problem?"

"No problem, Bill. I just don't want to impose."

"I said I'll take you."

Susanna weighed her options and realized she didn't have any. She had to get to Farida's this morning no matter what. So it was Bill Strong or nothing. "Well, if you're sure it won't be a bother," she mumbled warily and fell into step behind him.

He held the door open for her, and she got into the front seat of his car. He watched her slide down as low as she could in the seat, didn't say anything, but when he got in and started up the engine, he looked at her suspiciously. *Oh, for Christ's sake, was he going to give her a hard time?* "I pulled a back muscle," she said, avoiding his eyes. "It doesn't hurt as much if I sit this way."

He didn't reply as he pulled out of his garage and backed down the driveway. She slouched down even lower to avoid detection by her watchers, held her breath, and prayed that the top of her head wasn't visible in the car window. Bill drove up their street so painfully slowly that she wanted to scream in frustration and jam her hand onto the accelerator, but she restrained herself. He probably had a gun in here too. Her heart pounded so loudly that she was sure a heart attack was on its way. Squeezing her eyes shut, it felt as if she'd fallen into Dante's Inferno and at this very moment was traversing the ninth circle of hell. The seconds seemed to stretch out to eternity as they inched up the street and past the parked, dark-windowed SUV.

Finally Susanna felt Bill's car turning, and she knew that they had pulled onto another street. When she didn't hear any screeching tires or vehicles coming up behind them, her relief was palpable. She moved up in her seat to a more comfortable position, snuck a peek behind her, and satisfied that they had eluded her watchers, she counted the endless minutes to Alexandria.

Leesburg Pike seemed to go on forever with Bill Strong's temperate driving style, but he stayed focused on the road and, to her relief, "You're a Canadian, huh?" was his sole stab at conversation for the entirety of the trip. Once King Street had entered Old Town Alexandria, she asked Bill to pull over and couldn't jump out of his car fast enough, making sure to thank him adequately. Last thing she needed was to offend him or set him off in any way. Waiting until his car disappeared into the morning rush-hour traffic, she practically ran the couple blocks to Farida's.

Susanna had been living next door to a madman and didn't even know it. Thank God that's over, she thought. Then she remembered how Bill had left a bunch of cheap, gas-station red carnations on her doorstep after Michael's funeral, and such a sadness engulfed her that she ran even faster to escape it. Were we all just struggling to do the best we could? It had been a kind gesture. She decided it was debatable. By the time she reached Farida's row house on Princess Street, she was practically gasping for air. Obviously she'd been slacking off on her evening runs with everything that had been going on in her life.

Hammering on the door, Susanna glanced around nervously, not even sure who specifically she was looking for as there was an assortment that seemed to be tracking her now. When no one answered her knocks, she hurried around to the back, fumbled with the gate until it opened, and slipped down the path to the potting shed at the end of the garden. A cluster of yellow forsythias lit up the back corner of the yard, blooming behind an assortment of tulips in candy colors. She tried the door of the potting shed, but it was locked. Peeking in through the grimy window, she could see the shovel propped up against the old bench, but she had no idea how to jimmy a lock. Who would have imagined it was a skill she might need one day? Where was Farida anyway?

Susanna took a few steps back, then ran and flung her body at the shed door. Damn, that hurt. The door creaked but didn't give, and her shoulder and arm throbbed. She'd have to break the window and try to climb in. She picked up a stone from the flowerbed nearest her and threw it at the window. Nothing. She tried swinging her purse at the window. No good either. How was she supposed to get into that shed? Looking in the window again, she noticed the latch on the inside of the door. If not for the windowpane, she could probably climb onto something, reach in, and unlock the door from the inside. Casting around the yard, she grabbed an Adirondack chair and dragged it over to the shed.

She took off one of her shoes and started hammering at the window with the heel. On her third try, the window shattered, and Susanna jumped back as shards of glass flew into the air, grazing her cheek. She swore and wiped at the blood with the sleeve of her jacket, put her shoe back on, pulled the cushion off the Adirondack chair, and positioned it in the bottom of the window frame. Pulling the chair right up against the shed, she stepped onto it, and started to wriggle her body into the shed through the broken window. About half way through, she sensed some resistance and tried to maneuver around to see what was holding her back, but she was stuck. At the same time she heard the back gate bang open, and she froze, half in and half out of the shed window.

"Oh, Holy Krishna, what are you doing?"

Susanna's body sagged with relief at the sound of Farida's voice. "Help me, Farida. I'm stuck."

Farida hurried over. "Couldn't you have waited a few minutes for me to get back?"

"I didn't know where you were, and I've got to hurry."

"Yes, I can see that. How's it going?" Farida asked wryly as she helped extricate Susanna from the broken window frame. "What did you do to my shed window? Sanyjay's going to freak out."

"I'm sorry. I'll pay for a replacement."

"Were you followed over here?"

"I don't think so," Susanna said. "But I definitely risked my life. I got a ride over with my insane neighbor Bill Strong."

"You don't think so? Then we better get cracking." Farida unlocked the shed, and they hurried in, pushed the bench to one side, and Susanna picked up the shovel and started digging.

"No sign of you know who?" Farida asked.

"Who? The Feds? My attacker? The SUV with the tinted windows that has taken up residence on my street outside my house?"

"Your spy."

Susanna shook her head as she dug, and Farida took the shovel from her. They took turns and worked as fast as they could until they finally saw the dirt-covered plastic bag. Inside were the stolen classified stereograms and memory stick, the cause of all Susanna's troubles. They both stopped and looked at it. Susanna broke the silence. "I'm doing this alone."

"How will you get to the Post? Fly?"

Susanna looked at Farida.

"I've got Sanjay's car," Farida said. "He took the Metro to work today."

CHAPTER:
THIRTY-TWO

FARIDA MANEUVERED SANJAY'S INFINITI through the D.C. streets with nerves of steel and the speed of a Formula One driver. Susanna hung on for dear life and didn't breathe until they pulled up in front of the Washington Post. Farida screeched on the brakes and stopped in a double-red, no parking zone directly in front of the building. She turned to Susanna, and they smiled at each other.

"Never underestimate the power of women working together."

"All I can say is there's no possible way anyone could have followed us with you driving," Susanna said as she released her grip on the dashboard. "Jesus, Farida. You'll love Toronto when you come to visit. Everyone drives like you there."

A sharp rap on the passenger-side window made them jump. A parking warden was motioning for them to open the window.

"You're lucky I'm feeling generous today, ladies," he said. "Move it or lose it. Now."

Farida pulled up twenty feet further and stopped again. They were still in a red, no-parking zone. The women looked at each other. "Do we really have time for this?" Farida asked.

Susanna shook her head, and Farida shrugged her shoulders. They got out of the car, leaving it where it was, and hurried into the building as the parking warden stood watching them in disbelief.

When they entered the lobby, the guard at the security desk stopped them.

"We're here to see Barb Newman," Susanna told him.

The guard looked from one to the other.

"I believe she's at the International Affairs Desk," she added.

"Names, please?"

"Oh, sorry. Susanna Bailey and Farida Rafik. We have something for her."

The security guard looked through a black binder on his desk, picked up his telephone and punched in a number. After a moment, he put down the phone and looked at them. "Leave it at the front desk. That's here." He tapped the counter in front of him.

"What do you mean?" Farida said. "This is highly classified stuff. We're not leaving it with you."

"So don't." The guard closed his binder with a thump. "She is not available."

"Not available?" Susanna's mouth dropped open. After everything that had happened, after everything they had been through, this is how it was going to end?

Susanna and Farida looked at each other. They couldn't just leave the bag there. What if it never reached the woman?

"And now I'm going to have to ask you to leave," the security guard said as he started to come around from his station.

"Just a minute," Farida jumped in.

"Wait. Please call her once more," Susanna added. "This is urgent. Tell her I have something for her from Robert Crowell."

The security guard looked undecided, as if he was weighing her up.

"Do it. Tell her the name Robert Crowell," Susanna said firmly.

After another moment's scrutiny, he picked up the phone again and turned away from them as he spoke into it. They watched his back until he turned around, the phone still to his ear, and looked at them. "That's what they said. There's two of them here."

He nodded and hung up the phone. "Okay. Ms. Newman will be down in a minute. Follow me, and you can wait for her in a room down the hall here."

Susanna almost shook with relief. She placed the bag with the memory stick and stereograms onto the counter in front of the guard and pushed it toward him. Robert had said Barb Newman would know what to do with it. Now that the woman was on her way down, they could go.

"Just give her this package. Tell her it's from Robert Crowell. We have to go. Our car is" —

"Wait a minute," the security guard started to say as the elevator doors opened, and a tall, angular woman with short gray hair strode toward them before they had a chance to leave.

She looked from Farida to Susanna as she spoke, and her voice was soft and mellifluous. "Hello. I'm Barbara Newman."

They shook hands with her, and for a moment Susana felt an irrational stab of jealousy. She saw how a voice like that could work magic. How well did Robert know this woman anyway? She grabbed the package off the counter and proffered it.

Barbara Newman looked at it and then around the lobby. "This is from Robert?" she asked under her breath as she took the bag. "Do you work with him?"

"Not exactly." Susanna shook her head and turned to leave.

"If you'd just give me a minute of your time, it would help," Barbara said.

Susanna and Farida exchanged a glance. Farida shrugged. "You've got to tell somebody. Do you really want someone else going through what you went through these last couple days?"

Turning to Barbara Newman, Farida said, "But you've got to keep our names out of this."

Susanna nodded in agreement, and her eyes met Barbara's.

"Please," Barbara said to them. "Without Robert here, I need your help. I need everything you can tell me." After a beat Barbara motioned and extended her arm. "I've got a quiet place where we can talk."

Reiterating Farida's words, Susanna said, "But you can't mention either of us in connection with this whole thing in any way. Like Farida said, we must remain confidential sources."

"I can do that," Barbara Newman said and led them down the hall.

An hour later Susanna and Farida returned to the lobby with a nod at the security guard and headed for the doors. Susanna had given Robert the best gift she ever could have, and now at last it was over, the burden no longer hers. Or his.

They pushed through the doors and came out of the Washington Post building just in time to see a tow truck pulling away from the curb with Sanjay's Infiniti hooked up to the back. Their mouths dropped open. They looked at one another and then back at the tow truck as it merged into the traffic flow and disappeared along with Sanjay's car. Farida let out a deep sigh and shook her head in resignation. A man in a threadbare, pin-striped suit whizzed past them on a bike, balancing a banker's box on one knee as he pedaled. Fat drops of rain start to fall.

Pulling her sari over her head, Farida said, "To paraphrase one of your saints —"

"I didn't know I had any."

"Well, this one spent most of her life in India, and I know her because of this."

"Okay," Susanna said, looking at the overcast sky, fat with rain clouds. "We need to find an Uber or a cab."

"She said that we can do no great things, only small things with great integrity," Farida said. "We met the standard today, I would say."

Susanna looked at her. "I thought it was, 'We can do no great things, only small things with great love'?"

Farida considered the words and nodded. "That way is good too."

Squeezing Farida's hand, Susanna said, "Yeah, we did good. Thank you."

The rain was coming down seriously when they finally spotted a cab and hurried out to the curb to flag it down. The cab slowed and pulled over, its windshield wipers worked furiously. The cabbie rolled down the window and looked at the two rain-soaked women, smiling from ear to ear.

Susanna asked, "Can you take us to the Washington Impound Yard?"

Farida looked at her. "Sanjay's going to kill me."

The fog hung low and damp, and Susanna sat shivering on an elaborate concrete bench under the bare branches of the crepe myrtles that dotted the cemetery where Michael was buried. She had come to say goodbye.

"What's the worst thing you can think of, babe?" She spoke to his gravestone. "Don't be mad if I don't come and visit anymore. I'm not skipping town or anything like that. I gave the cops my new address and all." She was quiet for a while. "Things have been going on, but I'm sure you know — I mean, if you can see from wherever you are or if you even care anymore. It's been a while, I know."

The thick, gray fog wove between her feet, and she looked up at the barely visible tree branches overhead. "I'll always love you, Michael. But you know that too." She cleared her throat, thought about how to put words to her thoughts. "You think a person can really love someone more than once in their life?" Her voice had trailed off to just above a whisper. "Well, I do now, and it doesn't take anything away from my love for you. I had no idea. Wisdom is hard won, I guess, at least for me. So don't be mad that I've met someone. Funny thing is I may not see him ever again, but I'm happy, no matter what the future brings. I'm okay now. Oh, and I'm going home. Don't laugh. I know I had my heart set on opening the Maryland reporting office and it was a good idea, but I can do that up in Toronto too."

Rising, Susanna kissed her fingertips and brushed them along the gravestone. "I have to go. But we'll still talk, wherever you are and wherever I go. Promise." She started down the softly undulating path through a tunnel of overhanging trees, past a forest of gravestones to the parking lot when the roar of a loud truck startled her. Through the fog she could make out a garbage truck on the street that ran parallel to the cemetery.

The truck stopped, and two garbage men jumped down and started going through stacks of boxes on a driveway in front of a house. Someone had dumped boxes and boxes of books into the trash, and the men started to pick up random volumes and flip through them. One became engrossed in a book and stopped to read as the other one began heaving the boxes into the back of the garbage truck. Susanna stood mesmerized, watching them as a fine drizzle settled over her. After a few minutes, the reader took a handful of the books and tossed the rest, and they climbed back up into their cab. The driver turned on the crusher, revved the engine, and the garbage truck moved off slowly down the street and was eventually swallowed up by the fog.

When the spring storms came to Northern Virginia, they usually stayed around for a while. There would be no warning, no build-up, just a sudden deluge day after day. It was another one of the things about this part of the world that Susanna had never gotten used to. And the rains always stopped as suddenly as they started. A couple weeks later on a day when sheets of rain poured down over Arlington, Sanjay, Farida, and their two young daughters Jem and Leila ran from the parking structure over to the Ronald Reagan Airport terminal together with Susanna just as the downpour vanished. They waited for her as she checked in at the airline kiosk, and when she had insisted they go home, they refused. She turned to look at them, and the girls waved at her. She waved back, a lump in her throat, and her eye was caught by the large, scrolling electronic advertisements mounted on the wall behind them. An ad for a rum drink scrolled off the screen and was replaced by a smiling man with his arms around a cheerful woman in protective eyewear.

The man in the ad was helping her aim the gun in her hands at some unseen target. "Made with American Pride" said the writing across the bottom. "Seems like only yesterday your father brought you to the range for the first time. Those sure were good times – just you, dad, and his Smith & Wesson. Memories aren't the only things that should last a lifetime." Susanna stared, momentarily mesmerized, at the ad over the girls' head and shuddered at the imagined nightmare of her mother the gunslinger or a gun-toting Big Dave. This was just the sign she needed to reassure her that selling up and moving back to Canada had been the right move for her. An ocean of difference mere steps away.

Rejoining Farida and her family with boarding pass in hand, Susanna did a quick scan of the terminal. Even though she wouldn't admit it, deep down she still held on to the faint hope that Robert would appear, that she would look up to find him racing toward her, full of explanations and apologies, and sweep her up into his arms. Somehow it didn't feel like the end of the story for them.

She bent down and embraced Farida's girls and feathered

their heads with kisses as the lump in her throat grew and she covered it with promises of presents and phone calls. Farida took her hand and squeezed it hard, and Susanna squeezed back as she managed to hold off the tears.

"Susanna, Susanna, what I am going to do without you here?"

"Live longer," Susanna chuckled.

"Who would have imagined you ever leaving?"

"Stop it, for God's sake. Toronto is an hour's plane ride away. I'm not going to the other end of the world."

Farida pulled her close and whispered in her ear as they embraced, "If he tries to contact you through the office, I'll let you know right away."

Sanjay gave Susanna a tap on the arm. "Come on. You don't have a lot of time. Listen girls, I don't want any tears. You all wait for me here. I will escort Susanna to the gate."

Farida wrapped her arms around her daughters as she looked at Susanna. "Good idea. No goodbyes. Just text me when you land. "

As she headed for the gate with Sanjay, Susanna glanced back and gave them one more wave before placing her hand on Sanjay's arm. "Did Farida tell you about Robert?"

He studied her before saying, "I hope it doesn't upset you."

"No, not at all. I know at my age it's stupid but — "

"Since when does age have anything to do with finding your big love?"

"Wow, I never took you for a romantic, Sanjay."

He shrugged. "As long as your heart still beats and you are brave enough to keep it open."

"But I'd like to ask you something, only because you're sort of in the same line of work as Robert. Aren't you?"

Sanjay didn't answer.

"Don't worry. You don't have to answer that. But do you know anything about going gray, having to go gray, something like that?"

He nodded and waited for Susanna to go on.

"Well, here's the thing." All of a sudden the tears she'd been holding back threatened to burst like a dam. "Do you think I'll ever see him again, Sanjay?" This was proving to be more difficult than she hoped. "Do you think he's okay?"

"Two questions." Sanjay let out a loud breath and glanced around the busy terminal. He looked like a man who would rather be anywhere other than where he was.

He took Susanna gently by the arm and led her off to the side where they could speak without being jostled by passengers streaming past on all sides. He explained to her what it meant to go gray, that sometimes you had to hide in plain sight, blend in, until things settled down. Or sometimes agents had to disappear. Their covers may have been blown, the mission imperiled. Their life could be in danger from enemy agents. But since he didn't know any of the details of Robert's case, it was hard to say much.

He looked down at Susanna as she hung on his every word. "When an agent's life is at stake, when a mission goes awry, no corners are cut, especially with a valuable asset. But you're not even sure which agency he worked for, Susanna. So how can I give you specifics?"

"I understand." Her voice was barely audible. "He was a Naval officer. That much I do know."

"I work for the Feds. I don't know what his brief was or to whom he answered, but if he was a mission commander, he is definitely not disposable, and he can't just walk away either whenever he wants or when he's had enough. There is a protocol to be followed. Otherwise nothing works."

"So he's okay," Susanna said. "Nothing's happened to him; right?"

"If he were implicated in any wrongdoing, then that's a whole other wax ball. He would be taken away, debriefed. It could be a lengthy process." Sanjay paused. "And what happens after that, we won't go there because I don't know any of this fellow's particulars. And that's the way I want to keep it. Are you catching the sea drift of my situation?"

"Does that mean I'll never see him again?" she whispered.

"Not necessarily," he said. "But please remember, Susanna, good times, bad times, heaven is inside you no matter what."

Tears welled up in her eyes, and she wiped angrily at them. "You know, I owe him so much. He showed me my heart was still here and beating. I had forgotten."

Sanjay grew distressed. "And that's why I know you are going to be fine in the end." He hesitated. "If you are okay with it, I will hold you," he said awkwardly and put his arm around her and gave her a brisk hug.

"I will be, won't I?" The start of a faint smile played

over her face as the realization sunk in. Robert had given her the gift of waking from a deep sleep, and she had a lot of living left to do, with or without him. Even the pain of missing him was better than the numbness that had trailed her since Michael's death and long before that, if she were honest about it. Now there were plans to make, adventures to meet, cases to conquer.

"You've been a good friend, Sanjay."

"Farida and I, your sister and brother always."

"Always."

He dug around in his jacket and pulled out a plastic packet and gave her a tissue.

"I'm not crying," she said as she took it and dabbed at her eyes.

"That's good," Sanjay said, "because I know about my Infiniti getting towed. And I've been meaning to talk to you about that."

When Susanna laughed, he smiled with relief and said, "We really have to get going if you don't want to miss your flight." He took her by the elbow and steered her toward the line for the security check as people pushed past them. "Here, blow your nose." He gave her another tissue.

Susanna stopped and looked at him. "What hurts most is that I never told him that I love him when I had the chance." She swallowed hard. "And I do, with all my stupid heart. I really do."

He looked down at her. "You know what, Susanna? I'm sure he figured that part out."

"You think so?"
"Swear to God."
"Thanks."

CHAPTER:
THIRTY-THREE

A PALE LEMON SUN PEEPED OVER the watery horizon as Robert Crowell tossed and turned and sleep escaped his clutches. In his restless dreams, the barren road stretched endlessly before him, and the devil still whistled at his back. The gunmetal gray Navy destroyer cut through the churning seas as it headed for the Pacific atoll of Diego Garcia, a speck in the middle of the Indian Ocean, home to the United States Naval Communications and Support Facility, an essential link in the global U.S. defense structure, and the center of Covert Operations for the Western Hemisphere.

It was to this microscopic dot on the navigational charts that Robert was returning. No families, spouses, or dependents permitted on the island. To most of the world's population, it was invisible. You could not visit. You could not pick up a phone and call to say hello. You could not get a number from Directory Assistance. It did not exist.

Robert twisted on the narrow, hard bunk, clicked on the metal lamp above his head, and flipped open the volume lying on his chest. But the lines of print crashed around the page as the ocean heaved around him and thoughts of Susanna clamored for attention. He threw the book aside. His body, his mind, his heart, all of them hurt like hell, and he couldn't bear to think about the pain he had caused her. If only he'd been able to reach her at the inn that last day to let her know what was happening. If only she had answered her phone. It would have at least given him a chance for a speedy explanation and assurance that he'd be in touch soon as realistically viable. But that window of opportunity had snapped shut, and now the regrets gnawed at him.

Contacting her while he had sat in the Naval brig at Anacostia would have been the worst possible thing he could have done. It would have incriminated her further, brought her more trouble, and sucked her into a cesspit that could have taken years to climb out of. For her sake, he couldn't afford to make that mistake. So even though it had gutted him, he didn't try to contact her again. And when he sailed out without having spoken to her, it was the hardest thing he'd ever done.

Robert shifted on the narrow cot and shoved his hands behind his head. What would she do now? They had held him in the brig for 48 hours after accusations of a series of security breaches by the National Security Agency, with corroborating testimony from DIA operatives. Robert had punched back hard and taken it to the very top. The Vice Admiral of NSOC, U.S. Naval Special Operations Command, under whom he had served directly on missions into Afghanistan and Iraq and under whose purview he had been selected to go into the SSB, intervened. Robert's release was approved, the order was signed, and he was directed to return to Diego Garcia forthwith, a full debrief to be conducted there, followed by a disciplinary hearing if merited.

His secondment to the Strategic Support Branch was reversed on orders of the Vice Admiral himself and over protests from the Secretary of Defense's office. On that count, Robert's relief knew no bounds. He was finally free of the Intelligence gig. At long last he'd been handed his get-out-of-jail-free card. Silver lining big time.

And though the National Security Agency and the Strategic Support Branch pushed hard to keep Robert Crowell in the military jail or, at the least, have him transferred to a floating brig for the trip back, in the end the bastards had to bow to the top brass at NSOC, who held overriding jurisdiction and were able to spare him that indignity.

But anger still burned hot in his gut. He had served on the USS O'Brien and received the Meritorious Unit Commendation. He was stationed at Diego Garcia when they were the sole U.S. Naval base to launch offensive air operations during Operation Desert Storm. He had served as chief staff officer of Destroyer Squadron 15 before he was seconded to the Naval Special Operations Command, then the Defense Intelligence Agency, and finally the dark and murky Strategic Support Branch, under the Defense Secretary's direct control.

Now those pencil-pushing, fat-ass NSA bastards thought they'd get him into the brig at Charleston? Over his dead body. He had completed a couple dozen years of military service, and he would retire honorably from active duty when and if he so chose. And no motherfucker, thank you very much, was going to take that away from him.

Robert sat up in his bunk, and his bare feet started as they hit the cold floor. He could feel the slightest vibration as the ship battled the roiling waters. Unbidden, Susanna came to his mind again, laughing, full of amusement at some stupid thing he had said, and he broke into a slow smile, remembering all the promise that he saw deep in her eyes. Would it ever have been enough? How many endless nights had he lain awake, and when he did sleep, his dreams haunted him and teased, and he woke up hungering for her, hard with the need to bury himself deep inside her. He loved fucking her, and he loved making love to her even more. She had been his home at long last found, his refuge, when he didn't even know he'd been searching.

Now he would remain under a cloak of suspicion until the mission wrapped up, and if Susanna had taken the stuff to the press herself, he'd ride out the fallout from that. Let the highest bureaucratic levels at the NSA shove that up where the sun don't shine. Let the Secretary of Defense explain away the SSB, his shadowy little spy unit, what exactly they did and why they were not answerable to Congress. Let him explain their spying on whoever the hell they wanted or covering up whatever they felt expedient. Let him explain away collateral damage and Pegasus and brainless grunts like Big Red running free on the payroll, all footed on the taxpayers' graft.

So he would have to hang on and bide his time. And when it all faded into the dust heap of scandal and failed missions, then he would be able to contact Susanna again. By then he would have discharged his duty and paid the devil his dues. He would put in his release, and at last he would stand before her unencumbered, a free man, if she wanted him, if she would still have him. He would make her understand, forgive him. He groaned and dropped his head into his hands, resting his elbows on his knees.

Susanna was the one who had made him believe that just maybe there was another road, a different direction. He loved that she thought change was possible and that one noble act could erase countless slogs through the wasteland. God, he loved her. He told himself he didn't know her, but he did. He understood why she sometimes needed to put distance between them, and that was okay. He knew her better now than he knew the geography of his own soul, could feel her always beneath his hands, getting in the way as his fingers moved over the navigation instruments. Even when his ears were tuned in to the blips on the radar screen and his fellow naval officers stood at his side, it was always Susanna in his mind's eye, enveloping him as he drowned in the memory of the scent of her. And he didn't want to think of anything else.

He told himself he was headed for an invisible speck of an island half way around the world. His future was uncertain, and he had to be pragmatic. But she was the one who knew that Van was the man, that Everlast was true, and poetic champions compose. And she saw Robert like she understood Van. He had been known, and maybe that had to be enough.

But it was not. Would he ever see her again, or would he live out his days haunted by the loss? No. This time he was claiming a future for himself. With her. Until Susanna, he did not know if his heart still existed, but all that had changed in one moment on one day with a kiss.

Diego Garcia was still some 1,400 nautical miles away. The course was a turbulent one south of the Equator, and the waters at this latitude were fierce, unforgiving. The Indian Ocean was starting to toss the destroyer like an old metal tin, and his officer's cabin was starting to feel claustrophobic. He needed air. Getting up, Robert pulled on his pants. Shit, shower, and shave. Dress of the day. He needed to see the sky with a hard and sudden urgency. He had to get out of there. Lacing up his boots, he made his way to the upper deck and stepped outside.

The sky was there and beautiful. He inhaled the vast gray blue expanse, and his racing heart slowed. Would

Susanna wait for him? He wasn't sure, and right now there was nothing he could do about it. The whipping saltwater spray smelled clean and felt good. After a few moments, he could make out the familiar sea birds of the Indian Ocean, the shearwaters, the noddies and terns that punctuated the clouds and foreshadowed their arrival at Diego Garcia. Buffeted by the wind, the crew went about their duties on deck. The Quartermaster and the Master-At-Arms stood off to one side, having a smoke, and they nodded to Robert in greeting.

An albatross swooped down close, making him start, and then soared back up, airborne as it spread its seven-foot wingspan and momentarily ate up the sky. Robert swore under his breath and ducked back in and headed for the CIC. It was time to join his fellow officers.

CHAPTER
THIRTY-FOUR

A FORTNIGHT LATER WHEN MARCH was drawing to a close and back in Virginia spring was dancing its full-bloom jig, in Toronto snow and slush carpeted the city like a dirty rug, and chunks of ice still floated on Lake Ontario. The dredges of winter hung on.

Susanna and Marie walked through the LCBO, Liquor Control Board of Ontario, picking out wine for Marie's dinner party that evening. Susanna was walking through a section devoted to wines from France when she stopped dead in her tracks. In front of her stood a tall, pyramid-shaped display of Fat Bastard Shiraz. Her heart started to pound in her chest as she stared at it, and her thoughts flew to Robert and their time in Annapolis. A liquor store employee mistook her shock for interest and started explaining the origins of the wine and how lovely it was, all in a most amiable manner.

"Who would have imagined a Brit and a Frog, those sworn enemies of over a thousand years' standing, could work together harmoniously on anything," he asked conversationally, "much less the creation of a wine as fine as this?"

Without uttering a word, Susanna turned and fled the store, and the man looked after her, perplexed. Outside, as she gulped the ice-clean air, wrapped her winter coat more tightly around her, and waited for Marie to finish the shopping, her gaze wandered to the newspaper boxes next to a streetcar stop. Something caught her eye, and she walked over to get a closer look. The newspaper headline read, "Washington Denies Department of Defense Cover-Up." So now it was all done, finally finished. Susanna sucked cold air and looked up as a streetcar came trundling down the tracks and stopped in front of her.

A passenger got off, the doors closed, and the streetcar clattered off down the street. Through the rear window, she saw a lone man sitting in the very back. He was dressed in only a white, sleeveless undershirt and a winter Russian fur hat, and she could see his shoulders and arms, covered in dark hair like a pelt. His arms were flung out wide on either side of him, resting along the tops of the seats as though he was sitting at home on a hot summer day, master of his domain, oblivious of everything and everybody around him.

Susanna turned away and threw some change into the newspaper box and pulled out a paper and stood on the snowy sidewalk scanning the front page. "Two Iranian businessmen deported from United States amidst accusations of illegal spying sanctioned by Department of Defense." The wind ruffled the pages as she read. Something flew into her boot, and she looked down and saw that it was a dirty, flattened Crackerjack box covered in slush. She stared at it as the wind picked it up and hurtled it further down the street.

Marie came out of the liquor store with a carton of wine bottles and when she saw Susanna's face, she set down the box and hurried over to her. "What is it, cherie? You're as white as a ghost."

Susanna showed Marie the newspaper.

"Wait a minute." Marie looked up from the paper. "Is this what I think it is?"

Susanna nodded in response, and after a quick read, together they picked up the carton of wine and hauled it over to Marie's car. It was much too heavy for a person to carry alone.

The dinner party was an intimate and convivial affair, and when the conversation came around to the latest scandal in Washington, D.C., as promised, Marie and her husband Daniel did not mention Susanna's involvement. As the evening wore on and the wine bottles emptied and the candles burned down, Susanna found herself relaxing, and she was surprised to find that she was enjoying herself. Over coffee and the lilt of conversation, her attention was drawn to the tall, fair-haired man whom Marie had earlier introduced as Guy Byrne, a widower from Belfast, a lawyer who worked for the same law firm as Daniel but in their Irish offices.

Guy Byrne's wild and bawdy jokes kept the party in tears for a good portion of the evening. He wasn't exactly the picture that came to mind when one thought of a widower, Susanna mused as she glanced at him, taking in his lanky frame, the weathered good looks. But then did people look at her and say, "Ah, widow"? He was also a solid-gold dinner party guest, the kind every hostess counted on. He knew how to bring a little edge to the proceedings but never crossed into impropriety. And whenever he caught Susanna's eye, which seemed to be often, she noticed, he had the disconcerting habit of smiling at her. She would look away uncomfortably and shift in her chair, so not ready to go there. It was the last thing her heart desired. Surely Marie had not invited him for her benefit?

The party ended, and the other guests said their good-nights and wandered off to their homes on Toronto Island. Much to Susanna's chagrin, Marie and Daniel bundled up and escorted her and Guy Byrne together to the last ferry back to the mainland even though she would have preferred to leave for her new home on her own. A light snow powdered the ground and swirled gently around them as Marie hugged her and promised to come by with the kids the next day.

As the ferry approached, Marie's husband Daniel pecked Susanna on the cheek. "You're going to get through this all right," he said, looking her straight in the eye. "We're here for you now."

She nodded with a smile as a snowflake landed on her nose.

On the short ferry ride back to downtown Toronto, Guy Byrne flirted with her but not too much, and she found his soft Irish brogue soothing to her ears. As the glimmering lights of the downtown towers approached, the snow grew heavier, starting to obscure the view, and the wind knocked the breath out of them. When Guy wrapped a protective arm around Susanna, her body almost jumped, and she looked at him warily.

"Just to keep the wind's pummeling off you, Susanna," he said. "Honest."

"Okay. Thanks, then." She refused to meet his eyes, but his warm body felt comforting beside her. "Dinner was nice. I haven't laughed so much in a long time."

Guy's answer was swept away by the wind hurtling over the lake. A storm was blowing in. Susanna looked down into the blackness of Lake Ontario as the ferry inched forward, crushing a noisy path through the floating chunks of ice. When it docked at Queens Quay, they headed out to the street together to find a taxi. Guy flagged one down, opened the door for Susanna, and helped her into the back seat. He paused as her coat rode up her thigh, and she pulled it down hastily when she caught his appreciative look.

Guy slid into the back of the cab beside her. "I'm taking you home, Susanna."

She looked at him, her cheeks red and stinging from the wind. "Pardon me?"

A smile crinkled the sides of his eyes. "I wasn't being presumptuous. Forgive me. I meant I will see you home and then head back to my hotel."

A slew of conflicting emotions washed over her face as she looked at him.

"Are we okay now?" he asked, laughing.

A blush rushed up her neck into her cheeks to join the heat already there. "Of course. Yes."

He studied her a moment. "You are a bloody marvelous piece of work, Susanna Bailey," he said with his charming accent. "And I'm very glad to have met you."

"Excuse me, people, but time is money," the cabbie interjected, looking in his rearview mirror. "Are we going somewhere or not?"

"Yes, I believe we are," Guy answered.

The taxi pulled away from the curb, its heater blasting valiantly, and Susanna took in the Tamil Tigers sticker on the cabbie's glovebox, next to another one for the Toronto Maple Leafs, and the air freshener in the shape of a hockey puck dangling from the rearview mirror. Guy Byrne was a decent man, and she gave him a smile before turning her head away and laying her forehead against the frost patterns decorating the cab window. The cold crept under the collar of her coat and into her veins like a thief, making her shiver, stealing the warmth from her body, and she scratched an opening in the window with her gloved finger. No sooner could she see than the window would start frosting over again. She was definitely not in Northern Virginia anymore.

High up above, Big Dave downed another wee dram and let his despair belch across the winter sky, and Susanna heard thunder and watched the snowflakes whirl and swoop.

"You are always strong enough, little one."

What? You have got to be kidding, she thought. Big Dave?

Big Dave hiccupped and slurred platitudes of snow, and Susanna had an urge to drive her fist through the cab window. "Go away. I don't even know you, Big Dave. I never did," she wanted to yell, but she was in the backseat of a taxi on a downtown Toronto street blanketed in cold, where the headlamps and streetlights were blurry with snow, and somehow it didn't seem the city for it.

"*I only want you to be happy*," Big Dave Bailey wailed on the wind.

Oh, go away you maudlin, whiskey-soaked, cabbage-chomping bastard. Susanna turned from the window and gazed at the maroon-colored turban covering the cabbie's head. You just watch me, old man, she thought. The journey beckoned with or without your soul's true companion. There was a lot of living left for her to do. She caught her thoughts and stilled. She had done the right thing, for Robert and herself, and for now that had to be enough. It would be more than okay, and she knew that now like she knew breathing.

The cab slid treacherously down Queens Quay alongside the streetcar tracks while the cabbie cursed under his breath, and Susanna's thoughts wandered to Robert. *I wonder where you are tonight. Is your world gunmetal gray, or do you*

377

stand smiling at the churning seas? Is redemption sweet, my love, or bitter? She sucked in the cold air until it hurt, and she knew that, if she would visit with the sadness just a little more, it would ease. For if she could not bear the sorrow, she would not have felt the joy. And she also knew bone deep that their story was not yet over. It was not finished between them. Another crack of thunder reverberated through the night sky, making her jump.

"For the love of little baby Jesus," Guy Byrne exclaimed, laying his hand onto Susanna's coat sleeve, breaking into her thoughts and dragging her back into the taxi with his touch. "I didn't know you could have a snowstorm and thunder at the same time."

"This is Canada. The sky gets fucked up and drunk sometimes," she said as a smile played around the corners of her mouth.

Guy chuckled. "You're funny."

Susanna murmured, "It's in the shelter of each other that the people live."

"For sure."

She looked at him, taken aback. "You know that? What does it mean?"

"Sure. It's an old Irish proverb. Me ma used to say it all the time. We need one another, and that's okay. We are meant to love others and to be loved. Our very soul craves it."

Susanna nodded. "My dad says it too." She looked back out the frost-covered window and began to hum under her breath.

Guy leaned in closer. "Anything I would know?"

She sang the words softly, her voice hesitant at first. "J'arrive dans cette ville, qui ne meme pas ma ville. Je revien d'une village, qui est un beau village."

"Sounds like a café song," Guy said. "I didn't know you spoke French."

"It's from Quebec, one province over," she said and translated the words to English. "'I arrived in this city, which is not even my city. I returned from a village, which is a beautiful village.'"

"I've never thought of Washington, D.C. that way, but perhaps it is a little village-like."

"For some reason it was actually Annapolis that was on my mind."

"Ah." Guy cleared his throat, looking confused, glanced out the cab window and then back at Susanna. "Well, this most certainly is some crazy weather you've got in this wild country of yours."

Nodding, she turned away and began to clear the frost off the window again with small circular motions. And her hand froze. But the taxi kept moving. Robert Crowell stood on the sidewalk under a snow-covered streetlamp, at the edge of a swirling pool of light, hands in his pockets, while a black SUV idled at the curb behind him, releasing puffs of exhaust.

"Oh, my God." Susanna blinked vigorously, but he was still there. Her heart leapt to her throat. It was him. She could see him through the dancing snow. Robert's collar was turned up against the cold, shoulders hunched over, his coat much too light for this weather, and no hat covering his head.

"Wait, stop," she cried out, scaring both Guy and the cabbie with her outburst. "Stop the cab."

The taxi kept going. Guy craned his neck behind him. "What is it?"

"Stop, stop." Susanna thumped the back of the cabbie's seat with her boot. "Stop the cab. I have to get out."

The cabbie hit the brakes, the brakes locked, and the cab started sliding into the oncoming lane of traffic. The few cars on the road started honking at them. Spraying expletives, the cab driver fought with the steering wheel until he managed to swerve safely away and sideswipe a snowbank, bringing the cab to a stop. Then he turned and glared at Susanna. "No offence, lady…but what the fuck?"

"Just a minute," Guy started to say. "There's no need —"

Susanna opened the door, jumped out of the cab, and started running back down the street in the direction from which they had come. A lone pickup truck drove past, spraying her with slush. But now she couldn't see Robert anywhere. The black SUV was gone. The cabbie's angry exchange with Guy and Guy's placating words tumbled over the cold air like ice pellets. She took a few more tentative steps and looked around. Where was Robert?

She heard Guy's voice coming up behind her. "Susanna, what's going on?"

"I thought I saw someone I knew."

Silence and then Guy's voice again. "There's no one out

here." A pause. "We should get going. The snow is getting worse."

As Guy came up beside her, she turned to him. "Let me ask you something." She put her hand on his arm. He waited.

"Did you see a black SUV back there, you know, parked at the curb, about a block back?"

He thought about it. "I wasn't paying much attention, but I think so. Something big, headlights on, side of the road, dark, yes."

She sighed aloud. He looked around. "But I don't see it anymore."

"Thank you. What a relief. For a minute I thought I was losing my mind. I've got to get home."

Guy hurried her back to the cab. "Someone you know?"

"I have the feeling it's someone I'm about to get to know a whole lot better."

"And it makes you happy. I can see." Guy closed the door after her, then hurried around to the other side and climbed in. And their taxi disappeared into a haze of snowy white darkness, all the while watched over by the covert, clandestine eye of Intelligence, hugger-mugger and invisible as always.

When they pulled up at Susanna's west end, lakefront condo tower, she saw him right away. Robert Crowell stood outside the entrance to her building, waiting for her. She could barely hang on until the taxi came to a stop before flinging the door open and climbing out with a quick goodbye. The cab pulled away. Susanna wiped away the tears blurring her eyes as she walked slowly toward him.

As she drew nearer, Robert said, "Lovely day."

"Is it?" She reached him and stopped, and their gaze tangled. After a while she put out her hand and touched his face to make sure he was really there.

"Hell no, not really," he answered and grabbed her hand and pulled her into his arms. And after what seemed an eternity, he took a step back and brushed the melting snowflakes off her cheek and looked long and hard at her. "But it's the day I've been searching for my whole life and didn't know it. It just took me a long time to get here." He paused and ran his thumb over her lips. "But right now I'm freezing my ass off. Do you think we could go in?"

"You mean you don't already have the key to my front door?" she said, and they kissed. And the snow came down gently and sometimes fiercely for about another month, and they walked in it hand in hand every day and talked. And made love. And trust grew. Because that's how life is.

THE END

ABOUT THE AUTHOR

ALWAYS CAPTIVATED by the magic of words, and after careers in film production and court reporting, Virlana Kardash now lives in Canada, where she devotes most of her time to writing. Find out more at www.virlanakardash.com.

Made in the USA
Middletown, DE
10 November 2024

64235415R00231